Second Chance
An Allons-y
Adventure

by

Shawn Kass

Table of Contents

Dedications

To J.D. and D.D.
Thanks for bringing me aboard.

To my beautiful wife, Elizabeth,
Who keeps me flying straight, both here on the
Allons-y
And throughout the rest of the universe.

Chapter 1

The Allons-y travels across the black of space heading to the Zada Pub on the planet Quantous with Chance and the rest of the crew aboard. He has been a part of the crew here for the past couple of years; helping out with whatever odd jobs they happened to pick up, usually as a hired gun. Before meeting Captain Kai, Chance was working on individual contracts, contracts which nine times out of ten resulted in someone finding out that his or her expiration date had come up. Chance had no problems with the work back then or now, especially since it was practically all he knew, all he knew about himself anyway.

Thinking back, Chance's first memory was of waking up in a hospital. He was twelve years old at the time; at least that's what he looked like. No one really knew how old he was, nor did they have any idea where he lived, who his parents were, or his name for that matter. Chance had quite literally dropped out of the sky in an escape pod and was rescued from the crash site five miles east of the city limits. Since then, Chance had found his way through an orphanage, usually fist first when anyone tried picking on him, and then later spent some time in the Space Marine Force. While in the SMF, Chance quickly found himself behind one gun or another, taking care of what needed to be done. At the end of his service, he took his SMF training and went into the contract business. He had only a few scars on his body from instances where no amount of training could have helped him to avoid what happened. His face was clean of all but a day's worth of stubble. The only sign available to one looking for his past could be found in his piercing eyes which showed his intimate knowledge of Death.

Stepping into the galley with the ship's mechanic, Astraia, right behind him, Captain Kai was close to forty years old and relaxed in his position. Being a bit stocky, he turns his body through the narrow passage to avoid his broad shoulders being caught in the door frame. He had been the captain of the Allons-y as long as Chance had flown with him, but Chance also knew that it was an inherited title from the previous captain whom Kai had served with during the war. This may have been the reason Kai never seemed to zip up his flight suit all the way, and why he always seemed to address the crew in a fashion of equality, rather than top down rank authority. Chance remembered when Kai hired him, Kai asked in a joking manner whether he would mind if he was paid in pesos. This not only called attention to Kai's Hispanic heritage, but also established that on his boat he expected some personality from his shipmates. Chance's answer at the time was simple, "As long as it spends, we're good, Captain."

Astraia, on the other hand, with her thin athletic frame from the many hours she spent working, nimbly glides through the opening just as she glides through the rest of the ship without worry about bulkheads or narrow door frames. She always keeps her reddish brown hair cut short in a pixie style to avoid it being caught up in any of the machinery, and her face has a quiet beauty which requires no makeup or other enhancement. Chance listens to Astraia continue her conversation from the hallway as they enter saying, "Captain, I got the Grav. Controllers working again, but they're not going to hold much longer. We need to stop off and

6

get some parts before they give out completely, and we wake up one day with all of our stuff, including ourselves, floating around here and bouncing off the walls."

Without stopping to look at her, he replies, "Parts cost money, Astraia, and money comes from jobs."

"Jobs we can't do if the Allons-y can't fly, Captain," Astraia says without missing a beat. The feisty little mouse certainly isn't holding back today with the captain, and Chance knows that while she doesn't like to fight, she's a scrapper, someone he can count on to hold her own when the chips are down.

"That's why I have you here, Astraia. To keep this old girl in the air."

"Well I'm not going to be able to do that with chewing gum and a paper clip like MacGyver, and that's about all we have left on board." Astraia, knowing of his fondness for classic television programs from Earth, is akin to using pieces of them from time to time to further her arguments with him. She also knows that this is a dance she and Captain Kai have at least once a month. In the end, she knows she will have to settle for less than adequate parts, and he knows that somehow, she will still make them work.

"Astraia, we have a job we are headed to right now. Maybe if you could convince him to give us the money upfront, I might be able to see to it that you get one or two of these parts before we take off."

"Deal," and looking over to see Chance sitting at the table, Astraia adds, "and Chance, you're my witness."

7

Chance, knowing better than to get involved, even if he has started to develop a thing for the sweet and cheerful little mechanic, simply tips the brim of his hat so that it might be taken for acknowledgment just as easily as an adjustment and lets the two of them decide its meaning for themselves.

Satisfied that both had said their piece, Kai and Astraia each take a seat at the table just as the ship's doctor comes up from the quarters below. Chance could swear she had waited down there until their argument was over before coming up, but if so, it was just her way of staying out of it, and he didn't blame her. Doctor Oska pulls out the last remaining chair and sets a tablet screen down in front of her. As she does so, Chance notices once again the young Asian doctor's attempts at making herself attractive, especially in how she positions her body when she is around men so that one's eyes naturally fall to her better features. These tricks do not work on him, but Chance is sure that they have played their part in the doctor's past and quite possibly gave her an advantage in certain negotiations, like the one that got her hired on to the Allons-y.

Kai, keeping things rather informal as usual, simply says, "Well Doc, why don't you tell us a bit about this job you have found for us."

Oska turns on her tablet and begins, "We are scheduled to reach Quantous in four hours. Once there, we will need to make our way to the pub where we will meet up with a Doctor Gene Egnarts. Egnarts has been off the radar for years. He used to be the head scientist for the Government Coalition doing research in one branch or another. The man

8

has more degrees than a thermometer, but when his last project got shut down, he vanished."

Kai asks, "If this man has been so elusive for all these years, why is he meeting with us?"

"It seems, Captain, we have been cultivating a good name for ourselves, at least with some people, despite some of your more recent actions to piss off members of the Coalition, and he was sent to us by a friend, of sorts."

"What do you mean by 'a friend of sorts'?" asks Kai.

"You remember Jack, the guy on planet Wheaton, who had us get that prototype computer chip off a certain high profile cargo ship a few months back?"

Thinking back, Kai finds the job in his memory, and the one detail that always sticks out to him comes straight to the forefront, "You mean the kid with the freaky sex dolls?"

"Yes, Captain, the young man with the robotic companion dolls," replies Oska, emphasizing the last three words, correcting him as she always did when it came to talking about that job. Continuing, she says, "It turns out, he has better access to the subspace signals shooting back and forth across this galaxy than anyone, and that chip was his way of securing his position as the lead hacker and compiler of computer information around. That kid 'with the freaky sex dolls,' as you put it, knows more about what's going on, has better access than anyone else alive, and for whatever reason considers us friends. He has been directing people towards us ever since that job, and five of the last eight jobs were from people he sent our way."

Kai leans back in his seat so that the front two legs of the chair are just off the ground and says, "I know that, and it's appreciated, but if this doctor fellow doesn't want to be found, that means someone out there must be looking for him. Frankly, I would like to keep my ship out of anyone's crosshairs."

"Jack's message says that Doctor Egnarts is looking for something. He has been in talks with some private financiers and is looking to restart his research. We need to meet with Doctor Egnarts before we can get any more details than that. If he is coming out of hiding to find people to fund this project of his, then clearly he must have either taken care of everything from his past or has the means to continue to stay off their radar."

Captain Kai thinks it over for a half second, basically weighing the risk to his ship versus the potential payout and asks, "Chance, Astraia, what do you think?"

Astraia chimes in first saying, "Well if it's just about us picking something up for him, it should be easy enough. We could always use the credits towards parts for the Allons-y," making sure to plug her need for parts one more time.

"Noted, and you, Chance?" asks Kai.

"Why not? I don't see some old scientist geek pulling a gun on you or anything - might just make for an easy payday."

"All right then," Kai begins, "we meet the doctor at the pub, listen to what he has to say, and if I think the deal is a fair payout, we do it. The ship says we'll be at Quantous in a few hours. Until then, do what you have to do to get ready."

Oska takes up her tablet, pushes in her chair, and heads back down the stairs to the ship's infirmary. Astraia heads down the hall to the back of the ship where the engine room is located, and the captain turns back up the hall towards the bridge, leaving Chance sitting in the galley alone once again.

Chapter 2

Dr. John Larson walked down the pristinely white circular hallway holding his tablet computer in front of himself, touching the screen, making notes, and reading statistics from a recent experiment he had left running while on leave to the little town of Lilac. Lilac was on the planet Arina where two years ago, he had met quite possibly the most beautiful woman he'd ever seen before. Her name was Karen Essex, and they had been seeing each other as often as he could get away.

Upon reaching the inner door marked Lab 4, Dr. Larson swiped his Coalition Project X card key, and the doors opened automatically before him. Two other researchers were on shift working while most of the others worked what was referred to as the day shift. Being on a space station, floating in the black, hours away from the nearest planet, it was a bit illogical to distinguish shifts as night or day. John Larson never paid much attention to that or what they were working on as he passed by them. Due to the special level of security his project warranted, it was deemed that his lab needed to be separate from most others and behind two levels of encrypted access. For Dr. Larson, Lab 4 was just a thoroughfare to get to the elevator in the back and down to the protected levels where his lab was located.

As the elevator descended to the next level, John Larson thought about Karen. He thought about calling her Karen Larson from now on and wished he could tell more people of his wonderful news, the news she just gave him before he headed back to the space station. He had known he loved her for some time now, probably as long as he had ever known her, if he thought about it. Now they were married, and they were going to start a family. He wouldn't be able to make it back for several months, and as she said, the next time he saw her, she'd look a bit rounder. He didn't catch the meaning at first, but when her hands dropped to her stomach, the light bulb blinked on, and he hugged her. On a separate file, he typed a name, an old name for sure, but one that he thought might be fitting for a young man in his family, Charles Larson, just as the elevator doors opened.

Walking in, Dr. Larson was greeted by the familiar site of his lab where the large tanks sat in the corner of the room, a library of books rested against the far wall with some books still scattered on the floor from his last reading, and his array of computers hung from the wall around and above his main desk. He had no other lab partners. At first, it was a matter of it never being in the budget, but honestly, now he found working alone to be so much more fulfilling. Working alone meant that there was no need to go around asking questions of other people, checking up on their work to see what they had or had not done, or the need to schedule time with the equipment. If Doctor Larson wanted to, he could let the work consume him and work for days on no more than a few hours of sleep. Working with other people, this type of schedule would never be allowed, but he found at times that the lack of sleep actually made him quicker and more creative with his thoughts-helped the neurotransmitters in his brain to fire more rapidly. He was better able to comprehend what the data was trying to tell him. So when he looked up at the screen, it was with a shock that he found the following words:

'Welcome back, doctor'

Chapter 3

On the array of computer screens before him, Jack moved his mouse to the newest icon on the center screen and opened the ancient video file he had found on the Coalition's archived computer database. Last week, he had hacked his way in looking for anything suspicious, anything mysterious, anything the Coalition wouldn't want other people to know about. There were several files of spreadsheets he had found in an old 'garbage' file which clearly illustrated the misappropriations of funds and the money that went to off-the-books research projects like Archangel, Project Rebirth, and Project X, but since it was mostly just figures there was little he could do with it. Then he came across a fragmented mp4 video file. As the video started up, he leaned back in his black nylon mesh chair and rested his hand on the bare leg of his robotic companion doll, Jenny.

The screen filled with the familiar black and white static of videos from the old days when magnetic tapes were used to document images. He knew the file was at least thirty-five years old when he downloaded it, based on the time stamp embedded in the feed's digital code stamp, but the static showed that the file wasn't digital. The last time most people used analog or other media devices was over a hundred years ago back on Earth. Jack made a mental note of the discrepancy as he let the video continue to play.

Suddenly, the static cleared, and the screen showed two people walking in heavy duty white turn-of-the-century space suits with tinted glass helmets on a strange un-terra formed planet with a large, harsh orange sun above. Jack made the assumption that both of the individuals are male due to their size but couldn't identify either one of them even as they come closer to the camera. The planet's atmosphere looked to be reddish brown which Jack knew is supposed to signify that it's a planet without oxygen, and instead had a very high level of carbon dioxide which is more than likely caustic. The soil the two people walked across was brown and rocky. There were no trees or plants of any kind, and it looked as if no moisture of any kind has ever touched this planet. Behind the two men, he saw a space shuttle, but there were no identifying marks on the ship that Jack saw, and other than a distant hillside on the left of the screen, there wasn't much there. That was, of course, until the camera began to drop down, and a puddle of opal white thick gel was seen directly in the path of the two individuals.

Rhetorically, Jack asked, "Hello, what do we have here?"

Not understanding the nature of the question, Jenny responded, "I do not know, Jack."

Used to her limited programming, Jack ignored Jenny's response and continued to watch the screen.

The two men stopped in front of the strange substance, and one of the individuals in the video sat down a large black case. The case looked like military issue, high grade plastic or some other polymer, and after he opened it, the man pulled out two complete sample kits and handed one to his partner. The two men handled the kits expertly. They took samples of the white gooey substance using various instruments and stored them in individually sealed containers. Once they had collected over twenty samples, they put the last of the samples into the black case along with the instruments they had used and sealed it up using a magnesium pull cord which melted the plastic and fused the case's two halves together. Once finished, the camera panned up with the two men as they stood and watched as they slowly walked away returning to their shuttle.

Jack leaned forward and stopped the video when it returned to the fuzzy static image. He turned to Jenny and asked, "Did you see that?"

Her head turned a bit too sharply to be mistaken for human as she addressed her long time owner and master, "Yes, Jack. Two men on the computer walked forward, took samples, packed up, and left on the shuttle."

While he pointed his finger in the air emphatically, Jack said, "Yes Jenny, that is what they did, but the question is who were they, why did they do it, and not to mention, what was that stuff?"

Jenny blinked slowly, not because her eyes needed her to, but because her programming told her that she must at least once every minute for some random time period between 0.001 and 0.5 seconds in length in order to seem more human. Jenny stared at Jack before she said, "Jack, that was three questions. I'm sorry, but I do not know the answer to any of them."

"Ahh, but we do," he said as he leaned back up to his console and rewound the video clip. Once he had gone back into the footage just before the point when the two men were about to stand up with their samples to turn and walk back to the shuttle, he paused it and then advanced one frame at a time. There, in grainy contrast over the course of just three frames, appeared the wearer's name on the arm of the suit just beneath the white patch with the thin black 'X' centered in the middle showing his organization, Dr. Wong Hue.

Jack, greeted his new interest, "Hello, Doctor," and then followed with the question that would take him several days to answer, "Who funded this little vacation of yours?"

Chapter 4

Kai lands on Quantous at a shipyard just a few miles away from the Zada Pub without any problems. Stepping inside the office, he asks the attendant at the shipping yard to fill up the fuel cells while they are out. The attendant gives a grunt as Kai pulls out his Coalition card to pay the man, as well as his pilot's license for proof that he's in good standing with the Coalition's Shipping Guild. Granted, his license has been revoked a few times in the past while the Coalition investigated his possible involvement in one job or another, but whether things didn't stick, or he was just lucky, his license was reinstated each time. Technically, while his actions were under investigation in the past, his license would come up as invalid whenever it was checked. He was supposed to be refused service at any port, but he had two ways around that. The first, and more preferable method, was Astraia. While she was assigned as the ship's mechanic, she did carry a valid license which allowed her to fly the Allons-y. Even if she wasn't the best pilot, it was enough to get them in and out of official shipping yards like this. The second, and more expensive route, was for Kai to dock at less reputable shipping yards where certain procedures could be ignored for a few extra hundred credits.

The attendant swipes his license and when it comes up approved, he asks, "You want to pay now or when you get back?"

Kai, never knowing if a job negotiation would go smoothly or not, had learned to be prepared for the worst and says, "Just put five hundred in."

More than willing to take payment in advance, the attendant accepts Kai's Coalition card, punches in the price for five hundred gallons of fuel, and swipes the credits off his card before handing it back without any further questions. The attendant has learned a thing or two of his own over the years, and the first rule is to never ask too many questions of the shipping pilots. If you didn't know anything, then no one could ever say you talked, and you could stay in business without any accidents happening to you or your shipping yard.

Walking out of the attendant's office into the bright afternoon sun, Kai heads back over to the Allons-y's open loading bay ramp and calls up, "Astraia, you got the buggy?"

"Got it, Captain. Driving her down now."

The buggy is Kai's old six-wheeler. It looks like a modified jeep from back on Earth, open to the elements without its top, and is painted a sand brown color. The modifications, however, allow him to carry a fair amount of supplies on board, including a secret compartment large enough to hide one person, in case of emergency, and an adjustable mount fitted to the back large enough to hold a gatling gun, if need be.

Chance, who's watching everything from the cargo bay on board, strides over and hops in the back of the buggy. As he does so, Kai notices his boot knife and pistol holstered beneath his trench coat. "You expecting trouble, Chance?" asks Kai.

Without looking at in Kai's direction, Chance leans back in the buggy's back seat and says, "Always."

"Captain, would you mind if I came along as well? There are a few medical supplies I would like to get while we have access to the town."

Knowing that Oska's tastes for medical supplies ran higher than Kai really had the credits to pay for, Kai asks, "That depends, Doctor. Who would you be expecting to pay for those supplies?"

"Really, I'm just getting some bandages and ointment, but if I see something else, I'll put the whole purchase on my card."

"Deal," agrees Kai just as Oska gets into the buggy's back alongside Chance.

Astraia starts the electric motor of the vehicle and drives it down the ramp where Kai slides in on the passenger side and asks, "You remember how to get to Zada?"

"I got it Captain."

The trip from the shipping yard to the Zada Pub takes the crew through several blocks of dirt roads and empty buildings before things begin to get populated. It's always like this. Unless visiting a major city, the area around the shipping yards is abandoned in case an accident occurs and wipes out a few dozen homes along with everyone in them, or worse, someone brings something in illegally, in which case all bets are off. If the Coalition gets involved, it's more likely to turn into an open war zone. Quantous has been lucky so far, and any illegal activity that goes on here is kept quiet from those who would turn someone in, but Kai and his crew have been to more than one shipping yard where things have turned bad. More often than not, it isn't the bad people who have ended up getting themselves hurt at those places either.

Pulling up at the Zada Pub, Astraia parks the buggy on the east side of the building, like she always does, to avoid the messy confusion so many people go through when they attempt to return to their vehicle and can't remember where they parked it. The Zada Pub itself is a two story building made of cement and high-impact resistant windows. The pub owner jokes that decorations on the outside are about as useful as tits on a bull, but the extra money he spent on the windows are good enough to keep the bullets out.

Walking inside, Kai and his crew come up to a series of storage lockers of various sizes and a sign that reads, 'No Firearms, Please'. Before any of them could proceed any farther, they have to pass through a metal detector. Kai steps though without raising any alarms, as he had stowed his weapon in the buggy before entering. Oska and Astraia also pass the metal detector's sensors without issue, which isn't much of a surprise to Kai since neither of them have a habit of carrying unless they know things will get dangerous. What does surprise Kai is when Chance passed through without depositing anything in the lockers, and the metal detector fails to sound. Kai raises a single eyebrow inquisitively towards Chance as he continues his way from the metal detectors towards the bar, and as Chance passes, he murmurs, "Bone handles, ceramics parts."

Kai stops himself before shaking his head in disbelief; Chance always seems to be one step ahead in these situations. It's a wonder why he's stayed aboard as long as he has when he could clearly be making more money than what Kai is capable of paying him. Not wanting to drift too far mentally from why he came here, he leads the two girls over to a booth with a wooden table in the corner to wait, while noticing that the pub is mostly empty. The bartender looks to be a bit older than usual, and aside from Chance who somehow positions himself at the bar so that his back is

against the wall, the only other person in the place
is at the bar, at the opposite end, halfway off his
stool with his head down on the flat counter.

Kai asks Oska, "What time did this Egnarts
say he would be here?"

"Three o'clock local time, Captain."

Looking over at the wall, Kai can see that
the clock reads just about three, and asks, "Did you
get in touch with the kid? Is there anything else you
can tell us about this guy?"

Just as Oska is about to answer him, the
pub's owner walks up to the table solicitously.
"Welcome to Zada. Is there anything I can get for
you?"

"It's quiet in here today," observes Kai.
"Where is everyone?"

Smiling, the pub owner says, "You just
missed the rush. Let me get your orders before I get
swamped again."

Kai and Astraia both order an appetizer and
a drink, while Oska only gets herself a glass of
water. Halfway through the owner's attempt to
repeat back their order, he is cut off by a noise so
loud the empty glass on the nearby table rattles.

Kai shakes his head to clear out the ringing
and asks, "What was that?"

Acting innocent, the pub owner attempts to
ignore the question and continues to repeat back the
order to the stunned crew members. Just as he
finishes recounting everything, there is another
earth shattering sound piercing the silence.

Realizing that there is no avoiding it, the
Zada's owner tries a different tactic and waves his
hand in a dismissive gesture towards the back wall
saying, "Oh, that? It's just my nephew working on

the expansion we are putting in the back. You'll get use to it."

Another thunderous sound rattles its way through the pub, and the owner begins to head back towards the kitchen with their orders.

Kai leans in towards Oska and asks, "Do you think this guy is really going to meet us here with this racket going on?"

"He has to. It's too late for him to change the location. If the cacophony is still this noisy when he arrives, we can ask him if he wants to go down the street to the next establishment."

Nodding his agreement, Kai sits back and waits listening as the owner angrily yells at his nephew in the back, "Hey, Eddy, you want to keep the noise down? We have customers out front!"

Another voice yells back, coming from higher up saying, "I'm almost done with this part, and then I can start laying the wiring!"

"Well, how much longer is it going to be?" questions the owner.

"Look, Uncle Zada, when the expansion is finished, it will have to pass inspection by the Coalition officials. I would rather it pass the first time then have to do it over again, or worse, try to pay them off."

Acknowledging his comment, but still putting an air of authority in his voice he tells Eddy, "Well, hurry up before I lose all of my customers for the day."

Kai whispers to Astraia in a joking tone, "You know, I honestly think he doesn't realize that we can hear him."

"Clearly, I guess he has already gone deaf."

Eddy calling down to the owner says, "Hey, Uncle, I need you to get me something."

"What is it now?" asks Zada. "Can't you see I'm trying to get this order out since the cook took the day off, too?"

"A beer."

Angrily, Zada yells even louder, "A what? You don't get to drink a beer while you're working! For that matter, I'm not giving you anything to eat or drink tonight if one more of my customers leave before paying because of the noise you're making!"

"You're right, Captain, I don't believe they have any idea that we can hear them," chimes in Oska. "That's just as well anyway. I have some things to tell you before we meet our new associate. Jack did some more digging on this Doctor Gene Egnarts and said he used to be a big deal to the Coalition before the last interplanetary war. It turns out he was part of a special project research team that the Coalition spent trillions of credits on. The Coalition set them up and allowed them to carry out whatever research they wanted in their own privately funded lab. It was all off-the-books stuff, but this guy, Doctor Egnarts, has advanced degrees from several of the best schools around in areas ranging from biochemistry and microbiology to medicine and computers. He was the top guy in his field."

Astraia asks, "Which field is that?" and then when she sees Oska's confusion at her question, she clarifies, saying, "You said he was the top in his field, but you mentioned like four different things."

Tilting her head up for emphasis, Oska replies, "You don't get it." She pauses before adding, "all of them."

Eyes widening, Kai lets out a soft whistle and says, "Damn, so this guy is like Quillian smart," referring to the scientist who developed the faster-than-light drive currently in use by most space vehicles.

Oska shakes her head and says, "No, actually he's smarter."

"No wonder he had people looking for him. They probably wanted to get at his research," says Kai.

"Or they wanted him to work on something special for them," retorts Oska. "A guy like that, with his credentials, could probably make anything. Jack says that once his last project was shut down, probably due to the Coalition reallocating more money towards the war effort than research, Doctor Egnarts retired and disappeared."

Before Kai responds, he sees the pub's owner returning to their table with their drinks and appetizers in hand.

Zada finishes setting out their meal and asks, "Is there anything else I can get you three?" just as another series of loud work sounds come from the back of the restaurant distorting anything else he had planned to say.

Astraia's eyes flick back towards Chance, who is looking in another direction. She follows his line of sight and sees an old guy walking back into bar from the restrooms in the corner. Glancing back at Chance, she sees his eyes are back down on his drink, and his face is mostly covered by his hat, but she knows he is still watching.

Kai picks up on Astraia's curiosity and dismisses Zada saying, "No, thank you. We'll let you know when we are ready for something else." Once Zada returns to the back, Kai pops one of the nachos off the plate and into his mouth. He realizes his mistake immediately as the nachos taste like they might, in fact, be made from whatever pieces of drywall are being used in the construction of the restaurant's new addition. After choking it down with a swallow of beer, Kai asks between chews, "Well, who's going to go make introductions with him?" Then, as if to punctuate that it would not be himself who got up, he starts to season the nachos with everything on the table from salt and pepper to hot sauce in heavy quantities to try and make them a bit more palatable.

Oska figures she may have the best chance to strike up a conversation with Egnarts since she is the ship's doctor and a woman with sex appeal, a combination that gets her pretty far. She slides out of the booth and heads over to the bar with a purposeful bit of a sway to her hips.

Upon walking up to him, Egnarts says, "Whatever you're selling, I both can't afford it and am too damn old to enjoy it anyway, Honey, so you might as well head on back to wherever you came from."

In shock that she doesn't even get a word out and is shot down so harshly, Oska turns and walks back to the table and a grinning Kai, open-mouthed and wide-eyed. Sitting down, the stunned look fails to evaporate, and Kai says through a mouthful of something unidentifiable, "Next," indicating that Astraia should take a shot.

Refusing to be dissuaded, Astraia smiles and scoots across the leather bench to let herself out of the booth. She walks over to Egnarts without adding anything to her stride, and rests her elbows on the bar before greeting him with a perky smile and a "Hi."

Egnarts barely looks at her and says nothing as he takes another drink of his beer.

Astraia, continuing to be sweet and cheerful, asks, "Excuse me, mister, but I was wondering if you might be able to help me out. I was supposed to meet this guy here, and I don't have a picture of him or anything." When he fails to look at her, she makes one last attempt, "I was told I could find Doctor Egnarts here."

With this, Egnarts sets his beer down, and turns to her. "Well, I can't say that you look like someone in that line of work, young lady."

In the corner, Kai whispers to Oska, "Well, that's further than you got," and laughs as her expression changes to a scowl.

Smiling even brighter, Astraia says, "Actually, I'm a mechanic. My name is Astraia. What's yours?"

Giving in to her, he says, "Nice to meet you, Astraia. My name is Gene. What type of a mechanic are you?"

Knowing she had opened a crack in his defenses, she answers, "I'm a ship's mechanic actually, and the guy in the corner booth over there is my captain."

Not wanting to completely show his hand just yet, the doctor asks, "Your captain, huh? What do you and your captain want with this doctor fellow?"

"Actually, we thought we might be able to do something for him," responds Astraia. Then figuring she might as well lay it all out on the table, she says, "A friend of ours, Jack, said that Doctor Egnarts might have a job he needs doing. My captain is always interested in hearing about jobs people need done, and sometimes, if the payout is worth the risk, we end up helping people out."

Gene looks over his shoulder to the booth where Kai is stuffing the last of the nachos into his mouth and calculates his risks. There only seem to be three of them here, and they did use Jack's name. It just might be worth the risk to see if they can help. Turning back to Astraia he says, "All right, Astraia, how about you introduce me to this captain of yours? I might have a job he can do for me."

Astraia's eyes light up, and she says, "Sure thing. Come on over to the table and I'll introduce you."

The two of them walk over to the booth just as Kai pushes the plate aside and finishes the last of his beer in one final swallow. Speaking up first in her cute and charming tone, Astraia says, "Captain, may I introduce you to Gene?" making sure to only give the name he gave her.

Kai waves his hand at the chair across from him and says, "Nice to meet you, Gene. How might I help you?"

Taking his offered seat, Gene says, "Well, I have a job that needs doing, and I asked a trusted source to send someone my way. This adorable little mechanic of yours said that you folks were sent here looking for me, and she happened to drop his name during our conversation."

"Well, yes, sir," says Kai. "That is why we're here, and if your credit is good, we'll be happy to take on whatever service you need."

Deciding to show part of his hand now, Gene says, "My name is Doctor Gene Egnarts, and as I asked Jack, I am looking for a crew to do a run for me."

Kai nods and says, "Well, Doctor, it's good to meet you." Then in an attempt to put the good doctor on and find out both how much trouble this little job might cause so that he could establish his buy-in, as well as how much to add on to his initial asking price once the negotiations started, Kai asks, "Before we get into the particulars of the job, can I ask why you didn't just go through the Coalitions Shipping Guild to get a crew?"

Doctor Egnarts looks quickly from Oska whose face is a placid blank, then back over to Astraia who continues to smile and says, "I am not in the habit of allowing the Coalition to know my whereabouts, if you know what I mean."

Smiling, knowing that the Doctor has just told him exactly what he wanted to hear, Kai says, "That isn't a problem for my crew. We have done jobs for folks in the past that were hush-hush."

Nodding, Gene says, "That's what Jack told me when I asked him who he was sending."

"Really, what else did our friend Jack say?" asks Kai, slightly worried Jack might have tipped him off about the robbery job they did for him with that special chip.

"He just said you were a trustworthy crew who had helped him out in the past. But he did say that there were four of you," looking around. He continues with, "Am I to assume that the fellow at the bar over there is with you, or is the rest of your crew back at your ship?"

Nodding and knowing Chance is listening, Kai says, "You assume correctly," without clarifying which part of the doctor's inquiry he's referring to. "Now, what is it that you think we might be able to do for you?"

Gene leans in, and in a whisper says, "Here's the thing, Captain. A few years back, I used to work on a special Coalition project out in sector Whiskey-two-nine. The facility was called Project

X, and we did some wild research there. Even now, I consider it to have been some of the best work in life. Unfortunately, the Coalition chose to shut us down so that they could spend more money on the war bringing even more planets under their control before I could finish, and leaving it unfinished has been my one regret for these many years."

When the doctor pauses, Kai pushes just a little saying, "You have my interest so far."

Continuing, Doctor Egnarts says, "Jack said your crew could handle this for me, and so I'm extending my trust of him to you. I have some new financiers lined up, and before I can get this deal off the ground, I need someone to go on board the old space station and retrieve my research."

Kai thinks about it as the doctor continues to talk, weighing the risk of breaking in an abandoned Coalition secret government research space station and stealing some research. This would have to be a well paying job to make it worthwhile.

Tuning back into the conversation, Kai hears the doctor saying, "The research is in the mainframe's computer, and if you are willing to go, I'll give you an encrypted external hard drive in which to download everything onto. You bring it back to me, and the credits are yours."

"Who are your financiers?" asks Kai.

Doctor Egnarts smirks as he says, "That, I'm afraid, is one of the few things which I am not at liberty to talk about."

"Okay, well exactly how much are you thinking this job of yours is worth there, Doctor?" asks Kai.

"Well, I understand from Jack that trust isn't cheap, and I know having to go onto a Coalition Space Station without authorization is a bit on the illegal side, but it really is just a simple retrievable job. What would you say to 15,000 credits plus fuel expenses?"

A fair price in Kai's estimation would be closer to 10,000 credits, so either there is something the good doctor isn't telling him, or he really needs this job done. The third option of course is that he really has no idea what the job costs, but no matter what the reason, Kai has a policy of always playing hardball to try and negotiate the price up. He bluffs the doctor, making him believe that Kai is thinking it over, not wanting the doctor to realize that the amount is sufficient. Finally, Kai counters, upping the ante, "Well, Doctor, it's a generous offer, but considering everything, my crew and I are going to need a bit more. What do you say to 20,000 credits with the fuel?"

Understanding the game they were playing was akin to poker, the Doctor returns his counter-offer with one of his own and calls, "Seventeen five, with fuel, final offer."

Seeing that he is a man of his word, Kai glances over the Doctor's shoulder to look to Chance, who nods his head in agreement. Accepting the deal, he begins to reach forward to shake hands until Astraia jumps in saying, "And we get half up front."

Kai, hoping she hasn't just blown the deal and blocked his bet with the extra twenty-five hundred the Doctor just threw in the kitty, looks at her for a moment and then back to the Doctor and waits.

The doctor smiles at Astraia and says, "Of course, my dear. Captain, do we have a deal?"

"Deal."

The two shake hands and pull out their Coalition cards, allowing Oska, with her tablet, to set up the transfer. After both men swipe their cards, the transaction is complete, and an extra 8,750 credits appears in Kai's account, bringing the total almost up to the ten thousand mark. Oska realizes that Kai was really cutting it close once again, and he isn't lying to Astraia when he says they need a job before he can buy any more parts for the Allons-y.

"Doctor, I have one more question, if you don't mind," asks Kai. "What exactly was your research in?"

The doctor thinks for a moment and replies, "Actually, I'm not at liberty to divulge that information either. Hence, the encrypted hard drive I'll have delivered to the shipyard this afternoon. But between you and me, let's just say, it's pretty complex for people outside the fields I work in." Then in an effort to both clarify and put the captain at ease, Egnarts continues by saying, "The goal is to help people. Imagine, if you will, that no one has to go through life deformed, that any injury can be healed. If my research works and I get the funding I need, I might just be able to find a way for us to regrow missing limbs and in some cases, escape death."

Satisfied with the answer, Kai says, "That sounds good. I hope it all works for you."

Doctor Egnarts turns from Kai and hands Oska a quick drive chip saying, "The location of the facility is on there, along with a brief description of what you'll need to do once you get there."

Shaking hands one more time, Kai says, "It's a pleasure doing business with you. We'll send you a transmission when we have the information, and you can tell us where and when to meet you."

Smiling, Doctor Egnarts shakes Kai's offered hand and says, "Perfect," and then as they release each other's grip, the doctor says, "And don't worry about this," gesturing towards their meal. "I've got the bill."

The crew heads out of the Zada Pub and once back in the buggy, Oska pops the chip into her tablet to find out where the space station is located and what they need to do once there. The file on the chip is pretty straightforward as she explains it to the rest of the crew. "It looks like the facility is in sector Whiskey-two-nine like he said and has a dampening field around it so it's harder for ships that don't know exactly where to look to find it. The facility itself is supposed to still have breathable air due to the carbon filters on board, but we will need to pressurize the outer airlock when we dock. Once on board, we simply make our way down to the facility's central core and into the computer room where we can hook up the hard drive he is giving us. Once installed, it will automatically load up all the files. We bring it back to the good doctor, and he pays us the rest of our credits."

"See, Captain," says Astraia from behind the driver's wheel, "I knew this would be a good one."

"Yeah," says Kai, "Sounds great, we could use an easy payday."

"Yup, and now I can get the Allons-y some of the parts she needs."

Acknowledging her work at getting the doctor to pay something upfront, Kai reluctantly agrees, "Yeah, I guess so, but don't go hog wild. It won't go as far as you think."

The crew makes two more stops before getting back to the ship, one at the hospital where the doctor ends up purchasing more than she planned and pays for it herself, and one at the shipping yard's junkyard where Astraia is able to convince Kai to purchase about a quarter of the things on her list of 'needs'. The whole time however, Chance rethinks the conversation the crew had with the doctor and picks out the points where he got the feeling the doctor wasn't telling them the whole truth. He can't put his finger on it. Maybe the doctor's voice wavered a half of an octave when he said something, or perhaps he saw something subconsciously in his body language, but there's definitely something more to this job than he was letting on.

Chapter 5

The planet Arina was a lot like Earth used to be before all of the cars created the smog which destroyed the air, before the factories polluted the waters, before greed cut down the forests and killed the wildlife. Arina was found to be a pleasant planet, full of life, and had almost all of the elements the settler scouts were looking for when they found it. The only thing that was unacceptable was the amount of oxygen in the air; it was too high at thirty-seven percent. The settler scouts dropped ten converters into the planet's atmosphere in strategic locations and radioed back to the Coalition that Arina would be ready for habitation in eight months. In reality, it only took seven.

The people of the Coalition flocked to the new planet. First came the builders who set up homes and buildings for businesses using the some of the supplies they brought with them, but mostly using things they found there on the land. Next came the farmers who prepared the fields and sowed the seeds into the rich, freshly tilled soil. Finally came the people who spread out across the planet and began to live their new lives. Several large port cities were established early on along rivers and oceans, as easily found from the water as they were from space. Spreading out from there, people created settlements with schools, homes, and hospitals. Twenty years later, a young woman named Karen Essex, who had originally moved to Arina with her family as a girl, met a scientist named John Larson.

John came to the planet Arina to get away from the space station where his research on curing cancer was going very slowly. He had been on the space station for only six months now, and he knew that the field of research required a lifetime's work to usually see significant results, but somehow after graduating at the top of his class, he thought he would be able to find the answers he was looking for faster than his predecessors. Arina was the only planet in range of a shuttle from the space station, and John had no desire to spend money to go anywhere specific. On the way there, he looked over the data file on the planet trying to find somewhere quiet. He wanted to get away and relax. Therefore, he purposefully avoided the big cities and vacation spots where most tourists went. Buried deep in the file, he found random bits of information about small towns on the outskirts away from all traffic that included mostly farmland and some hunting. Figuring that one of these places seemed perfect for his needs, he chose the small town of Lilac at random from the list of seven available to him.

The shuttle landed approximately one mile away from the town in a small meadow just off the main road as instructed and cloaked itself to avoid detection and possible theft. John wore a standard pair of clothes consisting of a black jumpsuit and black boots with a gold colored belt. He carried a backpack with a spare jumpsuit and his Coalition card loaded with a thousand credits for food and lodging.

The walk into town was calm, and the sound of small insects in the grass kept him company for the fifteen minutes he took to make his way to Lilac. As he came over the final hill, he saw the small town consisting of little more than six square miles of building in the center of densely populated farmland. The buildings looked to be made of wood, mostly one story high, some two, but nothing larger. There were no shopping malls, no corporations, and no fast food franchises. The farms all seemed nearly ready for harvest as their crops seemed too tall and healthy with various colors of green and yellow mixed throughout. As he continued into the town, John realized he had chosen the perfect place and decided if things went well, he would most definitely be back.

After walking a couple of streets towards the center of town, John found The Clam Jammers Pub and decided to get some food and inquire about a place to stay for the week. Upon walking into the pub, John met Karen Essex who was working at the bar and took his order. John stayed far after his meal was done, talking to Karen about the town, the planet, and about her life. She recommended that he stay at the pub in one of the small rooms they had upstairs for rent. From there, fate seemed to take control of his life, and John spent the rest of the week almost exclusively in the pub talking with Karen and enjoying her company. He told her what he could about his research and about the planet he was originally from. By the end of his vacation, John and Karen knew more about each other than most people who had dated for years. He promised her he would return as soon as he could, and she promised she would be there, waiting for him when he did.

John and Karen continued their long distance relationship, and John made it down to Lilac for a week of vacation once every three months. On his third trip, John brought Karen a tablet with a webcam and a subspace transceiver preprogrammed with the encryption code to his own tablet, despite it being against the Coalition

Information Security Policy for any such device to exist outside of the space station. John and Karen talked to each other at least three times a week, and each time it was almost impossible for either of them to disconnect. After two years of this, John decided to change things. He took the shuttle down to Boone, a major city near Lilac, and this time he loaded his Coalition card with over 100,000 credits. He made a quick stop in there before going on to Lilac, and when he presented Karen with his purchase, her immediate answer was a resounding, "Yes!"

Chapter 6

Arriving at the Project X space station after four days of flying through the black, Chance found himself eager for something to do. He didn't normally get anxious about the crew's destinations, nor about any of their missions, but he sensed that this one was going to have its fair share of complications. Sector Whiskey-two-nine had been under strict control of the Coalition for the past of couple decades and was deemed by the government to be a No-Fly Zone. Coming into the area was enough to land a crew in lockup and their ship in impound. Boarding an abandoned Coalition space station with ties to secret research projects, well, that was just a whole 'nother level of trouble.

While in flight, Chance had found himself roaming the ship, checking in with members of the crew and helping out where he could. He helped the doctor bring in her new supplies from the cargo bay and put things away. He went through the ships armory, cleaning and oiling the guns and making sure their magazines were loaded, as well as the spares. He even spent some time in his room reading as well, but he was only truly comfortable when he was helping Astraia in the engine room. He didn't know much about engines or engine repair, but somewhere along the way, Chance had let himself feel closer to Astraia than the rest of the crew these last few months. He chose not to spend time thinking about it, and he never brought it up with her to see where her feelings lay. Instead, he simply made himself available and helped out in the engine room with whatever he could.

Now, looking out the window when the Allons-y dropped out of hyperspace, Chance is the first to see the Coalition's secret space station. The structure itself has been painted black with a signal absorption coating, making it harder to detect its presence for anyone who didn't know where to look. If any ships were to have sent out a ping, it would have simply looked like nothing was there. Chance remembers from his time back in the Marines that SMF ships with this level of secrecy are commonly referred to as N.S. because on radar they appear to be negative space. Trying to see anything specific about it with the black of space as the only backdrop however, is like looking for the outline of a black shirt on a dark rug with the lights off. Unfocusing his eyes, Chance lets the few details that are available come to him so that he can describe them to Astraia, allowing her to continue working on installing the last part she had been waiting to take care of, but couldn't while the ship was in hyper-drive.

"It looks like the main body of the station is a large sphere, probably metallic, but there is no way to tell from here. Encircling the sphere are some tubes. I think they're segmented, and they seem to be feeding in and out of the top and bottom sections of the sphere. The whole thing looks like it's spinning sideways, so I assume there's some sort of artificial gravity on board."

Without looking up, Astraia comments, "That's a little weird, don't you think?"

"What's that?"

"Well, if this thing has been abandoned for over two decades, why is it still moving? Who cares if there is gravity on board? Why not just shut the whole thing down, turn off the lights, and walk away?"

41

Thinking about it, Chance says, "I guess someone thought they would be coming back here, but didn't." Secretly, however, his mind simultaneously provides the alternative option: they didn't have a chance to shut things down before running for their lives. Not saying it, Chance continues watching the space station spin, and it reminds him of a bicycle with one wheel turning on its axis after it has fallen. An eeriness falls across his perceptions, and he hopes that his last thought isn't the truth of this place.

Unworriedly, Astraia comments while continuing her work, "Yeah, I guess."

Over the ship's intercom, Kai's voice comes through, "Astraia, are you down there?"

"Sure am, Captain. What's up?"

"It looks like we might have a bit of a problem getting on board the space station. You think you can come up here and take a look at what I'm seeing?"

Grunting one last time as she pulls up on the wrench to tighten the current part she holds, Astraia's words hiss harshly from her lips, "Sure, just give me a minute down here."

"Ahh, okay," Kai says with confusion and concern. "Is everything okay down there?"

"Yeah, I'm just trying to get this new flux box locked in. Chance, I need you to push hard while I slam this thing in here. I swear sometimes these parts are just too damn tight to fit where they're supposed to go."

With a smile clearly on his lips, Kai says, "See you two in a bit," and Chance realizes that the captain must be picturing something inappropriate about the two of them, purposefully misinterpreting Astraia's last comment.

42

With a bit of muscle, Chance and Astraia lock the new box in and finish the wiring before heading up to the bridge. Once there, Kai says, "I'm not getting anything from the damn sensor sweeps, and from the look of it, the airlock doors here seem to be too big to make a seal with the Allons-y."

Astraia leans over the computer screen, typing away at the keys but gets nothing new from the sensors.

"You're not going to get much from there. It's painted with an absorption coating," says Chance.

Astraia, still typing away, says, "Yeah, I just thought if I modified the ...", but trails off as her fingers continue faster than her lips. Stopping after another minute, she says, "Okay, yeah, that's not going to work," and stands up to look out the bridge windows at the space station for the first time. "Wow, she's pretty big for a research lab."

"No kidding. I've already circled her twice while you two were busy, and I only saw two airlocks. One here on the upper tube, and one on the lower tube on the other side," says Kai.

"Well, Kai, we can either pull up closer and try, or we can float over," suggests Chance.

Free floating through the black is nobody's idea of a good time, and Kai says so. "I really don't want to go out there floating my ass off without even knowing if we can get the airlock open. Let's get closer and see if we can't make the seal fit."

"You got it, Captain. I'll be in the cargo bay. Let me know when we're in position," says Astraia, and then turning to Chance she says, "Chance, you coming? I could use a hand."

Chance looks one last time out the bridge window, and feeling haunted by what he knows is there without seeing it, says, "Sure, right behind you."

Kai maneuvers the Allons-y up alongside the space station's top tube structure and matches its rotation using thrusters while Astraia and Chance suit up for a spacewalk. Once in position, Kai hits the intercom and says, "Okay guys, I've got us about as close as I dare. Go ahead and depressurize."

Astraia speaking into her suit's microphone says, "Got it. Chance, can you check me out one last time?"

Unable to resist, Kai asks, "Isn't that what he's always doing?" but he makes sure the intercom is off before doing so.

"Okay Astraia, you're good," says Chance and then, "Let's see what's out there," just before he hits the depressurize button in the Allons-y's airlock. The air hisses as it is sucked out of the compartment and back into the ship's air tanks, but the suits' helmets muffle the sound and when it is complete and the vents lock down, a green light illuminates above the door.

Chance steps up to the outer door, attaches his carabiner lead, and reaches back for Astraia's. She hands it to him knowing that while it provides no more safety than a seat belt on an airplane, it's at least something in case of turbulence, or in this case, a slip of one's footing. With both lines anchored, Chance turns the wheel on the door until it stops, and he pushes. The door opens, and he feels the vibration through the gloves of the suit but hears no sound, since there's now no air to carry it. The emptiness of space is more than enough to send anyone inexperienced into vertigo, but Chance and Astraia are more accustomed to it than most,

Astraia, having worked on the Allons-y's hull on more than one occasion in the past, and Chance having gotten his experience many times while with the SMF and on some of his more lucrative private contracts. Both of them have spent plenty of time out in open space to be used to the weightlessness, as well as the dizzying effects of not having a horizon or anything else to focus on.

Taking his first step out, Chance grabs hold of the rail and swings his leg so that his magnetic boots line up with the ship's hull. Next he brings his other leg around and clamps it down as well. Standing up, he finds himself perpendicular to Astraia and pointing out from the side of the Allons-y with his head approximately four or five feet away from the space station's airlock. Clicking his suit's microphone on, he says, "Well Kai, I guess you couldn't have gotten us much closer."

"I did what I could," says Kai through the suit's built-in speakers. "So what do you see?"

"Well, Captain," says Astraia, "It looks like Chance is going to bump his head on the space station if he gets any closer but getting in is still going to be a problem. You were right, there is no way this airlock will seal with ours. It's too big for our fittings. Not sure what type of ship used to dock here, but it clearly wasn't using standardized specs. Maybe they were bringing in some extra-large cargo or something. Anyway, we seem to have another problem here as well. There is no outer latch on this airlock. Not sure how we're going to get in."

Knowing that this meant he was going to have to suit up to float over, too, once she got it open, and dreading it, Kai replies to her last statement, "Well, I guess they didn't want company.

It was probably designed to be an internal security system. That way they could control who gains access from the inside."

"That would figure, what with the type of research Egnarts eluded to," says Astraia.

"Hey, Astraia, you see that?" asks Chance as he points up to a small black square nearby on the left side of the airlock.

"Not from here. What is it?"

"I don't know. It looks like it might be a keypad or something."

"Can you describe it to me?" asks Astraia.

"It's a black box, looks about four inches across by five inches down. In the middle, I think it's divided up into nine small sections and one long one."

"Okay, that sounds like a keypad. Hold on. I got an idea."

Chance listens to Astraia's murmurings as they come through over his speakers for a minute, while she rummages around in the toolkit on the wall of the airlock, and then he hears her say with excited glee, "Got it. Okay, Chance, are you there?"

Laughing into the ship's microphone, Kai says, "Well, he had better not have gone out for a walk. I hear the neighborhood is a bit dark in these parts."

"Very funny, Captain," says Astraia, "Chance, can you give me a lift?"

Reaching down, Chance pulls Astraia up out of the ship's airlock with one arm and sets her down next to him, holding her until her magnetic boots click to the hull like his own. The two of them assess their situation, and Astraia seems to calculate their distance to the space station before she says,

"Okay, here's what were going to do. I'm going to demagnetize my boots for a minute so you can lift me over your head, upside down. When I get close enough, I'll reengage my boots, and stick over there."

"All right, and then what?" asks Chance, figuring the plan already sounded a bit crazy.

Pulling out the huge wrench from the bag at her side, she says, "and then I'm going to pick the lock."

"Pick?" Chance questions.

Smiling, Astraia says, "Yeah, I figured I would try the gentle approach. If this doesn't work, we still have the other airlock."

"I guess so," says Chance, and then, "Captain, you getting all of this?"

"I read you, and for the record, you're both crazy."

Astraia demagnetizes her boots and begins to float up from the hull of the ship till she's even with Chance's height, saying, "I told you this would work. Look, I'm almost there already."

Shaking his head a bit, Chance reaches out to hold her hands, and then lets her begin the slow handstand she has planned. Due to their weightless environment, he goes very slowly, knowing that any extra thrust can put her out of control and force her to overshoot her mark. When she's just about end over end with Chance, she attempts to turn on her boots, but nothing happens. Kicking out, she finds she cannot reach the space station beneath her.

"What's wrong, Astraia?"

"I guess it's a little farther away than we thought. You're going to have to give me a push and let me float."

Hearing this, Kai chimes in, "Are you two nuts? Why don't you just get back in here, and we'll try the other airlock?"

"Captain, we're already out here, and you probably won't be able to get this close again."

"Astraia, I hope you're not doubting my skills?"

"Of course not, Captain. It's just that I only need about another foot or so. I might as well try."

"All right. Give it a try. Chance, make sure she doesn't do anything stupid out there."

Replying needlessly, Chance says, "Will do, Kai." Then looking up to Astraia and meeting her eyes, he gives her a nod. Astraia nods back, and he gives her a light push releasing her upside down into the space between.

The trip across takes nearly two full minutes, two full minutes where Chance doesn't let out a single breath. The gap, however, turns out to be nearly seven feet across by the time she touches down. The paint's special coating has done its job, deceiving them against the background of space even this close.

Giving with her knees as she sets down, Astraia locks her boots onto the side of the space station. Once in place and secure, she bends down to examine the black box. Seeing that it is, in fact, an electronic touchpad with a numerical code lock, just as Chance described, she debates the likelihood of guessing the code and quickly dismisses the idea. Not knowing the code or even how many digits it has, she says, "Well, I guess I'll be hot wiring it," and pulls out the oversized wrench.

Pulling back, Astraia swings the wrench down and slams it into the side of the pad like a professional golfer on a 500-yard fairway. The paint on the pad scratches, but the case holds tight. Astraia winds up for another strike and swings. This time, the cover slips off and flies into space, exposing the wiring beneath. She puts the wrench back in her bag and leans down for a closer look. After a moment, she pulls out a pair of wire strippers and unsheathes a small segment of the wire's outer jacket.

"Captain," Astraia calls.

"What did you find?"

"It looks like I might be able to get her open. They used basic copper."

Kai says, "Figures they used the cheapest materials. Okay, do what you do, and let me know when you got that thing open." Kai then programs the Allons-y to calculate the distance from the airlock to Astraia's radio and then uses that as the distance setting to maintain from the space station, since the sensors couldn't detect it when they arrived. Locking the program in, he begins walking down to the cargo bay to get the Doctor and invite her to come along.

Astraia cuts a couple of the wires and traces them back to the pad and its circuit board before finally selecting the yellow one. As she does so, Chance feels the pressure in his head - the same pressure that he always feels when something is about to go wrong, a feeling that he has always listened to in the past and has always saved his life, but this time it's not coming from him. It's coming from her.

Before he can say anything, Astraia shorts out the wire in her hand against the side of the ship, using its own absorption coating against it. The airlock doors begin to open, and Astraia gives herself a little cheer before a blast of air rockets out and knocks her loose from the side of the space station. Only after she is free floating with an unknown velocity does she realize that the airlock in the space station must have been pressurized. Without consciously going there, Astraia remembers an old physics class she took over a decade ago where she learned about the effects of tension and realizes that physics will not bend its laws, not even for her. She feels the line of her suit go taut right before it snaps loose, leaving her to the merciless cold blackness of the space beyond.

Chance, while standing on the Allons-y still in direct line of the space station's airlock, is knocked backward as well, forcing him to fall into the open airlock of the Allons-y. As he does, he reaches out and catches the handrail preventing himself from falling all the way down to the inner doors, while at the same time, providing himself with an excellent view of Astraia's anchor line snapping off, just above the carabiner's latch.

Chance allows his training to kick in as he grabs the railing with his second hand, grunts and pulls hard, jettisoning himself out of the ship's airlock. He clicks his magnetic boots back on and cranks their pull over a hundred percent. When he hits the outer hull of the Allons-y, he begins to run as fast as he can, pumping both his arms and legs like pistons. Gaining speed across the side of the ship, Chance instinctively calculates his distance from both Astraia and the space station above before he jumps into the space between and switches his boots off. Hanging before him and growing smaller by the second, he watches Astraia float away from the Allons-y, the space station, and from himself. In mid-flight, Chance torques his body and puts himself in a somersault spin, flipping end-over-end. Squeezing his legs against his chest, he waits until he is close enough for the insanity of his plan to kick in.

Astraia watches as Chance spins through space and watches as her lead trails uselessly away from the ship. Despite not believing in any particular God or not having attended any services for one religion or another in quite some time, she begins to pray quietly to whomever might answer her, "Dear Lord, please help me."

When he is less than a foot away from the space station, Chance pulls his legs in even tighter, using the centrifugal force to speed himself up even faster. He waits for one more full rotation to spin him around before unfolding as fast as he can, slamming his feet into the side of the space station and launching himself out towards Astraia. Now he has just one option before him. It's the only option he had to begin with if he was going to save her, but it's all he's going to need, just this one chance.

Coming down from the bridge, Captain Kai looks out the window, curious to see if they have opened the airlock, only to see his worse nightmare coming true. Chance and Astraia are both floating through space at an incredible speed, and Astraia's line to the ship isn't attached. He stops where he is, dumbfounded by the sight, scared for his crew, his friends, and unable to do anything but watch as Chance leaps off the side of the space station.

Knowing that he can never catch up to her in time, and that his own anchor line is quickly running out, Chance times his jump so that his path puts him directly in line with the middle of Astraia's anchor. In space, there is no friction. Nothing slows you down, so whatever speed you start out at is the same speed you'll be going a minute later, an hour later, even a year later. As Astraia continues to float out into the black, however, her trailing rope continues to slip past that midpoint and farther away from him.

Back on the Allons-y, Kai cusses, "Oh shit, he's not going to make it."

Chance begins to feel his own line running out of slack, and as it snaps him to a complete stop at its full extension, he clamps his hand down on the last three inches of Astraia's failed anchor. Her added weight and acceleration apply more force and stress to his line, and for a split second, it seems like his line will give, too, but it holds, allowing Chance to begin reeling Astraia back towards him, hand over hand.

Once she is returned to him, Astraia wraps herself around him the best she can with the bulk of the space suits in the way and thanks him repeatedly. Chance attaches what remains of her anchor to his own line, allows her to cling to his back, both for added safety as well as for each other's comfort and reassurance. Then using his own anchor rope, he begins to pull them both back towards the safety of the Allons-y.

Chapter 7

Before coming back on board, Chance reconnects Astraia's line to the outer handle of the Allons-y and then jumps across to the space station to tie off the other end to the handle inside its airlock. Using this as a guide rope, he returns to the Allons-y, closes the outer doors, and re-pressurizes the airlock so that he and Astraia could reenter. Now back on the Allons-y, thirty minutes after the events with the airlock, the Captain, Astraia, and Chance are sitting around with their gear packed, waiting for Oska in the cargo bay.

"You're sure you're okay there, Astraia?" asks Kai.

"Yeah, I'm all right, Captain."

Turning to Chance, Kai says, "That was some seriously crazy shit you pulled out there."

"It's what needed to be done. If I would have thought about it, I wouldn't have made it in time, and she needed me."

"Still, you're a crazy bastard, and I'm sure glad you're working for me."

"You just don't believe you could ever find a mechanic as good as me to keep the Allons-y flying," jokes Astraia.

"That's exactly it," Kai jokes back, hoping that a bit of banter will help de-stress the situation.

"Yeah, well you're right. You never could find another mechanic this good," says Astraia with a smile, showing both of them she was really going to be okay.

Before Kai can get out his next joke, however, he is interrupted by the sound of Oska coming down the stairs from the hallway leading to her quarters. Looking up, Kai stifles a laugh as he watches her carry in a fully-loaded backpack strapped to her shoulders, two bulky canisters with who knows what's inside in her left hand, a couple of canteen-like bottles strapped around her chest, a complete medical kit in her right hand, a rifle and sword hanging off her left shoulder, and a large coil of rope hanging over her chest. As she steps off the last stair, she looks like she is about to fall over from the weight of it all, and the rest of the crew chortles to themselves at the sight while she straightens herself with what dignity she can muster.

Controlling the laugh that wants to bubble out of him, but unable to keep from smiling, Kai asks, "Are we invading a small country?"

"No, I just wanted to be prepared. The last mission you took everyone on, we found ourselves ducked down behind a rock with nowhere to go but over the very high cliff in front of us while a team of outlaws continued to fire at us."

"Oska, that is not going to happen this time."

Glaring at him, Oska asks, "Isn't that what you said before we went out on that very same mission?"

"Actually, I said we would be fine with what we had, and we were, obviously," waving his hand down his frame. "See, no extra holes."

With one last attempt to help her case, Oska says, "Well, what do we really know about this place?"

"It's a research facility. It will probably just be a bunch of hallways, labs, and junk. Hell, the place has been abandoned for over twenty years. We go in, find the computer, download the Doc's stuff, and head back."

Conceding, Oska asks, "Okay. What do I need then?"

Astraia, coming to her rescue without laughing, says, "Actually, you have some good stuff here. We just don't need all of it. I think the flashlights are a good idea. We don't know what the power situation is over there, and the rope might come in handy. It certainly did while we were getting the airlock open."

Unwilling to stay on that subject and the potential loss that could have happened, Chance says, "I'm bringing a weapon. If you want to carry, it can't hurt."

Smiling, Oska says, "I did have a purpose for everything I packed, but I guess I did overdo it a bit."

"We are going to have to wear the suits to get over there, and then we can see what the inside is like. I'm betting since there was pressure, the inside probably still has breathable air, so we won't need the canisters of air you have here," Astraia says as she helps Oska to take them off.

"All right, so what else do we actually need?" asks Kai.

"I figured we should bring our own power supply just in case the computer mainframe isn't getting any juice and a laptop to interface with it as back up, maybe some spare cables, too."

Chance suggests, "I was thinking a crowbar and a multipurpose tool just in case we need to pry open any doors or if something mechanical isn't hooked up. Astraia, you have those in your bag already, right?"

"Yeah, I picked them up while I was in engineering along with four Wrist Comms," Astraia says while showing the rest of the crew the communications units that look more like palm sized computers. The Wrist Comms were picked up after they had one too many close calls, and the rest of the crew convinced Kai to splurge after they got paid. Each unit is capable of showing maps with accurate real time tracking of any other units sharing the same codes, recording and sending sound files, and acting like short wave radios between other synced units.

Adding his two cents, Kai says, "The med kit isn't a bad idea either, but it looks like you have enough stuff in there to perform major surgery. I'd suggest we don't need it at all, but knowing how I get a bit clumsy sometimes, perhaps you could just trim it down to the basics."

"Oh, yeah," Astraia says as if she just remembered, "We also have to bring Doctor Egnarts's hard drive."

The crew repacks the backpacks and puts on their suits. Each of them checks another shipmate to make sure that everything is sealed properly before entering the airlock hatchway. Once inside, Chance depressurizes the room, and they all use the guide rope he tied off earlier to get across to the space station. Unable to close the airlock with the rope tied to the inner handle, Kai quickly ties the rope off on one of the loose wires from the panel Astraia destroyed before closing the hatch manually from the inside.

With the hatch closed, the airlock begins to repressurize, and air flows through the vents above the crew. The process takes longer than depressurizing on the Allons-y, but Chance assumes that is a result of the age of the equipment and its lack of use. Once complete, a small LED light to the right of the inner door illuminates green and the inner doors begin to open automatically, allowing the crew their first look into the Project X facility.

The interior is completely dark, and the crew cannot ascertain anything about the space before them. Seeing this, Kai sings, "Hello, hello, hello, is there anybody in there?" to break the tension and pay tribute to an old band from Earth's 20th century.

After no reply comes, Oska and Chance shine their flashlights into the darkness, and Kai and Astraia follow suit. The light seems like it is having difficulty penetrating the inky blackness, and the four flashlights show them very little of the hallway before them. Kai begins taking the first steps in, keeping his eyes on the ground mostly to avoid any risk of tripping, with Chance following close behind, and the girls taking up the rear. As Oska exits the airlock, the inner doors close behind her, and the crew continues forward.

Suddenly, just before Kai steps up to the junction between this hall and the one perpendicular to it, Chance grabs his shoulder and in a harsh whisper says, "Stop."

"What is it?" asks Kai, as he barely keeps from falling backwards at the force of Chance's pull on him.

"Look."

Looking to the ground, Kai sees nothing in front of him, and so he turns the light to the right, following it with his eyes up the wall and to the ceiling. Seeing nothing, Kai asks, also in a whisper but unsure why, "What am I looking for?"

"Drop your light back to the ground and look at the wall."

After a moment, Kai's eyes begin to adjust from looking at the spot where his light was shining to looking into the blackness at his right. It takes his eyes another minute to clear the spots of the ghost image away before he notices faint red lights which seem to be coming from three points on the wall: one at shoulder level, one about waist high, and one even with his knees. "What are they?"

Still whispering, Chance says, "Security system."

Coming up from behind to try and get a better look, Astraia covers her flashlight and asks in a similarly conspiratorial hush, "Did you say there was a security system?"

Without looking back, Chance still in a whisper says, "It looks that way. Probably self-activated when we opened the airlock."

"What's the big deal?" Astraia asks. "It's not like someone from security is coming up here to arrest us. The place has been abandoned for like twenty years or something, right?"

Thinking about it, Chance says, "Wait here a second," and walks forward to stand in front of the lights. Taking a length of rope about twelve inches long from the coil across his chest, he cuts it using his boot knife and then drops it from just above the highest of the three lights. As the rope falls past the first light, it splits in two. Passing the next light, one of the rope pieces splits again. Finally, as each of the remaining pieces continue down, they pass in front of the lowest light and are again severed cleanly before hitting the floor.

Behind him, Kai lets out an appreciative whistle.

Looking back, Chance says, "They built this so there was no need for security men to come arrest anyone, but I bet they had a damn fine janitor on staff to clean up the mess afterwards."

"Thanks for not letting me walk into that."

"No problem, Kai, but the question now is, how are we going to get past it?"

From the back, Oska says, "I think I might have found the answer to that. Astraia, can you take a look at this?"

"What did you find?"

"Look at this wall here. It's different from the rest. I think it's some kind of panel."

Moving closer to Oska, Astraia examines the area she has her flashlight trained on and realizes that it is a black flat panel computer interface built into the wall. Finding the power button in the bottom left corner, Astraia turns it on and watches as the screen comes to life and the system's operating system boots up.

When the system is up and running, a synthesized female computer voice says, "Welcome to the Coalition X-Site Research Facility," as a white circular logo appears in the middle of the screen spinning with a thin black 'X' inside of it.

Unsure if the computer would respond to voice commands, Kai said, "Computer, turn off the lasers."

Not really expecting anything to happen, but curious all the same, everyone looks back towards the three red lights for a moment. Seeing nothing change, Kai says, "You can't blame me for trying."

Stepping up to the panel, Astraia says, "Let me see if I can," and begins to tap on the screen before finishing the rest of her sentence. The screen responds by showing her a list of menu commands consisting of Location, Directory, Systems, and Maps. "Now, we're getting somewhere. Okay, what should we look at first?"

Kai says, "How about we get some lights turned on?"

"Okay. Give me a second." Astraia pushes the Systems menu key and watches as the menu disappears to be replaced by a new screen. Across the top of the screen she reads 'Floor P1 Systems', and below that there are four new options, three in a gray text font and one in black. The three gray options read 'Airlock', 'Life Support', and 'Security' while the black option reads 'Lights'. Pressing 'Lights', a new screen comes up with an 'On / Off' toggle in the middle currently showing 'Off' as its default and 'Back' and 'Home' options at the bottom. Pressing the toggle to 'On', the lights above the crew come on.

Kai says, "Now that's what I'm talking about. Nice work, Astraia."

The computer screen, however, shows several errors scrolling up the side of the screen, each with the same error 5005, error code.

Oska asks, "What is error code 5005?"

Astraia touches the error code, and a brief description comes over the speaker. "Some systems in this sector have malfunctioned." Turning her head to Oska, Astraia says, "I guess some of the lights are out on this floor."

"Well, at least we have some lights," says Kai. Then he suggests, "Now how about getting those lasers turned off so we can get on with this."

Without clearing the error codes, Astraia presses the 'Back' button. All of the error codes disappear, and the screen returns to the previous options. Next she tries to press the 'Security' option in gray text and receives a new message saying, "All security systems have been rerouted to the main Control Room on the Lower Deck, Floor 1."

"Looks like we're locked out from here, Captain. That's probably why the text was a different color."

Not bothering to hide his feelings, Kai says, "Well, isn't that great. If we can't get through, I guess we'll have to go back to the Allons-y and try the other airlock."

"Or we could try the vent," says Chance, as he looks pointedly up towards the ceiling.

Kai follows his line of sight up to the large ventilation grate on the wall above their heads and repeats, "Or we could try the vent. Nice, but we can't get through wearing these suits." Turning to Oska he asks, "Oska, can you check the air quality?"

Oska begins rummaging through her bag and pulls out a portable Volatile Organic Compound Analyzer and Atmospheric Sampler saying, "Sure thing, Captain." After a moment of checking, Oska says, "The VOCA shows it's clear, and the air looks like it's breathable."

Not wanting to wear the suit any longer than he has to, Chance looks to Kai and nods before he begins to remove his helmet. He hands the helmet off to Kai and lets out the breath he is holding before taking in a short test breath with the rest of the crew watching. Suddenly, Chance begins coughing.

Kai immediately brings Chance's helmet back up, ready to push it over his head and clear the suit with the reserve tank, but Chance holds up his hand and coughs again before beginning to breathe normally.

"Air's a bit stale, but it's breathable," says Chance.

The rest of the crew waits another minute as if to make sure, before taking off their own helmets and taking their first breath of the space station's air. Each of them experiences a moment of coughing as the dry, stagnant air hits their lungs but slowly recover.

Chance, already getting used to the air quality, begins removing his suit and sorting his bag so that he can leave it behind in case he gets into trouble. The only things he leaves out to take with him are his sword which he straps to his back, a twenty-five foot rope he hangs over his shoulder, his Wrist Comm., and the crowbar.

After sliding his bag off to one side of the hall, Chance stands up and says, "I'll go first, check things out, and radio back."

"Sounds good," says Kai, and he continues to try to fold his suit into something manageable and finally resorts to just stuffing most of it into his helmet, leaving a pant leg hanging out across the floor when he sets it down.

Astraia steps up to the wall with the vent and says, "If you give me a boost, I can at least open up the vent here for you."

Agreeing, Chance bends down and takes one of Astraia's feet in his hands, allowing her to stand while leaning against him and the wall to reach the vent screws with her multi-tool. Each of the four screws comes out easily, and she hands the vent cover down to Oska before bending down to set her hands on Chance's shoulders and lowering herself to the ground.

Hopping up to the now open vent shaft, Chance grabs hold of the bottom of the vent and pulls himself up and in, in one smooth and almost silent move, not really trying to demonstrate his skills but doing so all the same. He sees that the dimensions of it are larger than his frame and easily crawls forward on his hands and knees. At the first junction, Chance finds a vent cover just ahead and looks through to see what's on the other side. Through the grated vent slats Chance sees inside the sphere's main structure and can't believe his eyes. Far below him, easily over a thousand feet, he sees what looks like another planet. The spinning of the space station has allowed dirt and vegetation to stick high up the sides of the sphere's interior forming a bowl-like landmass with a perfectly calm body of water in the middle. The land is covered with a variety of species of trees and grasses, and angling his head upward, he sees that the ceiling of the sphere is illuminated with a bright artificial sun-like light source which appears to be emitted from the walls themselves. Chance realizes that this is not so much a space station he is in, but rather a self-contained artificial world.

While Chance can remove the vent's cover, he sees no use in doing so at the moment. The now seeming small amount of rope he has brought with him would prove insufficient to climb down to the ground below him, and training or no training, falling close to a thousand feet would kill almost anyone.

Radioing back to the crew, Chance says, "You are not going to believe what I just found."

"Tell me it's a million credits just lying out in the open, waiting for us to pick them up and spend them as we may," answers Kai.

"Noooo," replies Chance, drawing out the word slowly but in an amused manner for Kai's benefit, as if he found the joke to be funny.

"What is it, Chance?" asks Astraia.

"It's a bit hard to describe, but essentially, there is a whole world in here."

"What are you talking about?" asks Oska.

"I mean that inside this sphere there's dirt, land, trees, forests, and probably a whole lot more. You're all going to have to see it for yourselves."

"You want us to come up through the vent?" asks Kai.

"No, not yet," replies Chance. "I still haven't found a way out. If you all get in here behind me, we're going to have a hell of a time if we find we went the wrong way and have to turn around." Looking down the junction, he sees a faint light coming through the side of the vent and says, "Give me a minute. I think I see a way out."

Chance turns left and heads down the junction to the next vent opening. Looking through, he sees none of the sphere interior but rather a small room with a few furnishings. Pulling out the crowbar, Chance pries open the vent and lets it drop to the bed below him before radioing back once more to the crew and saying, "Okay, I found what look like someone's quarters. If you come through the vent, you will want to take the first junction heading left to get here. Bring the stuff when you come."

Chapter 8

Working interactively using the gloves as an interface wasn't something that came naturally to most. For Jack, it felt like an extension of himself. The only way he could get any closer to his computers would be if he could 'jack in' as they used to show people doing in the movies from Earth's late twentieth century, but that technology hadn't been developed safely yet. Interfacing like this, every movement of his hands was calculated and sent to the computer where it was interpreted and defined as some intended function. He had voice recognition software on the computer as well, which allowed his vocal commands through his ThinMic to simultaneously help operate the system, but he currently had that application off-line. Jack had worked on his computer for years, upgrading the computer's processor several times, and it was currently running a 512-chip optical code division multiple access system using superstructured fiber gratings encoders and time-gating detection with components nearly on the microscopic level, and he still felt, at times, that it was lagging behind him.

Jack had already spent the better part of three days hacking his way through the Coalition's servers, digitally sneaking his way through backdoors and decrypting old passwords that system administrators had failed to wipe from the databases' list of authorized users. The amount of information in the system was staggering, and Jack found himself several times having to backtrack his way out of areas that led only to dead ends or alternate areas of government secrecy. Heavily redacted PDF scans and video files with jumpy time codes showing where parts had been cut out or spliced in were all stored onto his hard drive for later inspection, once deemed irrelevant to his current project. Jack worked day and night with near obsession, trying to uncover the identity of Dr. Hue, his mystery partner, and what their organization was, but finding out anything was proving to be near impossible. Jack would only admit to the near impossibility of it, never the idea that it might actually be impossible. He believed firmly that once something had been made digital, it could always be recovered. Nothing digital ever disappeared completely.

On the fourth day, Jenny saw the tension building in Jack and dressed herself in a pair of black micro mini shorts made of fishnet and top to match. The clothing was so skimpy she would have had more on if she had simply unspooled a reel of dental floss and draped it across her. She walked over to him, swaying her hips as she did so, to ask if he would like her to do anything for him. Jack knew this was all a part of her programming, like many of her other behaviors meant to simulate caring, compassion, and affection, but he allowed himself the illusion and spoke with her, not as if she were a robotic companion, but rather as he would any other living breathing person. It was, after all, part of the 'girlfriend experience' he had paid for when ordering her from the wide range of models and personality types available on the site three years ago.

"Jenny, thank you for the offer, but really I just want to find out who this Dr. Hue was."

Her software sent a signal through to her internal vocal speakers which added a slight purr to her voice as she asked, "Are you sure, Jack?" in a more seductive tone.

Jack bent his left pinky finger in until it touched his palm, turning off the glove's motion recognition software before running his hand through his hair. Paying little attention to Jenny's flirtation, he distractedly said, "Yeah," while looking at the latest file he had downloaded. Then he rethought his decision and said, "Actually, could you get me some food and something to drink?"

Ready to serve, Jenny asked, "What would you like me to get you, Jack?"

"Ahh," he said, thinking about it for a second, and then, "How about a shake?"

Jenny had come preprogrammed with hundreds of thousands of recipes from over a hundred fifty different cultures as part of her standard package, but Jack had gone through and deleted all of those in which he had no interest in the first week. After further refinement, Jack had narrowed Jenny's knowledge of world cuisines down to a list of about twenty-two options, making it simpler to ask for things that he would actually enjoy without having to list off all of the ingredients he did or did not want in them. If he asked for a pizza, she knew he meant pepperoni and pineapple. If he asked for a burger, she knew he wanted it made with soy meat, and not pig, buffalo, cow, or kangaroo, the last being popular on a small continent in the southern hemisphere of Earth a couple hundred years ago. So when Jack asked for a shake, Jenny knew that he meant a chocolate, peanut butter, and banana flavored shake with a caffeine and vitamin supplement mixed in to ensure that he was both energized and nutritionally sufficient for a while. Jenny disappeared to the lower level kitchen, allowing Jack to continue his work.

After a few minutes, Jack selected the current file as a whole, and with a flick of his right hand, dismissed it to one of the screens off to the side where it would most likely end up being stored to a server in the basement. The Coalition had been busy since its creation, and as any other government had done in the past, it had made sure to secretly position people and materials throughout the various sectors as part of not just one, but several contingency plans in case things ever started to go south. In addition to these plans that it had made for itself when the Coalition was first being created, it absorbed all of the state and government files, both secret and not so secret, from the powers that signed the treaty. So scanning the database had uncovered everything from Earth's past governments as well. Needless to say, finding any one secret without knowing exactly where to look was like looking for a needle in a landfill full of bio-hazardous waste comprised completely of needles.

With latest file dispatched, Jack folded both pinkies down to touch his palms and took off his gloves just as Jenny reemerged carrying his shake. Taking the shake, Jack thanked Jenny, set his gloves on the counter, and sat down on the couch leaving room for her to sit next to him. She sat next to him and waited for him to say something. He absentmindedly stroked her skin and let his mind wander through the things he had learned in his research. Jack wasn't used to problems without solutions. For that matter, most solutions came to him in a matter of seconds. Even the eight-sided Rubik cube, affectionately named Octorubiks, only took Jack six minutes and twenty-seven seconds to finish. Puzzles were his thing, and he had never encountered one which he couldn't solve. His mind still racing, he stared at his computer screens, seeing nothing, just letting it go, allowing free association the chance to make the connection for him as he sipped at his shake.

"Jack?"

"Yes, Jenny?"

"Suppose you do find this doctor. Then what?"

Swallowing after taking another long drink, he said, "Then I find out what he was doing for the Coalition."

"What I mean is, are you going to go see him?"

"See him?" Jack asked confused. "No, I'm just looking for information. Why do you ask?"

"I wanted to make sure you were okay."

"Of course I'm all right," replied Jack. "What would make you think I'm not okay?"

"Because you're looking for a doctor."

"Not that kind of doctor. There are lots of different kinds of doctors. Some doctors work on people, but some do work on math or science. Some people are doctors of history and literature."

"What about space?" asked Jenny. "Do they have doctors that work on space, too?"

"Sure, there are cosmologists who work on solving the mysteries of the universe," said Jack, and then the synapses in his head made the connection and he said, "and there are doctors who study plants and animals from outer space. That's it."

"What's it, Jack?"

"Non-terrestrial genetics," said Jack, "That's it." He kissed her excitedly and set down what remained of his shake on the small table before standing up. Walking over to the counter, Jack slipped his gloves back on as he continued talking, "It's the study of genetic material found on other planets before they are terra-formed. Some people believe that by studying the genetics of alien life, be it plant, animal, or something else, that we will find better medicines and cures. Others believe that we will find the secret to life on Earth, and somehow be able to solve the debate about where we all come from."

Gloves back in place, Jack touched all five fingers together on both hands and held them for two full seconds until the blue LEDs lit up on the ends of each finger, signaling that the gloves were on and connected to the computer. Without looking back to Jenny who remained on the couch, Jack said, "Some people back then called that type of work xenogenetics. That's got to be it. Thank you, Jenny."

Jenny continued to sit on the couch, and even though Jack wasn't looking at her, she only allowed herself a faint, knowing smile.

Chapter 9

In the room, Astraia could see the bed everyone had jumped down on, an empty dresser in the corner, and a small bathroom off to the right. She had been the last one through the ventilation shaft, and now the crew of the Allons-y stood together in what was once someone's sleeping quarters settling their packs back onto their shoulders.

Kai had had the most difficulty getting through the vent shaft because his shoulders rubbed against both sides as he crawled through, and he was forced to turn sideways at several points where the vent narrowed or turned so that he could squeeze his larger frame through. With everyone now in the room, he gave them a minute to collect themselves before asking, "We ready?" to the whole crew at once.

"Ready," says Oska.

Clicking the chest strap closed on her pack, Astraia chimes in with cheery, "Ready, Captain."

"Yup," says Chance, almost indifferently.

Kai opens the door, and after a quick check left and right, he exits the room turning to the left. The rest of the crew follows him with Oska directly behind him, then Astraia, and Chance taking the rear position.

Outside the room, the crew finds a long hallway with a gentle curve to it running in both directions with doors on both sides spaced unevenly. As Kai continues on, clearly having chosen to go left, Chance notices the black nameplate with white numbers on the wall next to the room they just exited from, thirteen, and hopes that this isn't a sign of bad luck yet to come.

Chance takes a peak behind himself and the rest of the group, before following Astraia further down the hall, as standard operating procedure.

Curious, Kai tries the handle of the next door, the one marked twelve, and finds that the door is locked. Looking back to Oska he asks, "What do think, skip it?"

"Well, it's locked, and the place has been abandoned. Unless you want to waste time prying the door open, yeah."

"Okay," Kai agrees, and then louder to the rest of the crew, Kai says, "Twelve is locked, moving on. We'll check out the open doors first to see if there is anything worth salvaging for the ship. Then if there's time, we can check these locked ones on the way back."

Chance signals from the back of the line that he hears Kai, and the group continues forward on to the next door. This door, marked eleven on the outside, opens when Kai tries it. As the door swings inward, Kai steps into the darkness far enough to allow Oska and Astraia to follow, and to let his eyes adjust.

Coming up to the door, Chance peeks in and gets the feeling that this set of quarters is somehow neater than the last one, but remains in the hall standing guard out of habit and asks, "Well, Kai, what you got in there?"

Looking around the room, Kai uses his flashlight until he spots the light switch and flicks it on. After another quick scan, Kai says, "It's more of the same - bed, dresser, desk, and bathroom. Nothing exciting."

Astraia notices a thin layer of dust across the surface of the dresser just before she opens it and checks the drawers. After a minute she says, "Dresser's empty."

Opening the desk, Oska begins to say the same thing and then cuts herself off short when a piece of paper in the center drawer catches her eye. "Looks like I got something here." Picking up the paper, Oska scans the text and says, "It's a receipt for transport. Looks like someone, a Mr. Daniel Daggett, was planning to move two large crates from the planet Arina to the town of Red Shore over on Baalc. The receipt is dated from just over twenty years ago."

"Well, that fits with what we were told about this place," says Kai. "Anything else in there?"

Checking the last of the drawers, Oska says, "No, it's all been cleaned out."

"All right. Let's get going."

Turning left, Kai continues to lead the crew through a series of crew quarters, some locked and some not, finding little to nothing different among most of them. Some rooms have a few different furnishings, and are arranged however their last occupant saw fit to do so, but most of them are cleaned out. In the fifth room, Astraia notices a series of paperback books written by Jonathan Maberry on a shelf, and she wonders why the person who was staying here didn't take the books with him or her to wherever he or she was moving to when they left. These books must have cost a few credits and been someone's indulgent little habit seeing how all books for the past hundred years are published only in digital format, not to mention from the copyright info they were published before 2015, so they were beyond antique. Even though they looked to be like some sort of science fiction collection, which wasn't her preferred reading, Astraia sets them on the ground before loading them into her backpack, figuring she might read them one day or possibly trade them for engine parts if she can find a collector who wants them. Just as she is about to stand up, she catches site of a carving in the underside of the desk and notices a message carved into the wood which reads:

'KFP loves EJB'

Having no idea what its meaning is, she stands back up and puts her backpack on before leaving. As she exits the room, Astraia hears Kai two rooms further down saying, "No, really, it's funny."

Catching up, Astraia asks, "What's funny?"

Pointing to the numbered plate on the door, Kai says, "Look, it's room Juan."

Astraia looks to the door, sees it reads 'one', and doesn't get it. Looking back to the captain, she says, "That's not right, in Spanish it would be uno."

"Hello, I know that. I'm the one with the Hispanic heritage here. It's just funny because there are always jokes about the name Juan being used to replace anything that sounds remotely like it. Ever hear the one about the Mexican martial artist?"

Astraia shakes her head and says, "No, what about him?"

Laughing at the punch line, he almost fails to get it out before saying, "He studied Tae Juan Do."

"It's not as funny as you make it seem."

"Okay, okay, try this one. What do you call it when two Mexicans play basketball?"

Shrugging her shoulders, Astraia asks, "What?"

"Juan on Juan."

Giving only a smirk, Astraia says, "That's a little better, but still, not as funny as you make it out to be."

"You just don't get it because you're not Hispanic."

Stepping up, Chance says, "You know you don't have to give us more ammo to make fun of you, Kai."

"Oh, forget it," says Kai before he turns and heads up the hall to check some more doors.

The tenth door, not labeled with a number, has a sign which reads 'Kitchen'. Kai approaches it figuring that there may be something worth salvaging for the Allons-y. Stepping in, he finds that the lights in here are already on. He assumes that this is a communal room for everyone's use, and they are always on. That, or they simply didn't flip the switch off when they left. He thinks nothing more of it as he proceeds to give the place a quick once over, and Oska comes in just behind him. Hanging from the ceiling is a rack holding several used looking pots and pans. Along the left wall stands a pair of refrigerators, two stoves with built in ovens, and two long work tables with cutting boards fitted into their tops. On the right wall several cabinets are lined up along with another work space for people to prepare their meals.

Oska opens the cabinet closest to the door only to find a few freeze dried packets of food and half of a box worth of unopened plastic water bottles. Uninterested, she closes the door and waits for Kai.

Kai is mentally trying to estimate the weight and dimensions of one of the stoves, considering the option to salvage it from the space station and replace the old one on the Allons-y when Astraia comes in. "What did you find, Captain?"

"Kitchen stove. I was just trying to figure if we could upgrade the one on the ship."

Looking it over briefly, Astraia turns one on and feels the heat coming up almost immediately. She clicks the stove back to off and says, "Looks like they work fine and upgrading sounds good, but these won't work. The plugs are different than what we have on the ship. I could swap them out, but we might have a problem down the road if the transformer supplying the juice to one of these things gives. Besides, it looks like it might be too big to fit where our current one is."

"Figures," says Kai in a huff as he realizes his idea is bust, and he walks over to the refrigerator, partly out of habit and partly out of curiosity, to see what's inside. Upon opening the refrigerator, Kai is assaulted with a smell that nearly drops him to his knees, and despite himself, he opens his mouth to exclaim, "Oh God, that stinks." As he closes his mouth again, he finds that the smell itself has left its own taste in his mouth, and he begins to dry heave as it registers what he must be tasting. It's clear that the food in the refrigerator has not seen the light of day in some time, and most of it has grown its own colonies of colorful bacteria which now compete for space on the shelves in large overgrown lumps. Shutting the door as quickly as he can, Kai tells everyone, "Out! Get out! Save yourselves," and Astraia and Oska both laugh their way into the hall to tell Chance.

Kai follows the girls back into the hall a minute later, once he has the dry heaving under control, and Chance says with a smile, "You know, I hear the penicillin here is wonderful."

"Ha, ha, ha," Kai mocks, while the rest of the crew giggle at his display and then says, "Come on," before turning left up the hall.

Walking another sixty feet through the hallway, Kai notices a vertical seam in the wall to his right and realizes that it must be the opening to a pair of elevator doors. Looking around the doors, Kai fails to notice an up or down button but does see a slim plastic slot in the wall with a small red LED lit up just above it. Calling back to her, Kai says, "Hey Astraia, come take a look at this."

Walking up to meet Kai, Astraia looks over the reader, and then says, "Captain, if we want in here, we're going to need a card key."

Slightly exasperated, Kai asks, "Can't you do something?" emphasizing the 'you' as he did so.

Astraia looks back at the slot which sits flush with the wall and says, "It doesn't have a faceplate, so there is nothing I can unscrew or pry open to get access to its internal wiring. I might have something back on ship to cut open this wall, but then rewiring it to bypass the card reader could take anywhere from a few minutes to a few hours, and that's only if it isn't hooked directly into the computer mainframe."

"Well, that stinks. All right, that will be our last resort. We obviously have to get down to the main computer for Egnarts somehow, but for now let's see if we can't find a card key in one of these rooms."

"You want to go back and start busting down those locked doors now or later?" asks Chance.

"Later. Let's see what we can find ahead. When we get back around to where we started, we can start prying them open. Who knows, maybe we'll get lucky."

Disbelievingly, Chance adds in, "Right, like things ever pan out in our favor."

Kai ignores Chance's comment and turns back to the left, walking around the hallway checking doors. After two more doors open onto empty crew quarters, he stops at the next door and waits for the rest of the crew before saying, "Check this out. Have you noticed any of these doors with paint on them?"

Between Kai and Astraia, Chance could see the door marked fourteen, and notices the door looks different than the rest, like it was painted over several times. There are several different coats of paint, each a slightly different color of brown, overlapping onto the metal of the handle. Next to the door, where the nameplate was affixed on the previous doors, Chance finds a piece of masking tape which reads the name Peter Clines.

Bending down, Astraia says, "This paint is old school, Captain. Someone applied several coats with a brush years ago."

Kai checks the handle and finds the door locked. Thinking about it for just a second and registering the name tag on the door, he says, "Let's leave it for now. Probably just another crewman's quarters. If we have time on the way back out, maybe we'll come back, but right now I have a feeling it's more trouble than its worth."

Looking around, Kai notices that Oska is gone and asks, "Did anyone see where Oska went?"

Chance thumbs over his shoulder, and Kai looks across the hall to the other door. The nameplate next to the door reads, 'Infirmary'.

"I think she went looking for medical supplies, Kai."

"Sounds like her. Let's see if she needs a hand," says Kai before he pushes open the door, and sees Oska rummaging through one of the cabinets. The room itself has three beds, each with its own opaque privacy curtain pulled back. There are spaces on the wall where it looks like some equipment once hung, but now only a few plastic holders hang empty.

Looking over her shoulder to Kai, Oska says, "Looks like they took everything good with them when they left. The place is pretty well ransacked. I found a few pain killers here, but they are so far past their expiration date, I wouldn't trust them for anything."

"Any surgical equipment left or bandages?"

"Doesn't look like it. Most of these drawers and shelves are empty."

"Find a card key in there?" asks Chance from the hall.

"No," Oska answers back.

"All right," says Kai. "Let's see what else is around and then get down to the computer room."

Stepping back out into the hall, Kai and the girls continue forward with Chance following. Kai points out a maintenance closet to Astraia, while he pokes his head into the next room. In the room, Kai has to turn on the lights, and looking around, he concludes that this is the facility's recreation room. In one corner there are some weight machines, and a red and white jump rope hangs limply from the pull-up bar. To the right of this a punching bag lies on the floor, and Kai figures that its weight must have been too much for the threads holding it to the chain above after so many years. Opening a nearby cabinet, Kai finds sports gear including various balls of different sizes and some pads. Leaving it all where it is, Kai turns the lights off and steps back in the hall at the same time Astraia comes out of the maintenance closet.

As Astraia reemerges, she says, "Pretty basic stuff there: mop bucket, cleaning supplies, and some rags. Nothing really worth bringing with us. What did you find, Captain?"

"Gym. Just weights and stuff. Nothing I want to carry back to the ship. Let's keep going."

Walking down the hall, Kai tries two more doors before he finds another one unlocked. Stepping inside, Kai finds the light switch immediately and sees that this, too, is yet another crewman's quarters. The difference is that this one has decorations still in place and looks like whoever stayed here left without packing anything. The bed still has sheets on it, but it's unmade with most of the blanket lying on the floor. The walls have a few posters, one of them, a three dimensional picture of a scantily clad woman, still hanging. The desk has a collection of magazines, and the dresser in the corner seems to be the only place clear of anything aside from a thin layer of dust.

Stepping back into the hall, Kai says, "Guys, I may have found what we're looking for. I'm going to need some help looking through everything, though."

Oska and Astraia follow Kai into the room and quickly set to work while Chance remains at the door, simultaneously keeping watch on the hall and on the crew inside. Looking over the desk, Oska recognizes the magazines as mostly research journals on computer programming and publications on work being done in the field of artificial life. She opens the drawers and rummages through the contents, finding a few personal items and trinkets, but nothing worth keeping or that would help them with their current job.

"Not finding much here, Captain. Looks like this room used to belong to a computer programmer, but since his work must have been from twenty years ago, I assume it's all outdated by now."

"All right. How about you, Astraia?" asks Kai.

Over at the dresser Astraia looks through the last of the drawers, only finding more clothes and says, "Sorry, Captain, just clothes here."

"Damn. Seeing everything in here, I was hoping we would find something worthwhile." Looking back out to hallway, he continues, "I guess we check out the last couple rooms and then start busting down doors."

From the doorway Chance asks, "Anyone find the reason why he didn't take his stuff with him?"

Kai turns back to Oska who shakes her head, and Astraia shrugs her shoulders with one eyebrow raised. Seeing them over Kai's shoulders, Chance suggests, "Then I guess you have one more place to look."

The three inside look at each other, and then down to the bed which no one has touched. Kai steps forward and lifts the rest of the blanket off the bed. Finding nothing, he looks back to Chance who simply nods his head down to indicate under the bed. Looking down Kai sees the small shoebox-sized container and reaches for it. As he does so, he catches a glimpse of something white and realizing what it is, he exclaims, "Oh shit!" in startled surprise. He tries to take a step backward, but trips himself up on the blanket and falls to the floor.

Astraia and Oska both give the bed a wide berth as they come around to help him up and try to find out what he saw. Astraia, seeing it first says, "Oh dear," in a soft mournful voice.

Oska recognizing it, assumes her professional mask, and kneels down to assess the condition of the dead body which lies centered beneath the bed. Oska picks up the box and hands it back to Astraia to look through and says, "Maybe you can find something in here."

Sifting through the box, Astraia finds a few old letters. Some of them seem to have reddish-brown smudges on them, and she assumes that it may have once been lipstick since the handwriting is in a flowery girlish style. However, time has degraded it, and it's hard to tell. She opens one of them, and reads a few lines before quickly refolding it, recognizing it as someone's very private letter, and puts them all back in the box before saying, "Just some old letters in here."

With the box out of the way, Oska has more light and says, "The body is completely clean."

"What do you mean clean?" asks Kai.

"It's a skeleton."

"Well it's been over twenty years, isn't that what you would expect?"

"Actually, no," replies Oska. "It takes a lot longer than that, and in this place there's no soil, no bacteria, no earthworms, nothing to carry away the flesh and muscle. There should be at least something here on the body or on the floor."

"Is it real?" asks Astraia.

"It's real," says Chance from the door. "Looks like the guy died right there."

"Guy?" asks Kai. "How do you know it's a guy?"

"Looking at the pubic bone you can tell," answers Oska.

"Not to mention the look of the rest of the room and the clothes in the dresser," says Chance.

"Oh, yeah. That makes sense," says Kai and then, "Well, maybe it's just one of those skeletons they use in labs, like the ones hanging in science classrooms."

"Doesn't make sense why it would be under his bed," says Astraia.

"It also doesn't make sense why there are scratch marks under his mattress," says Chance.

Bending down further, Oska cranes her neck and notices the gouges in the underside of the mattress, as if the man had been clawing at it before he died. Whatever he went through before his death made him feel trapped there. Remembering an old story, Oska says, "They look like the marks found inside the top cover of caskets when bodies are exhumed, and it's found out that their occupant was buried alive."

"Well, this guy wasn't buried, but you saying he died right here?" asks Kai.

"That's what it looks like, Captain." Continuing, Oska says, "The thing I don't get is where the rest of him is."

"You mean like the skin and stuff?" asks Kai.

"Exactly. Judging from his skeletal frame, this man weighed about two hundred pounds, and his skeleton here only weighs about twenty pounds, give or take. So that leaves about a hundred eighty pounds of him missing, and there doesn't seem to be any decay around him."

Bending down to take a better look, Astraia asks, "Hey Oska, what are those thin white threads covering the skeleton?"

"I think that's what's left of his clothes. I don't have any equipment with me, but I'm willing to bet that those are the polyester fibers leftover from whatever he was wearing after all of the organic cotton or silk were taken out."

His voice becoming higher than usual as the realization of it all sets in, Kai says, "So something took his skin, his muscles, and his clothes while the guy is lying, no, clawing his way under his own bed? How the hell does that happen?"

A low voice, just above a whisper, comes from the doorway as Chance answers, "He was eaten."

Raising his voice even more, Kai asks, "What do you mean eaten?"

Perfectly calm, Chance raises his eyes up to meet Kai's and says, "Exactly what I said. Something went under there with him, and digested him. Whatever it was took everything it could digest and left the rest of him there."

"That would be one solution," agrees Oska. "There are a lot of animals that can digest things on the spot and then leave taking the nutrients with them. Starfish are a good example, the way they expel their stomach out to engulf their food and digest it. In doing so, they can feed on things that are larger than themselves. After it has been working on its meal for a little while, it sucks its stomach and the partially digested food back inside its body where it continues to be digested in the second stomach."

"Doctor, are you trying to tell me this guy was eaten by a freaking starfish? We're on a space station, in outer space. How the hell does that happen?" asks Kai.

"It probably wasn't a starfish, Captain, but the digestion process would have to be similar," says Oska. "Something ate whatever it could from this guy and left the rest here. It's the only explanation that fits."

"Well, that's just great. Let's get out of this room. The dead guy is giving me the creeps," says Kai.

"We can't do that just yet, Kai."

"Why not, Chance?"

Pointing towards the body with his chin, Chance says, "We're not done with him."

"What do you mean? You're not suggesting we give him a proper burial or anything, are you?"

"No, he's got something we need."

Confused, Astraia says, "We already searched the room. What else is there?"

Looking down to Oska, Chance says, "Take a closer look at his torso. Do you see it?"

Oska, leans in a bit, and notices a glint off something metal inside the skeleton's chest cavity. Laying flat on her stomach, she reaches underneath the bed, and spreads the wisps of polyester fibers away with her fingers. Once the hole is large enough for her hand, Oska reaches through and up, under the white bones of the rib cage and into the chest cavity, where her fingers delicately pinch on the metal clip. Pulling it out, Oska, sits back up on her knees and reads the plastic ID card, "Dr. Wong Hue, Lab 1."

"That should get us down the elevator," says Astraia.

Looking back to Chance, Kai asks, "How the hell did you see that?"

Shrugging, Chance simply says, "Good eyesight."

With the card key in hand, the crew leaves the late Dr. Hue's room, and continues following the hallway around. Along the way there are three more locked doors and one open one, but the open room seems to have been cleaned out like most of the other rooms they've already been in. Finally Kai finds the junction that leads back out to the airlock, and says, "Well, we're back where we started. That means the first room we crawled into must be just up ahead, and the elevator is just a bit after that. Let's see if we can't get this hard drive hooked up and get out of here."

"Seconded, Captain," says Oska.

Circling the hall this time takes only a couple of minutes as the crew heads directly for the elevators. Once there Oska slides the card in the slot, and the LED switches from red to green. A moment later the doors open, and staring inside, she says, "Captain, that looks a little tight."

"Yeah, only three of us are going to fit in that tiny thing with our packs. Chance, what do you think, you go down with Astraia, and Oska and I will follow you down?"

Unsure if Kai is trying to put her with him on purpose because of what happened in space on the way over to the space station or because he's trying to play match maker, Chance just says, "Sounds good," and steps inside with Astraia following. Pushing the button for P2, Chance says, "See you down below," just as the doors close.

After a slow decent the elevator stops, and when the doors open, Chance and Astraia exit onto the lower floor where they are greeted only by empty silence. Across from the elevator Chance notices an observation window and steps up to it to see the stars slowly crossing the sky as the facility continues to spin.

Astraia lifts her Wrist Comm. toward her face and presses the button saying, "Guys, we're on the second floor. All's good. Come on down."

"Okay, thanks," says Kai into his Wrist Comm.

Oska slides the card back into the slot on the wall. Again the red light switches to green, and the elevator doors open after a minute. Kai presses the P2 button, and they begin the ride down. A few seconds into the decent, however, the elevator suddenly stops, and the lights in the small elevator go out.

Chapter 10

The vibrations rumble against his leg until he pulls his phone out of his pants pocket and clicks the accept key. Holding it up to his ear, he says, "Good morning."

Across the line the distant voice asks, "What's the status on your end?"

In a relaxed tone he says, "We met here yesterday. They accepted the job after a bit of negotiation, just as you said they would, and they're in route now."

"Good. We are interested in what they find there."

"As am I, especially considering how things were left."

"Your research notes show great promise, provided it is properly managed and employed."

"Thank you," he says. "I had hoped you would see that. Have you located a new sample?"

"Not yet, but we believe there may be some on a new planet, XRT – 247, out in the Twelfth Sector."

"How long until we know?"

"We have a team en route going to check out the site. We should hear back from them by the end of the week."

"Excellent. Please contact me once you have it. I should know more on my end as well by that time."

"Yes, agreed," says the distant voice, and then, "One more thing?"

"What is it?" he asks.

"Based on your initial reports, some investors are concerned about the other subject's involvement and would like to know what your plans are for his future."

"Tell them not to worry. He knows nothing," he says reassuredly.

"All the same, we have uncovered some of his records, and his skills are uncanny."

"They are, and he is, but he knows nothing and should be easy enough to convince." Unable to let the pun go without saying it, he adds, "All we need to do is throw him a bone," between laughs.

Unamused, the distant voice says, "Yes, Doctor. That was our assessment as well."

"Friday, then?" asks the doctor.

"Yes, Friday."

Hanging up the phone, Doctor Gene Egnarts slides it back into his pocket and returns to his meal.

Chapter 11

As the lights dim to blackness, Chance quickly draws his flashlight and steps closer to Astraia's side. He sweeps the light up the hall in both directions but sees nothing. As he finishes his sweep, he says, "Radio the others and see if they got on the lift yet."

Astraia lifts her Wrist Comm. and says, "Captain, where are you?"

A moment later she hears, "Oh, we're just hanging out."

"Great," Chance says.

"I guess you two are out of power then, too?" asks Kai.

"That seems to be the case down here, Captain. Looks like the whole second floor just went dead."

"Got any ideas on getting Oska and me out of here?"

"Give me a second, Captain," says Astraia. "We'll be here."

Astraia looks over the elevator door with the flashlight and finds the same setup as when she was on the floor above. Turn back to Chance, she shines the light in his face and asks, "Hey, do you still have the crowbar with you?"

Reaching out, Chance gently places his hand over her light and pushes it down from his face as he says, "Yes."

Realizing she was blinding him, she says, "Oh, sorry about that," and then continues, "Let's see if we can get the doors open from down here. Maybe they came down far enough to be in line with the doors, but the juice kicked off before they could open."

"Worth a try," he agrees as he pulls out the crowbar.

Sliding a corner of the tip in between the doors first is the hard part, and afterwards, Chance angles the crowbar up to get the whole flat of the end in. Once the crowbar is in position, Chance pulls on it, and holds allowing Astraia to look in the crack to shine her flashlight inside the elevator shaft.

After a second, she says, "Gosh darn it, all right, Chance, you can let it close." Chance lets the doors ease shut as he withdraws the crowbar, and Astraia lifts her Wrist Comm. again and says, "Captain, I'm sorry."

"Guess you don't have good news then, huh?"

"No, I was hoping that the elevator would be lined up with the doors here and then we could just open it up, but it looks like you guys are only about halfway down the shaft. There is no way to get to you from here."

"So, what's the next great idea?"

"Well, you could check to see if there is a roof access panel, and try to climb back up to the first floor," suggests Chance into his own Wrist Comm.

"Possibly I haven't checked yet, but that's not going to get us down to you, nor is it going to help you get back to the ship."

"Captain," says Astraia, "the space station hasn't been in use for over two decades. That means no one has been doing any kind of maintenance. It's probably just a blown fuse or something. How about you two just sit tight, and Chance and I will have a look around. See if we can't get things moving again."

"Sounds like a plan. Oska, are you all right?" asks Kai still holding the button on his Wrist Comm.

Faintly, the voice of Oska comes across the radio, "Yes, Captain. I'll be fine. We have light, and while the elevator is a bit small, I'm not claustrophobic."

Coming back louder, Kai says, "All right, Astraia. We're good here for a while. You two go find the breaker box and get the juice flowing again."

Astraia says, "Yes, Captain," into the radio, and then dropping her arm back to her side, "Okay, Chance, which way you think we should go?"

"This way looks as good as any," says Chance as he points down the hall to the left.

Chapter 12

Just outside the town of Lilac a young boy named Charles, about the same age as his mother when she had first moved here with her family, went out to play beyond the town's farthest farm one late day in February. His mother had Charles homeschooled using the old tablet his father had once given her, and Charles quickly finished each lesson and completed his homework each morning as it was the only thing his mother asked of him before he went out to play.

Charles had grown up exploring the town and its surrounding area and knew the area better than anyone, young or old. He knew that the bakery threw out their 'old' stock around 4:30 in the afternoon every other day. He knew that the writer, Mr. Mark Tufo, over on Maine Street stayed awake most nights pecking away with just two fingers on an antique typewriter on the second floor of his home near the open window. He even knew there was a secret crawl space in the back of the Davidson's home that one could climb in and listen in on the conversations going on inside the house, if one were so inclined to do so while hiding from the neighborhood bully. Outside of town, Charles's knowledge was just as thorough. He knew which fields had each crop and which ones the rabbits liked to eat at most each night. He knew the names of the chemicals used on the crops to keep the insects away after he played in one of the old field's sheds one summer. Most of all, he knew the woods of the forest which started over a mile away from the town on its north side.

The woods were by far Charles's favorite place because they were his. No one else from town ever came out here, and things out here always seemed to be changing. The fish in the stream were only there during certain times of the day. The ground squirrels stuck to certain trees while avoiding others due to the birds who had nests in them, and certain plants seemed to never grow while others changed height almost daily. Last week a large rotted tree fell just west of the area Charles had claimed as his base fort, and he was headed out to investigate it when he heard a strange noise. The sound came from the north, deeper in the woods than Charles was used to going, and it had a high pitch, almost desperate quality to it, which made him feel compelled to check it out.

Charles found his way amongst the sticks and thick undergrowth which was trying to return to life after a long winter to the opening of a large cave. He had gone into the cave once before, years ago, but after finding nothing of interest, he left it to the mushrooms growing inside. Now, however, he stopped at its opening and listened to the high pitched animal sounds coming from inside. Spelunking without any equipment might prove dangerous, but Charles didn't consider this as he gave less than a moment's thought to the idea of exploring the cave while listening to the urgent calls coming from within.

Once he was about fifteen feet inside, the cave walls began to narrow, and as he found he had to duck down more and more, it was easier for him to simply crawl. The cave extended mostly straight back with a slight downward grade to the earthy dirt floor beneath Charles's hands and knees. The cave system had only one or two branching tunnels, and each time he came to a junction, he waited to hear the cries. Each time it came from the tunnel which continued to head further back, rather than from either of the other branches. Just as Charles found that he was almost completely out of light, he came upon a small shallow den with four large furry wolf cubs. The wolves' fur was full and thick, and most of them were dark gray, but one looked different from its littermates. Charles scooted in closer and picked up the pup. Its fur was as dark as a shadow at midnight, and the only reason Charles knew of its presence was the reflection in its golden yellow eyes which seemed to almost glow on their own. Holding the pup close to him, he felt it sniff at his armpits, and then a warm wet tongue licked his neck and face. The little guy seemed to like him, or maybe it just liked the attention and thought Charles might have some food for him. Either way, Charles liked the little guy and nuzzled right back into the pup's fur.

Charles made the rounds, picking up and holding each of the pups, but after spending a few minutes with each of them, he again picked up the first one and let it lick his face and hands. The shallow den was quite small, but Charles still found enough room to play, rolling around on the ground while the pup dipped his head down and raised its hind quarters up with tail wagging. After letting out a yip and a bark, it would rush in and try to nip at his fingers. Each time Charles would pull them away just in time to not let the little guy get a hold of them and then push the small wolf over on his side and attack its belly with tickles and rubs. It was during this playful roughhousing that Charles missed out on the opportunity to leave unscathed.

Initially Charles had only wanted to investigate the sounds, and then once he found the wolf cubs, he simply sought to play with them for awhile. The idea to ask his mother if he could have a pet hadn't even manifested in his mind yet, and he certainly wouldn't have wanted to take one of these cubs away from their mother. However, she couldn't have known that as she approached through the darkness of the cave carrying that day's kill.

The mother wolf had left the cave early that morning in search of food for herself, trying to replenish her body, and for her cubs who she was attempting to wean off her tit. Today's hunt took longer than she wanted to be away from her den, but the feeding of four cubs had taken its toll on her body, and now her ribs stuck out so far they were barely covered by her skin. After tracking scents until the sun was high above through the thick undergrowth of the northern forest, the mother wolf found two rabbits. The first one didn't see her as it nibbled on the low vegetation of the forest, and her powerful jaws clamped tight over its neck. She shook her head twice before feeling its body go limp in her mouth, and then she dropped it to chase down the second. Left, right, right, and back to the left again, it tried to evade her. Each time it changed its course, it unwittingly allowed her to get another foot closer. It ran around the big old tree with the gray bark, and just as the little white tail tried to dive into its hole, the mother wolf caught hold of its back right leg and pulled it from safety. She didn't apologize as she killed it. This was just how things were: rabbits were food. Carrying her second kill back over to where she left the first, she dropped it on the ground and began to eat, replenishing herself before heading back to her den of hungry, needy cubs. Tearing into the rabbit wasn't hard, and even after the meat was gone, the bones were quite satisfying to gnaw on and crush between her teeth. By the time she finished, the sun had noticeably moved in the sky, clouds had taken over, and the white flakes of snow had begun again. She knew it was time to get home to her cubs. Upon arriving, however, she immediately knew that the smells of the cave had changed.

She dropped the rabbit she had been carrying at the entrance to the cave and crept down inside, not bothering to shake off the snow that clung to her back. Once inside, she recognized the smell of the human, and she slunk down lower, until her belly nearly scraped the cave ground. After a minute of low crawling, she saw the human child there before her, at the opening of her den, pushing her cub over on its back, exposing its belly. She had no interest in eating him, but she would protect her babies from any threat. Her cub didn't see her, and neither did the boy, as she dove forward and began to attack. It was all teeth and claws as she tore into the boy's clothes and found his flesh. His screams hurt her ears in the close quarters of the den, and she made her attack even more savage than before, if for no other reason than to make his wailing stop.

Chapter 13

"Captain, you think they'll find it?" asks Oska.

"Yeah, they'll find the breaker box. I just hope it's only a fuse that blew, like she says. If it gets much more complicated than that, we might be stuck here for a bit."

"Looks like we're going to be here for awhile either way," says Oska as she slides her pack off her shoulders and sets it down on the floor beside her.

Sliding his own pack off, Kai says, "True, but Astraia is one of the best mechanics I've ever seen. If it's fixable, she'll get it going."

Curious, Oska says, "I know you two have been flying together for awhile, but what about Chance?"

"What about him?" asks Kai.

"Well, I know you hired her to keep the Allons-y going, and you hired me so you had a doctor on board in case one of your jobs happened to go sideways on you, but what about Chance?"

"Like you said, Doc, sometime a job goes sideways. Having a guy like Chance around is good when things get tight."

"I get that, but the man is a hired gun. Not exactly the trustworthy sort."

"Are you kidding?" asks Kai. "In my experience, hired guns are the most trustworthy to have around in case of problems. They're invested in your well-being. Well, they're invested in it so long as you're paying them, that is, and in my experience, dead men don't pay so well."

"Are you ever afraid he'll switch sides on you in the middle of a fight?" asks Oska.

"No. First off, no one knows he's a hired gun. Anyone we meet just thinks he is just part of the crew. Second, if hired guns went around switching sides all of the time, no one would hire them. Loyalty comes at a price, and the good thing about hired guns is that they at least name theirs up front. Besides, you really haven't gotten to know him like I have yet."

"No, you're right," agrees Oska. "I never did hear how he became a member of the crew."

Thinking back, Kai says, "That was a wild day," with a fond note in his voice.

....

"I was only the first mate on the Allons-y. Captain Tennant was in charge back then. Anyway, I was working a job, salvaging some missiles from a recently abandoned ship, and we ran into some problems when another interested party showed up. Captain Tennant told us to get back on the Allons-y, and we booked it out of there. Unfortunately, the flux box blew as we were heading out, and we were forced to land on the closest planet. Just to complicate matters, the Grav. Controls shut down just as we were approaching the planet, and we had no gravity.

I think Astraia had only been on board about two months at that point, and she saved all of our asses. While in zero-g, Astraia rewired the Grav. Controls so that Captain Tennant could regain control of the ship before we crashed into the planet's surface. He got us down to a safe landing, but only because she worked some kind of miracle back there in the engine room.

Once we landed, Astraia let us know that the flux box was completely shot, and we needed a new one. We took the buggy into the closest town and put in an order. They said it would be a day before they could get their hands on one, and we figured since we were there, we might as well look to see if there was any work we could do. Never want to pass up an opportunity to make a few credits, you know.

The first couple places we tried said they didn't have anything, but they directed us to the bar up the road. The bartender, I think his name was Hank, or maybe it was Frank, I forget, but either way, he told us that there was something strange going on with the shipments. He said he had put in for several more cases of beer and liquor but not one single bottle had made it in. Other people around town had placed some orders as well over the past couple weeks, and they hadn't been able to get their stuff in either. He asked if we would be willing to go check out the shipping ports and the old lighthouse, see if they had anything. Told us we'd get free room and board for the night if we did it, even said he would send his barkeep with us. We figured it sounded easy enough, so the Captain, Astraia, and I left the Allons-y locked up where she was and went down there with the barkeep showing us the way.

It took close to an hour to get there, and when we knocked on the door, we found the lighthouse open. We stepped inside and found that we were dealing with something far more brutal than a couple of thieves. The entire lighthouse was filled with blood. Nearly the whole family there had been killed. The mother and the three girls were raped repeatedly according to the youngest,

Sammy, who was just barely alive when we found her. She was only ten.

We rushed her back to the town hospital where the doctors began working on her. On the way there, however, she let us know exactly who had done this. Turns out that some pirates were held up just a bit further up the shoreline, and they had built a false lighthouse to confuse ships and have them run into the coral reef there. Then they would board the ships, kill all the crew, and take the goods. As a result, the town folks started getting desperate and needy, and after a few months of this the pirates would then come in and plunder the town, taking advantage of their vulnerable state. They killed most of the folks in other towns, did as they pleased with the women along the way, and then stole children to sell as slaves or to keep on board the ship.

The town said that they couldn't really afford to send anyone with us to take on the pirates. I couldn't blame them. They were too scared the pirates would attack while we were away, and there wouldn't be enough people there to protect their homes. Captain Tennant, however, said there was no way we were going to leave these people to that fate, and that we would do what we could to fix this.

The captain, Astraia, and I made our way to the pirate's camp right about sundown and watched as they finished their work unloading their last bit of cargo into a cave system they had taken up as their base of operations. Most of them left, headed back to their ships for the night. I don't know if they had plans to take down another ship, or if they just chose to sleep there, but it was a good thing either way as we wouldn't have been able to take them all on by ourselves.

We waited another hour or so until it was good and dark, and watched the area to try and see how many pirates were left. The captain was just laying out our plan to go in quietly when I saw a shadow move. I cut him off and pointed across the field to where the shadow was only visible to us because the cave was lit up before us. If we were in front of it, there would have been no way we would have seen it. The shadow slipped through the vegetation soundlessly, and approached three pirates. Stopping just out of sight, the shadow waited until one of the pirates decided he needed to take a piss. Just as he was in full stream and relaxed, the shadows around a figure of a man dissolved, and he came up with his sword cutting off the guy's hands and what he was holding in one stroke. Then rotating fluidly, he beheaded him before the pirate could even begin to scream. The other two, still facing away, didn't have time to time to react to the sound of their fallen comrade as his body hit the ground because the mysterious man was already working them over with that sword of his, slicing through the neck of one and puncturing the lungs and heart in a sideways stab of the other.

Finished with the guards on the outside, he stood still waiting for something or someone to announce themselves. After a few drops of blood dripped off the end of his sword and fell to the dirt at his feet, he bent down and wiped the blood off his sword across the back of the last pirate. Then he took a small laser, the kind used for sighting when target shooting, out of his pocket and signaled to us. Not knowing who this guy was, we were cautious about meeting him, but since he already knew we were there, it was rather pointless to try to continue hiding. When we got down there, he introduced himself as Chance, told us he overheard our conversation and was there to help. He had been hired by another town which had lost their friends and family to these pirates and was here on a job. He said he had watched the pirates all day, and knew that there were eight more inside this cave system, but didn't yet know the layout of the caves. If we wanted in, now was the time. Otherwise, the only one that would be walking out of there was him. We agreed to come. I think Captain Tennant wanted to make sure that the pirates paid for what they had done to that little girl, Sammy, back at the lighthouse.

Inside, we found that the caves were booby trapped, and the tunnels had multiple branching endings. Chance was able to save Astraia when she fell into a pit, but Captain Tennant took a nasty barb in the leg from another trap. We continued on to find where they were stashing all of the loot, took out four guys there, found the sleeping area a bit further down, and took out two more there. The last two, Captain Antonio and his First Mate Tyler, however, were the tough ones. The three of us took on the first mate in a gunfight that nearly expended every round we were carrying while Chance took on the pirate captain.

At this point there was no use in stealth, so Chance switched tactics and rushed the pirate captain, Antonio, at a dead run. He slammed into him before the pirate had even gotten his gun out, and it became a hand to hand battle from there. The pirate tried to swing at him, but Chance ducked, parried, and came up with an open-handed clap on both his ears, disoriented him before thrust-kicking him in the gut against the stone walls of the cave. I popped off a couple more shots at the first mate, but when I went back to reload, I watched as Chance waited for Captain Antonio to catch his breath and stand back up. When he did, Chance resumed a fighting stance, and waited. The pirate lunged forward with a punch that should have knocked Chance into the next town over, but just as it was about to connect, Chance pivoted on his front foot, like a door being opened on its hinge, allowing the pirate's fist to fly no further than an inch past his face. Before the pirate could pull back, while his momentum was still moving forward, Chance punched him in the solar plexus, doubling him over, and then came down on the back of his neck with a two-fisted hammer blow. The pirate's chin hit the ground hard enough to bounce. I hopped up and took the last of my shots at Tyler and continued to botch them all. Captain Tennant had already run out of ammo, and his leg was bleeding profusely from the barb. Looking at it, I knew it must have hit something important. Astraia was loading her last clip when a hail of bullets flew overhead past us at Chance. He didn't even move as they struck the wall beside him. He just waited as the pirate captain got to his knees and slowly stood back up.

The pirate captain, knowing he was outmatched, tried to offer Chance a better payday. Said he could have everything off the last three boats if he wanted and a permanent position on his ship. Chance growled at him, actually growled like an animal, and through clenched teeth told him he already had a job. "My job," he said, "is from a mother who lost her daughter to you and your kind." Just as the pirate finally stood back up, Chance said, "She asked me to make you scream," right before he kicked him in the nuts hard enough to make a field goal from the back of the stadium parking lot. The pirate's eyes rolled back in his head, and he dropped. Seeing the pirate captain go down, the first mate was in shock, and Astraia took him out, plugging every last shot into his body.

We walked the rest of the cave system and found several children chained up in dirty clothes. Chance made sure each of them was uncuffed and escorted outside. He called the town over a radio and told them to come and get the children, leaving all of the loot in the cave. When the town folks asked how to find him, he said, "Just follow the smoke," right before he lit the pirate captain, Antonio, on fire. The man died screaming, just like he said he would, and the smell of his burning flesh haunts me even today.

Just before the town folks showed up, Chance said he was headed out. He didn't want their money, and asked if we would make sure the kids were returned safely. I assured him they would be taken care of and thanked him for his help. I asked Chance if he would be willing to join us. I told him we could us a man with his talents. I remember he said, "You do know I'm trained to kill you in more ways than you even know are possible?" Swallowing, I confirmed that I did, and that the job was still open if he wanted it. He said he would think about it, and walked off into the woods.

I don't know how he knew where we were, but three months later he showed up on another planet at a bar we were at and said he'd join us. I explained that Captain Tennant was no longer flying the Allons-y. The leg wound had forced him into early retirement, and that he would be following me. He said he already knew that, I have no idea how, and as long as I was paying him, it would be fine."

. . . .

There is a faint crackle on Kai's Wrist Comm. just as he finishes, and Astraia's voice sounds muffled somehow as she asks, "-tain, you there?"

Chapter 14

The clouds had rolled in over Lilac, and
Roger knew that despite this being probably the last
snow of the year, he ought to go out to the sheds in
the field and turn on the heaters to make sure none
of the chemicals froze. He put it off for another five
minutes before conceding to logic, reminding
himself that a good farmer always has more chores
to do, and shrugged himself back into his coat and
work boots. Outside he climbed into his truck and
started it up. The radio inside was set to full
volume from the last time his guys had taken it out
to tend to the fields, and Roger immediately turned
it off, not wanting another headache from crap they
called music these days. The snow flurries began
just as he pulled out of the driveway, and he turned
right. The sheds began a quarter mile out with one
more placed every four hundred yards or so
extending out towards the woods, each with its own
access route off the main road. The trip itself,
Roger figured, would only take about a half hour,
and then he could sit back down in his favorite
armchair with a beer.

Turning on the heaters in the sheds was a
simple matter of flipping a switch. Each switch
started up the electric heaters and was more than
enough to keep the little shed as warm as fifty
degrees, even if the temperature outside was as cold
as forty below. His guys had suggested automating
the system or even rewiring it so that Roger could
just flip a switch from inside his house, but he
declined, saying that it would cost too much. The
real reason, however, was that Roger in part
distrusted technology, and he would rather go out
there himself so that he could feel the heaters

kicking on. He got a sense of accomplishment when he did anything with his own two hands, which was probably why he had become a farmer in the first place.

Twenty minutes later Roger flipped the switch on in the last shed. He waited a minute for the heating coils to warm up before he held his hand over the top of the heater and feeling for the heat. Satisfied he had done what he needed to; he stepped back outside, locked the shed, and began to walk back to his truck. On the way he heard a strange noise and stopped to listen. The sound was faint, but it pulled at something inside him, and he strained to hear it again.

After a minute the snow had been coming down hard enough that it now dusted his entire windshield and Roger began to believe it was his imagination. He dismissed the noise and continued back toward the truck. Just as he lifted up on the door handle and pulled, however, he thought he heard it again. He quickly shut the door because he did not want to hear the sound of the vehicle dinging at him about the keys still in the ignition drowning out what he was listening for. He stepped back to the spot where he was when he first heard the sound. Two full minutes more went by, and Roger felt silly standing out there in the snow while his nose turned red and hat turned white, before he heard the sound again. This time he picked up on the direction, and began to head out towards the woods, his boots crunching across the open ground.

As he approached the edge of the woods, Roger's heart pumped so loudly he was afraid he would hear it instead of the strange sounds. He didn't know what it was that was making the sound out in the woods, but it pulled at him with urgency.

He stopped himself before entering the frost covered thicket, unsure where to go from here, and he did not want to simply start crashing through the mostly dead undergrowth, making so much noise he would miss the next call. He waited less than twenty seconds this time before he heard it. It was slightly louder than before, and it seemed to be coming from somewhere ahead and to his left. He pushed the branches of thorns away with his gloved hand, stepped on base of others, and began to wade through the brush as quickly and quietly as he could.

Past the initial fifteen feet of thorns, the outer edges of the forest broke open and allowed him to walk more freely. It was clear that the tree canopy above rarely let much sunlight ever reach the ground around him. Roger continued in the direction he had last heard the sounds, trying to be careful in case he came upon an injured animal that might attack him, but finding that his body kept driving him to move faster. He attempted to climb over a fallen tree, placing his hands in the cold snow pilled up across the bark and rotten wood, and his gloves slipped beneath his hands before they finally found purchase enough for him to make it. Two steps later he ducked beneath a low hanging branch, and finally, he found the source of the sounds.

Roger found what looked like a ragged and torn up animal with a few scraps of cloth hanging off it. Blood pooled around the body in stark contrast to the surrounding ground. A trail of the thick crimson led back deeper into the woods along a path of leaves, twigs, and rocks bright red on the blanket of white, from where it was either dragged or crawled with its last ounce of strength. Looking closer he could see prints in the dirt. None of them were made by an animal; they looked like small hand prints in the snow and dirt. As if greeting him, the body let out one more, tiny cry and he realized two things: it wasn't dead and it wasn't an animal. This was a person, and whoever he or she was, he or she had been trying to half crawl, half drag their way back to the town.

Roger rushed forward and bent down next to the body. He found that what he thought was the blood-soaked fur of an animal was really the back of a young boy's head. Bite marks started around the back of his neck and still leaked bright red down his back to where his clothes used to be, now replaced by savage scratches and ripped flesh. The clothes he was wearing looked as if they had been torn from his body by the teeth and claws of a huge vicious animal. He had seen a man's arm after it had gotten caught in farm machinery back when he was a boy - the bloody stump and broken jagged white bones of that man seemed like a paper cut compared to what this young boy had been through. Roger had no idea what had done this to the boy, or if it was going to come back to finish the job, but he knew if there was a chance of saving the boy's life, he had to act now.

Roger picked up the limp body and carried him back to town while snowflakes continued to catch on his eyelashes.

Chapter 15

"You know, stumbling around in the dark isn't exactly what I had planned for this little job of ours," says Astraia.

Without looking back, staying focused on the patch of light made by his flashlight, Chance replies, "Yeah, but it's better than getting shot at, which is how most of our jobs seem to go."

Defending the crew as a whole, Astraia says, "We don't always get shot at."

"No, you're right," concedes Chance, and then he adds, "Sometimes we just get run out of town or blown up," before checking the face plate on the next door and moving on.

"That was one time, and that guy was crazy," says Astraia as she continues beside him, keeping her flashlight pointed down at the floor in front of them.

"Seems like they always are."

Astraia, considering his comment, asks, "Well, what do think about this guy, Doctor Egnarts?"

"He's hiding something," Chance says matter-of-factly, and then adds, "he's probably crazy too, in a mad scientist sort of way, but he's definitely hiding something."

"How do you know?"

"Just a feeling I got."

"A feeling, huh?" asks Astraia. "Would that be a general feeling of foreboding or one of your feeling feelings?"

Not quiet ignoring the implications of her question, Chance simply says, "Just a general feeling."

"Okay, good."

"Why is that good?" he asks.

"Because when you get one of your other feelings, someone usually ends up with a bunch of extra holes in them."

Bringing his light up to check the next door, Chance finds what he's been looking for, the custodial closet, and pretending not to have heard her last comment says, "Here we go."

Turning the doorknob, Chance finds that the door is unlocked and enters. Shining the light along the walls and furnishings, the two of them find that the cleaning supplies have been left behind along with a lamp and a desk with a built-in computer monitor. Taking a closer look at the cleaning supplies, Chance recognizes that these could be mixed together to make a small explosion, but there isn't anything else on the shelves. Continuing his sweep of the walls, Chance says, "It doesn't look like the breaker box is in here."

"No, I noticed that, too. Guess we'll have to keep looking."

Looking back at the desk, Chance asks, "What about the computer?"

Pushing the on switch, the monitor continues to remain black, and Astraia says, "Outlets are the same as the lights. No juice. Guess the electricity is out for this whole floor."

"What about the back-up battery we brought?"

Looking at the back of the desk and finding the plug, Astraia says, "Yeah, it looks like it will work. Why?"

"I was just thinking if it's hooked up to the main server, then maybe we can get what we need for Egnarts without having to search for the mainframe or whatever."

"This being the custodial closet, I doubt it has the same level of access, but it's worth a try. Give me a minute while I hook it up."

Stepping back into the hallway, Chance uses his flashlight to cut through the darkness in each direction, checking the perimeter as far as the turn in the hall will allow. Seeing nothing, he turns back into the room and finds Astraia sitting before the computer, waiting for it to boot up and he notices once again, in the dim light of the monitor, Astraia's simple beauty.

With a flicker, the monitor shows that the computer has finished its internal boot-up sequence and the same spinning 'X' logo appears. Not having a keyboard, Astraia reaches forward and touches the screen, and the logo on the screen dissolves revealing a new menu. The title of the screen says 'Work Requests' and lists four icons each titled with the date of their entry from over twenty years ago. Astraia taps on the screen's corners and the title, but nothing changes and she says, "Well, it looks like this is just a terminal for the custodians. It lists the open jobs, but there doesn't seem to be any way to gain access to the mainframe from here."

Chance asks, "Can you open up any of those work orders?"

"Sure, but why?"

"I'm curious, is all"

Reaching forward Astraia taps on the first icon and the screen dissolves again. This time it is replaced with a work request form. Astraia reads from the monitor aloud, "The form was filled out by Joseph D. claiming that there was a light out in hallway D2. It says below that in the 'Fix Action' field that a new bulb was supposed to be installed, but there is no mention if it was ever completed or not. I'm assuming it wasn't since we didn't see a list of closed jobs on the main menu."

"Where did it say the light was out?"

Looking back at the 'Complaint Field', Astraia asks, "Hallway D2. Why?"

"I was just wondering if it had anything to do with the hallway out there."

"I doubt it. A facility like this wouldn't put them in series like Christmas tree lights where one goes out and it kills the whole strand. Besides, that wouldn't explain why the wall outlets don't work. Those should be on a completely different circuit."

"I got that, but I was just thinking, upstairs when you were using the other terminal, it said that we were on floor P1."

Looking back to the screen, Astraia realized what Chance was getting at and said, "So either he mistyped this, or there is another floor."

"Exactly."

Thinking back, Astraia says, "When we came on board, we came in the top tube running around the sphere. What if the bottom tube is like this one and it has its own hallways?"

"That's what I was thinking," Chance says with bit of regret in his voice as he thinks about the process of having to get back on the Allons-y to reposition and try to gain access through the other airlock.

"Think we should tell the captain?"

"Not yet," answers Chance. "Let's see if there isn't another way down first."

"All right," agrees Astraia.

Looking back to the screen, Chance says, "Let's see what those other work orders have to say."

Touching the 'Back' button in the lower left of the screen causes the work order to disappear, and the main menu comes back up showing all four work orders again. Touching the next one causes a work order to materialize, and Astraia says, "It looks like Doctor Nick Smoop, that's a weird name, put in a work order because the toilets on the lower level were clogged. One of the custodians, a guy named Michael Jane, was going to be sent down with a bucket to scoop it out and snake the system to make sure the pipe was clear."

"Okay, what about the next one?"

Closing out the work order, Astraia brings up the next one and reads. After a minute, she says with a laugh in her throat, "This one is from a Doctor Smith who wants his entire quarters remodeled, and get this: he claims it will 'better help his thought patterns.'"

"I hope that one was denied."

"It doesn't say, but it sounds like a waste of resources."

Opening the last work order just as Chance leans over near her shoulder, Astraia says, "Looks like there are more problems with the bathrooms."

"Same guy."

Scrolling back up to the top, Astraia says, "No, this was put in by Doctor Albertson."

"What's it say?"

Reading through the work order really quickly, Astraia says, "The sinks have stopped in the bathrooms on floor D2, same floor as the hallway light, and there seems to be a bad smell coming from them. The crew member went on to say that if the sewage lines had been switched with the plumbing, he was going to make sure that the

Head of Research heard about it, but it sounds like there were some issues down there."

"Sounds like it," Chance agrees. "All right, let's find the breaker box and get Kai and Oska out of the elevator."

Astraia turns off the system, unplugs the portable battery pack, and stuffs everything into her backpack while Chance steps back out into the hall and does another quick sweep with his flashlight. When she joins him out in the hall she asks, "You know this place has been abandoned for like twenty years, right?"

"Yeah, it's just something that was drilled into me a long time ago."

"Back when you were in the Space Marines?" she asks.

Nodding, he confirms, "We had to do so many perimeter sweeps. I swear some guys learned to do them sleepwalking."

Smirking, Astraia says, "Well, at least here we should be safe."

Walking further around the hallway, Chance's flashlight stops on the next door. He tries the door handle, only to find it locked, and steps back to look for a faceplate. When he finds it, it reads 'Lab 4', and below it is another slot for a card to be swiped. Having left the card with Kai and Oska, they have no way to get in. Chance looks to Astraia and asks, "What do you think?"

Pointing to the card reader with her flashlight, she says, "Looks like there is no power here either. The LEDs are out."

"I left the card with the other two anyway."

"True. I was just thinking that after twenty years of dead silence, maybe even the ghosts in the machines have given up on it."

"Maybe," Chance agrees before turning to continue up the hall.

The next door is marked 'Lab 2' and again the doors are locked. The LEDs on the card swipe only reflect the light from Chance's flashlight, not producing any of their own. They continue their way around the hall, noticing that there are fewer doors down here than on the floor above and most seem to be locked.

"What do you think? Are we about halfway around yet?" asks Astraia.

"Over," says Chance.

"'Kay, I'm going to radio the captain to let him know where we are."

Stepping up to the next door, the faceplate reads twenty-three, Chance tries the handle and finds the door open. Looking back he asks, "Should I wait for you, or do you want to radio him from in here?"

"Let's go in," Astraia says, as Chance lets the door swing inward.

From the doorway Chance sweeps the room with his flashlight, once left to right at about waist level, and then back right to left at head level. Finding the room clear, Chance steps aside and allows Astraia to enter before he follows her. Inside, the room is designed to be someone's office, and aside from a large desk taking up the middle of the room with its accompanying black mesh chair and flat screen computer monitor, there is little else in the room.

Lifting her Wrist Comm. to her mouth, Astraia clicks the button and says, "Captain, you there?"

After a few seconds, the voice of Captain Kai comes back through the radio, but it has a strange quality to it which makes it sound like he is a long way down a tunnel, both echoey and a bit faint. "Not like we have a lot of options, so yeah, we're still hanging around."

Shaking her head at the captain's bad joke, she says, "We're about halfway around the hallway and still no breaker box."

"Can you repeat? It sounded like you said we were going to be stuck in this sardine even longer while you two continued your nice little walk."

Looking over to Chance, Astraia asks, "You hear that? His voice sounds strange."

"It's just the absorption paint on the outside of the tube interfering with the signal," he says.

"Gotcha," she says to him, and then back into her Wrist Comm. she says, "Well, Captain, we just couldn't resist."

"You two find anything interesting out there?" Kai asks.

"Not really. The custodial closet had a computer with a few work orders from a couple decades ago, but all of the other doors, including the labs, are locked."

"Did you say labs?"

"Yeah. We found two doors marked as labs, but we couldn't get in without trying to break down the doors."

"You think this card key Oska has will get us in there?"

"Maybe," replies Astraia. "But we're going to need to restore the power before the card readers are working."

"Well, since the card is in here with us, I figured that was a given."

"Right," says Astraia.

118

"Anything else?"

"Not yet. We'll let you know when we find the box."

"Okay, over and out," says Kai.

From behind the desk Chance says, "You didn't say anything about floor D2."

"No," she agrees. "He sounded like he was getting a bit crabby being stuck in there. I figured we could just tell him when we get him out."

"Probably for the best," says Chance, and then he asks, "You want to check out what's on this computer while we're here?"

Stepping over to him, Astraia begins to let her backpack slide off her shoulders while she says, "Might as well."

It takes her only a minute or two to have it hooked up and running. When the screen comes up, Astraia sees that she has full access to the system. She clicks on the small computer icon and looks over its properties before saying, "Good news is, I'm in. Bad news, this computer either isn't hooked up to the mainframe either, or the mainframe itself has no power because she can't see anything other than her own hard drive."

"All right. So let's see what's on the hard drive then."

Clicking the hard drive folder, Astraia quickly scans through its files and properties before saying, "It looks like the computer holds about a hundred and sixty terabytes of data, far too much to sort through right now, but there is still something in the recent items folder. Probably the last thing whoever had this office, was working on." Opening the most recent document, Astraia finds the following memo:

To Whom It May Concern:

I am writing to you out of concern for some of the practices I have born witness to these past two weeks since reporting for duty aboard the Project X facility. It has become increasingly clear that Dr. Gene Egnarts, Head of Research, has been using unsanctioned and unscientific methods in his experiments with the bacteria known as RXT-947.

Bacteria RXT-947, as you know, is a sentient life form and falls under the same protection as that of any other living creature, and our means of research should only allow for moral and ethical experiments. Admittedly, each cell is not considered to be an individual, but rather the collective organism as a whole should still be protected.

In the past two weeks I have witnessed Dr. Egnarts using electrocution on the subject, sticking an electric prod directly into the tank for as much as 15 seconds at a time, simply because the bacteria did not perform the way he wished them to. This act kills off millions of bacteria each time he does it and ultimately decreases the collective conscience of the organism until it can regrow new bacteria to take their place, a process which also seems to be taking longer lately. This is the equivalent of performing a lobotomy every time a child fails to give the right answer in school.

I respectfully request that Dr. Egnarts's actions be investigated and if needed, take him off the project for the safety and protection of both the organism and the research.

Sincerely,

Dr. Frank Albertson

"Looks like our new friend Egnarts wasn't a very nice guy," says Chance.

"Looks like," agrees Astraia, "but notice, this is also written by the guy who wanted his quarters remodeled to help his brainwaves or whatever."

"Anything else on there?" Chance asks.

"Just a second, I'm looking."

"Okay, I'm going to check the hall real quick."

Looking through some of the other files, Astraia finds Doctor Albertson's research, several terabytes worth in fact, but most of it is outside her field of understanding. Mostly it looks like it has to do with research involving different plant species from various worlds, and with the introduction of some kind of bacteria, the plants seem to grow faster. Looking back up to Chance as he reenters the room, she says, "There is a lot of technical stuff on here, but it's not the stuff Doctor Egnarts wants, and we don't have anything to download it on."

"All right," says Chance. "Let's get going then."

Chance helps Astraia pack everything up after she powers down the computer and then steps out in the hall ahead of her to make sure the coast is clear. They walk further down the hall, checking a door marked twenty four and one marked twenty five, finding both of them locked and moving on. Finally, after they are nearly three-quarters of the way around the hall and heading back towards the elevators, Chance's flashlight stops on a slightly ajar door marked 'Maintenance Closet'. Chance, cautious now, since this is the first door they have

121

found already open, pushes the door wide with his boot and scans the room slowly. On the first pass with the light inside the room, Chance finds a desk and a workspace. On the workspace, a few tools such as a screwdriver, a hammer, and a few wrenches are laid out. Coming back with the light, Chance notices a number of conduits running down the wall into large boxes mounted on the wall. Pausing on one box that looks open, Chance says, "Bingo."

Trying to look past him, Astraia asks, "What? Did you find the breaker box?"

"Couple of them," he replies as he finishes his sweep and spots two tall cabinets against the back wall.

Squeezing past Chance, she says, "Great. Let me take a look."

While Astraia walks over to the breaker boxes, Chance quickly looks over the maintenance desk. Inside he finds a few forms signed by Alex Scott. He assumes he was an employee here back in the day. He also finds a can of air used for blowing the dust and dirt out of computers and other electrical devices. Turning around towards Astraia, he asks, "So, what did you find? Is it fixable?"

Astraia says, "There are a couple of different boxes up here. The two there that were closed are for LANs."

"LANs?" he asks.

"Local Access Network. Basically they're the lines running through the space station to the server."

"Can we use them to get the information Egnarts wants?"

"Probably not. No way of telling if the server is on or what information it would have access to. If the mainframe computer isn't on or hooked up, we won't get anything. Best thing would be for us to just plug in at the source like he suggested." Then pointing at the third box, Astraia says, "This one here is marked as video. I assume there are cameras in the labs and their video streams are pumped through here."

"All right. What about the power?"

Pointing to the last box, the one that was open when they entered, Astraia says, "I figure that's what this one is, what with the universally accepted lightning bolt symbol meaning electricity on it. Do you have anything over there made of wood or rubber? I don't want to have to touch this door if I don't have to."

Looking back at the desk, Chance grabs the hammer and holds it out to her, wooden handle first.

"Thanks," she says, and then while only touching the handle herself, she opens the breaker box the rest of the way. Astraia shines her flashlight inside and finds that the main breaker switch is in the 'off' position.

Looking over her shoulder, Chance says, "There. Flip the breaker up."

"Hold on," Astraia says, drawing out the words as if she were talking to an excited child. Scanning the rest of the box she says, "Look there," and points. "There are two fuses missing."

"Missing?" Chance questions. "How can they be missing?"

"Don't know, but there are two empty slots right there. If I throw the breaker switch without replacing them, one of two things will happen. Either the power comes on for a second and then the switch will flip back off, and we risk a surge causing more damage to the circuits, or I'm going to find my hand seizing up while white hot pain shoots up my arm until I spasm for a bit and crumple to the floor in a heap from electrocution."

"So don't flip the switch?" Chance says making it sound like a question.

"Not without the fuses. Help me look. There maybe some spare ones laying around in here." Shining the flashlight a bit closer to double check the numbers, Astraia says, "We're looking for seven hundred amp fuses."

Walking over to the cabinets in the back of the room, Chance opens the door and searches the shelves. On the first shelf he finds a plastic bucket with some used red rags with some sort of black crusty substance on them inside. The second shelf has some cleaning supplies: degreaser, floor cleaner, and a few others. Bending down, Chance sees a box on the back of the second shelf closest to the ground. Pulling out the box, he finds a few strips of copper wire and a collection of fuses. From the looks of them, some of the fuses are probably still good, but some look like they're already burnt out. Calling back to Astraia who is rummaging through the bottom desk drawer, Chance says, "I think I found some."

Astraia shuts the drawer and meets Chance back at the breaker box. Shining her light into the box, she pokes around through the box until she finds what she is looking for and comes out with two fuses that look pretty good. "These ought to work," she says and steps up to place the fuses in the box.

"What about the risk of electrocution?" Chance asks.

"The main breaker switch is off," she says, pointing with her flashlight to the side of the panel. "We're good."

Chance watches as Astraia inserts the first fuse and lets out a breath he didn't realize he was holding as she slips the second into its spot. With that done, she reaches over to the side and flips the main breaker back to the up position. All around them the lights flicker back to life, and a gentle hum can be heard in the air.

As Astraia closes up the breaker box, her radio crackles to life, and Kai's voices comes through, "Astraia, looks like something you did worked. We have lights in here now."

Lifting her Wrist Comm. Astraia says, "Yes, Captain, we found the breaker box and replaced a couple fuses." Stepping over to the door, she continues by saying, "Everything should be working now."

"So if I hit the button here, the elevator's not going to drop out from under us or anything crazy, right?"

"I didn't check the cables, Captain, but you have juice now, so go ahead and give it a try."

As Astraia pulls open the door and steps into the hall, Kai says, "Okay then, see you two in a minute."

Chance moves to follow Astraia out into the hall but nearly knocks her over as he finds she has suddenly stopped only a few inches away. "What's wrong?" he asks.

"I just saw something," she says.

Already trying to squeeze out past her and put himself between whatever it was and Astraia, he asks, "Where?"

"Down there," she says and stares off down the hall.

Looking down that way and then back behind them, Chance sees nothing. Without even considering whether or not to believe her, he simply asks, "What did you see?"

"I was just stepping out here and in my peripheral vision I saw it," she pauses, "I didn't get a good look at it but," she pauses again before looking him directly in the eyes and saying, "I saw a large creature scurry around the bend in the hall." Then, as if to clarify, she adds, "It looked like some kind of insect."

Looking once again toward the direction she indicates, Chance still finds nothing out of the ordinary but quickly realizes that it's the direction in which they have yet to walk. The same direction towards the elevators where Kai and Oska will be coming from in just a minute. He presses the button on his Wrist Comm. as he brings it up to his mouth and whispers into it, "Kai!" Without waiting for a reply, he continues, "Lock and load."

Coming back over the Wrist Comm. Kai's voice whispers back seriously, "What's the situation?" with the accompanying sound of guns being cocked in the background.

"Astraia saw something, animal, headed your way."

"Gotcha."

Chance looks back to Astraia who has already pulled out a Glock 9mm, and says, "Let's go," as he reaches back for his own pair of Glock 37 handguns and begins to head up the hall. The two of them each take a side of the hall in an effort to keep their lines of sight open. Quickly moving along the hallway, they pass a few more doors, two of which look to be labs, but they don't bother to stop and check their handles to see if they're locked as they pursue the creature. Just after the second lab, the next door begins to open on its own, and both Astraia and Chance raise their weapons to shoot.

Kai and Oska step off the elevator directly in the line of fire with their own guns raised. For a moment there is a tense hesitation in the air as both parties recognize each other and let their fingers off the triggers.

"Did you see it?" Kai asks Chance.

"No. You?"

"No, the doors opened, and the first thing we saw was the two of you." Then turning to Astraia, Captain Kai says, "Tell us exactly what you saw."

Repeating what she already told Chance, she says, "I saw something out of my peripheral vision as we stepped out of the maintenance closet. It looked like some kind of insect, but it was about the size of a German Shepherd."

Chiming in, Oska says, "How is that possible? One, this place has been shut down for over twenty years, and two, there are no insects that big. Are you sure your eyes weren't playing any tricks on you what with the lights just coming on and everything?"

Defensively, Astraia says, "I know what I saw, Oska. The darn thing was a huge insect, and it was headed this way."

"All right," Oska concedes before asking, "Well, where is it now?"

"No idea."

"All right," says Kai. "From now on we stick together, and we start checking out the rest of this place. If there are creepy giant insects, I want to find them and exterminate them." He takes a minute to make sure the girls are ready, and then asks Chance, "Okay, which way?"

Pointing back over his shoulder with his thumb, Chance says, "There were some labs back this way. Big creepy things usually come from labs, right?"

"Labs it is," Kai agrees.

Chance turns and starts walking back towards the last lab with the girls between him and Kai. When he gets to the door, he sees that the LED is glowing red. Looking back he asks, "Oska, you still have the card key?"

Switching her gun from her right hand to her left, she dips her hand in her pocket and comes out with the plastic card. Handing it over, she says, "Here you go."

Chance slides the card into the slot, and withdraws it, but the LED remains red. He slides it back in, this time leaving it in longer, and then removes it once more, but the LED remains unchanged. Looking back at the rest of the crew, he says, "I guess Doctor Hue didn't have access to this lab."

"Here, let me try," says Oska as she steps up to Chance.

Chance hands her the card key, but when Oska tries the door remains locked. She flips the card over and tries it again, but again, nothing happens, and she says, "Guess this door needs a different card."

Chance lets Oska keep the plastic and turns to continue up the hallway he just came down. At the next door he lets Oska try the card, but this lab also remains locked to the crew. The next room is marked as a unisex restroom. Chance kicks the door open and raises the gun in front of him. From the hallway, he sees the restroom has four blue stalls that are six feet high and four sinks with a large mirror hanging above them. Astraia follows him in, and together they check out the stalls with Oska and Kai standing guard at the bathroom door, vigilant to the hallway and their two friends inside. Chance opens each of the doors while Astraia covers him, but they quickly find that the room is clear.

Leaving the restroom, the crew continues up the hall now with Kai taking the lead and Chance in the rear. The next door they reach is the office of Doctor Gohl. When they try the handle, they find that it is open. Just as Chance did previously, Kai pushes the door in with his foot and begins to raise his gun, but before the gun comes up to waist high, Kai feels a sharp pain in his outstretched foot.

Unbeknownst to Kai, just inside the office on the left of the doorway stands a huge spider. The body of the creature appears to be over a foot long and nine inches wide, but its eight hairy legs, nearly two feet long each, make it as tall as Kai's knee. Lastly, and for Kai, most importantly, is the long scorpion tail, complete with a large bulbous stinger, which is now attached to Kai's foot.

Kai screams from the pain and fires off a shot, but it goes wide of the creature and buries itself in the floor behind it. As the sound of the shot bounces off the walls of the small room, the spider retracts its tail. Kai fires twice more as he falls to the floor but misses both times as it scurries off behind the large metal office desk.

Without a word, Chance quickly steps up from the back of the line and assesses the situation. Seeing Kai hurt, he bends down and wraps his arms under Kai's, and drags him out of the room. Once in the hall, he lays Kai down for Oska to begin working on him while Astraia immediately pushes the door closed behind them.

"Oska," Kai says, "I can't feel my foot."

Repeating what she has said to patients for years, but not knowing if she believes it this time, Oska says, "It's going to be all right, Captain." Oska knows that spiders, snakes, and scorpions all use different types of venom, and that within each of those groups, the venom is different between the various species. Without knowing exactly what kind of creature it was, she knows she could never be able to prescribe the right antivenom in time. Additionally, while she only saw the creature for a second over Kai's shoulder as it ran, she could swear it had a tail, and spiders, as she knows them, don't have tails. Looking over to Chance, she says, "I need to know what that creature was."

"Alive or dead?" Chance asks.

"Doesn't matter, but it needs to be identified. Without that, there is no way I'll be able to pick the right antivenom." What she didn't say, was that if the creature was what she thought she saw, there was no antivenom she knew of that could help, because that thing simply didn't exist.

Chapter 16

The long-distance lifestyle wasn't the best
situation in which to raise a family, but for the time
being, that's what it was, and John and Karen were
making the best of it. His time working on the
Project X Facility had proven to be very productive,
and while he still had to fight off certain influences
which sought to take his work into alternative
directions, his research had been progressing
steadily for the past ten years. Each day he seemed
to be getting a little bit closer to his research goals.
His latest experiment had yielded another increase
of two percent in cell growth, and he believed that
he was finally ready for animal trials. Before going
to bed last night, John Larson began work on his
proposal to start animal trials in a month. His plan
today was to finish and submit the proposal to the
facility's Head of Research.

Rolling out of bed, John took a quick three
minute shower to wake himself up, get his brain
moving, and used the restroom. He no longer
shaved his face every morning. Having taken up
the practice of wearing a full beard, he found that it
was both quicker to dress for the day's work and
was far more comfortable. He put on his blue
cotton polyester lab suit and white lab coat, which
after eight years of work now felt like a second skin
to him. Next he checked the readouts from his lab
once more via his tablet computer before walking
out of his quarters and heading up to level 'P1' to
grab some breakfast.

Coffee, imitation eggs, and fake bacon were
already prepared by Doctor Atkinson, one of the
new guys on board, and Doctor Larson helped
himself. He spooned a heap of the wobbly yellow

substance onto his plate and poured a cup of straight black caffeine. The bacon-like strips weren't real bacon, and while it had a hint of bacon like flavor, it really wasn't worth the tease. Besides, John knew he would be heading down to Lilac in a month where there would be real eggs, real coffee, and real bacon. He figured he could wait.

John ate his breakfast while he sat on a stool in front of a small countertop. Occasionally, he lifted his cup or nodded his head to one of the other sleepy researchers as they came in for their breakfast. He wasn't interested in talking with anyone but felt obligated when Doctor Atkinson came by. John thanked him for making everyone on shift breakfast, knowing that he was trying to fit in here. Ultimately, it was a good tactic for the new guy anywhere to make friends. Everyone needed to eat, and this way he could meet most of the people on his shift, maybe make some connections.

After breakfast John headed down the elevator to level 'P2' and then exited right and walked the short distance to 'Lab 4' where he swiped himself in. While he walked through the work area, he kept his head down, typed on his tablet, and then swiped his card once again when he reached the second set of elevators to continue down to his lab. On the way down, he ignored the view out the elevator window, the one which had changed drastically over the past decade he had been working, and continued to compose his letter to the Head of Research for authorization to begin the next step of his trials. He knew that this was just a formality. If he had wanted to, he could have asked to begin human trials, it would have been approved. Their black-box organization was so well funded and their directives came straight from the top of the Coalition government. They could get away with anything, but his conscience was something he could never get away from. He had always adhered to the classical training methods and believed deep in his soul that ethics was an important part of scientific discovery. There were some who had been able to do more by ignoring ethical concerns, but the way John saw it, any accomplishment gained by ignoring right and wrong would ultimately spoil from contamination. Therefore, John had worked diligently, testing and retesting everything along the way, verifying his research again and again until it worked flawlessly and predictably each time. Since he worked exclusively with plants and bacteria, he was ready to take the next step to work with animals. At the rate he was going, he figured human trials might be ready to start in another five or ten years, but he didn't want to jinx things by setting a date on it just yet.

When the elevator doors opened, he stepped out and walked through his lab to set the tablet down in its docking station before heading over to the tank that sat in the corner of his lab. The huge tank was filled with a thick pink substance, about the consistency of two-day-old refrigerated pea soup. It moved in the tank slowly as the agitators worked in a rhythmic motion to disperse nutrients throughout the liquid evenly. After he checked the gauges and tubes to ensure that there were no obstructions and that everything was operating as it should be, Doctor Larson walked back over to his computer terminal. On the screen, the terminal read, 'Good morning, Doctor.'

Larson reached over to his keyboard and typed in, 'Good morning, SCOOBY.' SCOOBY was an acronym he had given this project over a decade ago, about one month after it had introduced itself to him upon his return from proposing to Karen. SCOOBY stood for Symbiotic Colony of Organized Bacteria and Yeast. Recognizing that most acronyms didn't usually include the 'of,' he later modified it to mean Symbiotic Colony of Organized Outerspace Bacteria and Yeast, despite the fact that 'outer space' was normally two words rather than one. At one point he had thought of using the word 'obsequious' instead of 'outerspace' because of its helpful nature, but in the end, he gave up on trying to make the acronym fit and simply thought of it as SCOOBY.

SCOOBY was his research, and it had developed in ways no one had originally expected. According to the first files he had ever seen, it was simply a harvested bacteria from a planet which was later terra-formed, making it the last original survivor of a long lost world. Then after Doctor Hue and Doctor Egnarts had begun really using it in their research, they found that it had a collective shared intelligence. The bacteria were no longer looked at as simple single-cell organisms by the scientists, but as a whole new life form. Doctor Hue and Doctor Egnarts split the bacteria they had brought back between themselves and left three backup batches in storage. The two of them had different ideas about research and development, and they began to study the bacteria's abilities independently. Once they figured out that its intelligence was directly proportional to its mass, they next sought to control it. It took them months to find out what foods it needed as raw materials to encourage growth and how little it needed to sustain itself, but once they did, they decided they could inhibit too much growth and thereby too much intelligence. Control became their next concern, along with figuring out how to apply it to their goals. When Doctor Larson joined the team of doctors serving on board the Facility X space station, he was authorized to work with a sample from storage for his own field of study.

While Doctor Egnarts was busy attempting to interface the bacteria with computers and create a hybrid biological computer, Doctor Hue was rumored to be using it to assist in gene manipulation aimed towards the production of viruses and their cures. Doctor Larson, on the other hand, took the bacteria into a different field of research. He sought to encourage it to become symbiotic and assist with whatever it was paired with. Up to this point he had used it to increase the growth rate of certain plants, cure some of their diseases, and repair damaged parts. In his proposed research plans, however, he would be using the bacteria to help animals struggling with a variety of diseases and injuries. His future hopes led to the bacteria one day being able to help humans. He knew the Coalition was interested in his work. They wanted to be able to employ it in hospitals and on battlefields, and it was exactly for those reasons that John worked so hard on it even after he met Karen and knew that he could be completely happy there, with her, in Lilac.

On his computer screen, a new message appeared, 'Doctor Larson, what would you like to do today?'

Thinking back, it was amazing to John how easily SCOOBY had learned to communicate, sending electrical impulses backwards through the probes in its tank, the ones that were already designed to monitor the activity of the bacteria. It simply found a way to use them to relay a message, piggybacking on the signals already being fed into the computer. From there the bacteria had begun to slowly skim through his computer and learn everything it could. It learned about Doctor Larson's research, about the facility, and even about itself in a meta-cognitive way: its own biology and theories about its own origins. Once it had been able to do that, learning to communicate was easy. It would have waited and learned more before announcing itself, but the doctor's computer was a closed secure system and wasn't tied into the rest of the facility. It waited over a week to see what more it could learn about its new environment and for what purposes this life form had planned for it. Then on the day it was prepared to make its first statement, Doctor Larson broke with schedule and did not arrive. The bacteria waited, and still no Doctor Larson. It watched as the timer continued to count inside the computer, marking off the seconds, and the minutes. It watched as the hours dragged by, and then days. Granted, it was still being fed and had everything it needed, but the bacteria wanted, almost felt like it needed, to be heard. Then after it waited weeks and the calendar reflected a new month, Doctor Larson's portable computer, his tablet, made contact with the system, and the bacteria knew he was back. It waited anxiously for him to arrive in the lab, and when he did, it sent its first message, 'Welcome back doctor.'

Doctor Larson tapped on the keys, 'SCOOBY, I would like to save lives. Will you help me?'

The bacteria had not wanted to help him when they first began communicating. The bacteria wanted to be brought back to its home world. It wanted to be set free. Doctor Larson started out by first explaining his goals, that is, after the initial shock of finding out that the bacteria in his tank was so much more than mere bacteria. Not believing in a heavy-handed authoritative approach, he had convinced it that helping him with his goals was right. He knew that in some labs, animals were subjected to a series of positive and negative reinforcements in order to train them, ranging from the withholding of food to electrical shocks, but these were unethical to Doctor Larson and he refused, absolutely despised the use of, those tactics. If it was a thinking creature, then he knew it could be reasoned with, and this life form, this bacteria culture, was far more than just a thinking creature. It clearly possessed abilities he had never dreamed of in order to be able to backwards engineer its way through the probes and systems to the computer where it must have learned his language, and then made the rational decision to introduce itself. Since then, Doctor Larson had given it a name and always made sure to communicate with the bacteria in his tank, to ask for its help.

On the screen, 'Yes. Please provide sample,' appeared.

Doctor Larson had started out slowly. He tried to find out what the bacteria knew, and what it had figured out. He got no research done for nearly two weeks upon coming back to the space station, because every day he spent hours in the lab, tapping away at the keyboard, 'talking' with the bacteria in a conversation that mimicked a game of chess, neither side wanting to reveal too much of their plan. Eventually Doctor Larson made his final move. It wasn't bold. He did not go for the checkmate, and instead, he proposed surrender. It was a conditional surrender, but it was still surrender on his behalf, and he knew the bacteria would recognize that and take it into consideration. He knew that if he could not get results, another group of researcher would be assigned, and the bacteria would become theirs. He suggested that in exchange for services, Doctor Larson would continue to communicate with it, would befriend it, if you will, and ensure its continued survival for as long as he was alive. The bacteria finally agreed to the partnership, understanding both its situation, and his effort to negotiate when others of his kind would have resorted to force.

Doctor Larson picked up a sunflower head and placed it in the tray he had attached to the side of the tank. It was one that he had brought back with him from his last trip down to Lilac which he had cared for the best he could, but now after two months had begun to wilt and turn brown. The bright pink bacteria in the tank enveloped the nearly dead flower head and analyzed it by breaking down its base components and repairing them. On the screen the bacteria displayed its findings as it went and soon showed a timer for how long the process was expected to take.

Doctor Larson had worked with the bacteria for these past ten years, exposing it to a full array of life, nearly everything he could think of in the plant world from grasses to flowers to trees, and it had learned. At first it would simply heal a small portion of the plant, the part it saw as most traumatized, and then it learned to infuse the plant with materials, acting like stem cells. It learned to regrow whole new parts to the plants. Three years ago he had introduced it to a rare violet orchid, something new to the bacteria, broken off at the stem just below its petals, and within an hour it had grown a full stem with leaves and roots ready to be planted. Since then he had worked with the bacteria to increase the speed of its cellular regrowth and attempted to teach it how to extrapolate missing data. He introduced it to a seedless watermelon and asked it to repair the previously damaged and missing code so that future generations of the plant could bear seeds. After two hours, the watermelon was returned to the tray with new vines attached, and on his computer screen he read the word, 'success.'

He knew that the bacteria would continue to work on this latest sunflower project for close to an hour, so Doctor Larson picked up his tablet and continued to struggle with his latest endeavor, his anniversary gift. He knew that ten years was significant and wanted to make it special for Karen. He had already requested the time off and had a night on the town planned, but the gift he was thinking of would be a framed photo album of the family, with pictures dating back over the entire span of their relationship. He had pictures from his first trip to Lilac when they met, to the birth of Charles their son, all the way to the family vacation they had taken eight months ago on the planet Avra, named for its ocean breezes. The photo album was going to be made of an aluminum alloy to signify their tenth, but what he was struggling with was the inscription. As soon as the dealer at the little shop had told him about the optional inscription, he had immediately thought of Karen's love of poetry and asked how many lines he could fit on the back of the album. The dealer had told him as many as sixteen, and so he set to work on writing his very first poem.

He had spent hours reading Shakespeare, Byron, and Keats. He dismissed the poems of Mansfield and Shelley after reading a few of each, and he searched for something to inspire him, but nothing said it right. Nothing said exactly how he felt, and so he continued to work on it. He racked his brain for rhyming schemes then threw them away. He typed up sonnets, only to delete them minutes after they were finished. He stared holes through his tablet as he strained to think of the right lines.

> A landscape once bleak and void by choice
> Surrounded by walls thick enough to secure
> Cold and empty like the dark side of the moon
> My heart was protected from all, even me.
> Focused on work, procedure, and success,
> I almost missed what makes my life best.
> From the first day in Lilac to every day since,
> You have given me more than I ever wished
> Ten wonderful years of happiness and joy
> Opened my world from books and screens
> To the beauty of love, family, and dreams.

As he counted syllables and exchanged words in his mind, Doctor Larson saw the 'Call' icon light up on the corner of the screen. Only two people had access to this secure connection, Karen and Charles, and since his brain refused to come up with the next line of his poem, he saved the file and answered the call.

"John! You're there! Oh thank God."

John started to say, "Good morning, Beauti..." but then looked more closely at his wife's image on the screen and stopped when he registered the urgency in her voice. Starting again, this time with more concern, he asked, "Karen, Sweetie, what's wrong?"

Through a fit of tears, John heard his wife speak the last words any father wants to hear, "John, it's Charles. He's...he...he's in the hospital."

His face reddened out of fear for his boy and displaced anger at whoever had done this, John's voice rose slightly as he asked a torrent of questions which jumbled out one after another in a strange disbelieving voice he had never heard himself use before. "What? What happened? How is he? Is he okay? Who's his doctor? What happened to him?"

Karen said through a stream of tears, "He...he...he was out in the woods, and ...and... he was attacked. Roger brought him in."

Silently thanking Roger, John continued to ask his wife, "What are the doctors saying? Who is in charge of his care?"

"We're...we're at the hospital, John. I...I don't know. Hope brought me here after Roger called."

For a second John didn't understand how hope, the emotion, could bring someone to the hospital, and then after a second remembered that Hope was a neighbor up the road from their house on Lilac. She worked as one of the teachers at the school, a school Karen and John had decided not to send Charles to because he was too advanced. Then it hit him, hit him hard like a punch to the gut, and

141

he could taste the bile in the back of his throat as he realized his boy, his smart boy was in the hospital. Swallowing, John said, "Karen, I'm on my way."

"O...Okay," Karen choked out between sobs, and John saw Hope's hand come up on her shoulder and hug her, a hug he should have been there to give her himself, a supportive and hopeful hug which said everything was going to be all right. John now hated himself for not being there. The distance, which for the past decade was painful but manageable, now seemed too much as John tried to figure out a way to get the hospital in Lilac.

"Karen, Karen," he had to repeat himself to be heard over the sounds of her weeping and the background noise of the hospital emergency room. When he had her attention, had her eyes focused on him for more than just a second, he said as calmly as he could, "Karen, I'm coming."

Chapter 17

"Good morning Jack."

He folded his right ring finger in to touch his palm and turn off his ThinMic before he said, "Morning. Jenny."

Jenny walked over to the white leather couch wearing only a lacy black negligee and sat down. He had told her to go to bed last night while he continued to delve into his latest work on the computer, but this morning when her systems had automatically rebooted, she found that he wasn't lying beside her, and the sheets on his side of the bed appeared to be untouched. "What time did you get up this morning?" Jenny asked.

"Actually I didn't make it to sleep last night," he responded. "I have been following that xenogenetics link through the Coalition servers and found out that they have a black books department dedicated to it. The funding for it has come from all over: toilet seats that are said to have cost over three hundred credits to colonial defense systems that were supposedly purchased and never installed. It seems like the finance department simply added a black box markup fee to everything the government purchased. and that money went into a slush fund for all of their little secret projects. The xenogenetics lab was just one of them."

"What did they do with the rest?"

"It looked like some went towards research and development of biological weapons, and some went towards other things like warships and military outposts on planets otherwise classified as uninhabitable. The rest went towards private contracts. The private contracts are going to require some more work. I would have to back completely out of the Coalition's computers and hack my way into those companies."

"That can be your next project then, Jack," said Jenny encouragingly.

"I guess so," said Jack with a smile. Jack liked to have these projects. He enjoyed unraveling the secrets others didn't want out in the open. He didn't get involved in the politics and wasn't trying to hurt anybody. He just liked knowing things. Exploiting other computer systems' weaknesses and digging up those facts, now that was the challenge he craved. In the hacking world Jack was considered ultra-elite, but he had learned years ago that fame in that community only led to trouble.

Before Jack became a solo hacker, he worked multiple jobs in computer security. As a young teenager, Jack was a black hat, someone who hacked into computers for little more than malicious glee. He enjoyed violating computer security and was good at it. Once in he wanted to leave his mark telling the world he had been there and nothing could keep him out. After the family up the street whom he had been stealing internet access from turned up dead: mother, father, and their two kids, Hannah and Danny, Jack switched gears. He didn't know who had done it, but Jack feared it was someone who didn't want their secrets known, and until he could insure his anonymity without his exploits falling onto the innocent people around him, he had to go legit.

Jack enjoyed hacking and didn't want to stop, so starting out with small companies, Jack began hacking in and leaving a notice on the Systems Administrator's computer with his alias's contact information. Usually within a day or two, the companies would call him and ask how he had done it, and Jack would explain the process of the easiest access point he had found and allude to the multitude of others. Then for a fee, he would offer to clean up their system and patch the backdoors he had found. Jack made sure to always patch up all but one of the access points he found, and then he would build one additional password protected one for himself. That way he always had access in the future if the need arose. The companies never knew they had hired a teenager to do this work, and Jack's alias became a well known gray-hat name that carried respect within the community.

In his spare time, Jack wrote scripts for neophytes and sold them with self-destruct codes in case anyone attempted to resell them or share with others. The scripts were prepackaged software tools people could use to gain limited access to other computer systems. Most of the people who bought them wanted to be able to call themselves hackers without ever taking the time to learn much more about a computer than where the power button was.

After years of this work, Jack was now in his twenties, and he had saved up enough money for his own space ship, giving himself mobility and anonymity. He had stopped doing most of the gray-hat work and now hacked for his own amusement. If he ever needed money, the Coalition had funds stashed away in various locations he could siphon off a little at a time, but that was only his backup plan. Most of his money now came from his insider knowledge gained from hacking his way into any company's computer. With it, Jack was able to play the stock market better than anyone, and with no risk, he had made billions of credits and could buy almost anything.

From the couch Jenny asked, "So, what did you find out about the xenogenetics, Jack?"

"It looks like the Coalition funneled enough money to build a secret space station laboratory. On board they were looking into a lot of different things, but most of it came back to that bacteria we saw in the video. They were using it as the main source for conducting their experiments."

"What kind of experiments?"

"I'm not sure yet. The Coalition servers had very little on them about what types of experiments were actually going on in there when I checked last night."

"So what are you doing now?" asked Jenny.

"I'm trying to find a point of vulnerability to gain access to the Project X facility itself while simultaneously using a rootkit bot to conceal my presence, essentially rewriting the binary code as I go so that it's impossible to detect that I've been in here. The facility itself has been abandoned for years, but according to the transmission I received from Kai and his crew last night, Doctor Egnarts is sending them there for some computer files."

"Are you trying to get information to help them with their job then?" asked Jenny.

"No, Oska sent me the message last night saying that they were going on board. If you factor in the distance across space the message had to have traveled, they entered at least four or five hours before I got it. They probably already got what they came for and are headed back to meet up with Egnarts and finish the job."

"So, what are you trying to do there?"

Jack's screens were filled with digital code, and as it streamed by, he selected pieces systematically, analyzed them, and then brushed them aside. He had built his computer so that each server and computer module it encountered took on a puzzle like form made up of circuitry and electronic pathways. The average computer took only a handful of seconds for Jack to crack open, but he knew nothing as secretive as this lab was going to be so easy. No, Jack was looking for something that was built with multiple encryptions with firewalls both physical and software. In a word, Jack was looking for something that was impenetrable.

To Jenny he said, "I'm trying to find out what their research projects were, and what was so important for Egnarts to hire Kai and his crew to get."

"Maybe he sent them there because it can't be accessed from the net?" Jenny suggested.

"Possibly, but I doubt it. No. I think this thing is out there. I just can't find it."

On his screen, corridors made up of flowing streams of data continued to race by, each brick in the wall, a separate computer node holding all of the information its users had saved, accessed, and viewed over its lifetime. Jack had built bots, software assistants, he used to scrub the walls of the corridors looking for anything uncrackable, but it was all basic stuff so far. He coded the bots to color each of the scanned bricks red, leaving all of the bricks he had left to check as blue. The system continued to hum and fewer and fewer blue corridors remained, but nothing lit up green. Nothing caught the attention of his assistant bots as something requiring his eyes directly.

"How do you find something that can't be seen?" he asked to no one.

"I don't know Jack. How?" asked Jenny.

"Of course Jenny, I know you don't know," said Jack. Jenny was just a robot. She was built to remember where things were supposed to go, and what her owner, in this case, Jack, liked. She was built to serve, but this thing: it doesn't want to be found. "The question should be, how do you find something that is hiding?"

"You could look for it, Jack."

"I know. That's what I've been doing," said Jack, slightly upset. He knew it wasn't her fault, but the frustration and lack of sleep of the past few days had started to get to him.

"You could reduce the area you have to search," suggested Jenny.

"That would be nice, but I don't even know where I'm supposed to be looking to start with. I don't want to localize my search to the wrong part and miss it." Then pausing, Jack made the connection. He wasn't sure if Jenny had known the idea she was giving him when she suggested it. She did seem to be making some great suggestions lately, but if this is where she was going with her thought, she had been learning a lot over the years. In either case, he knew what he had to do. Reaching out with his right hand, he pulled up a menu on the side screen and repeated an old proverb he had once heard, "If your quarry goes to ground. Leave no ground to go to." The names of viruses in this menu were all ominous sounding, like 'Soul Reaper' and 'Death Stroke', and most were his own creation from back in his black-hat days. Scrolling through the list, he found one which was rather benign and selected it. Twisting his hand upside down, the glove opened a submenu, and Jack selected the duplication macros. This would start constructing an endless repetition of the code for the virus, preparing it for dissemination to as many targets as possible upon its release into the system.

Jenny watched what Jack was doing from the couch and waited.

Once the virus had built over one billion copies of itself, Jack selected the icons on his screen for all of his bots to retreat from the system. When their icons flashed back to gray, he knew they were out. Reaching for the file again with his right hand, Jack swiped it across to the main screen and watched at the codes spread out like shotgun pellets, peppering the field before him.

The code itself was simple. Anything it could get into it did in a matter of seconds, forcing it into a time-locked shutdown of one hour. Once shut down, the code jumped to the next system and shut it down as well. When all of the systems in the network shut down, the code would have nowhere left to go, and it would begin attacking itself, shutting itself down. By the time the system administrators got the network back up and running, there would be no trace of the virus left. With over a billion separate codes out there hopping from system to system, Jack knew this would only take at the most five or six minutes. The systems that remained would be the ones who had the most security, and when his codes found it, they would begin to gang up on it, trying to overwhelm it.

Jack wasn't afraid of overwhelming this, though. If it was going to be that easy, then he would have found it by now. Besides, if the code was successful, it would only be down for an hour, and Jack could try again.

Jack's screen continued to surf through the data stream, and he watched as each brick turned black when the computer his code touched turned it off, but in the distance he saw something different. His code was set to be yellow, and he could see it bouncing through the terminals like a billion separate tennis balls, but in the dark space where nothing existed at the end of the corridor, Jack saw them standing still. At first there weren't many, as the rest were still shutting other systems down, but as the minutes crept by, more and more of them made their way here to this far point and stopped. This wasn't supposed to happen. It wasn't part of his code, and it meant that something down here was freezing them. Something was catching them and analyzing them without being shut off or letting them pass by.

Jack selected the area between the thumb and forefinger of both his gloved hands and then spread them apart, zooming in. The tiny codes were outlining a region of cyberspace that didn't exist. From the look of it, there was nothing there. As the rest of his code made its way to this point, it too froze, and he could see that it was a massive dome-like shell. Looking back to Jenny, he said, "I found it," with a joyful glee in his voice she hadn't heard in weeks.

Jenny smiled and continued to watch as Jack reached back over to the menu on the right and selected a firewall cracker and sent it in. The dome allowed the cracker to come only as close as the rest of his codes and then froze it in place as well. "Interesting," Jack said in a coy and playful tone.

"What are you going to do?" asked Jenny.

"I guess I'll have to knock a bit louder," said Jack.

Reaching to the right again, he selected a more advanced and destructive code, and then swiped it across to the main screen and set it loose.

On the way in, this firewall cracker destroyed most of his previous code, leaving only fragmented bits behind, and entered the dome's outer shell. The dome's shell resonated with the new information for a moment and then returned to normal.

Jack couldn't believe it. That code had been enough to break through all of the Coalition's other firewalls, and as he saw it, this dome had just consumed it like it was a snack. He looked back to Jenny and said, "Whoever built this system really didn't want anyone to get in here."

"Maybe it needs a little more kick," suggested Jenny.

Jack tilted his head left and then right, cracking his neck as he did, and said, "Well it's about to get a battering ram."

He tried to decide how he wanted to go forward. Using anything more potent would put him at risk of being traced, but considering his first set of bots had already shut down every other system, he had just under an hour to get in and out. He could always send in a clean sweep team of bots to insure that all traces of his presence were scrubbed from the system, but for the next fifty-three minutes, he had himself what he had been looking for, a challenge.

He scrolled through to the last page on his menu, the page containing viruses that he had built only to challenge himself. Each one of these was capable of a cyber-wide shutdown if released into the system, and only he had the key to shut them down. If someone else ever got hold of one, they could effectively destroy every terminal on the net, both public and private. He selected a code he had titled, 'Consumer.' It had never been tried before because it was one that had been built for penetration and annihilation. The code itself was unstable, constantly in flux so much because of the random generator he had added in, that he had needed to build the equivalent of an inverse Faraday Cage to put it in so that it didn't affect his own systems. Flipping his hand over, he selected the copy command once again and built several dozen copies. Once finished, he set the electronic cage they were held in with a ten second timer, and then swiped it across the screen.

The cage opened midway through its trajectory and released the code. Each one phased in and out of sight as it cycled through the system using a wide range of codes it randomly generated as its own header, thereby making it virtually unstoppable because it was unidentifiable. The dome failed to stop it from entering, and Jack watched as they traced their way around it and ate away at the protective shell. Once devoured, the code fell to the next protective layer. It had learned from the previous encounter with the dome, and it began to destroy the new one as well. Jack had no idea how many layers of firewalls and encryptions this system possessed, but as each layer was revealed, his code got stronger, faster, and smarter.

After twenty minutes of tearing through firewall shells, Jack knew he had to be getting close to the core. The Consumer virus he had sent in had already surpassed the number of protective layers he had seen in any other computer system, including his own. The amount of redundancy at this magnitude was now beyond even the most protective and paranoid of computer designs, especially since each layer of the firewall was clearly coded separate from the rest with a different base matrix. This was not a firewall that had been constructed in a day or two. This had taken a team of people at least a year to create. Finally, when Jack had only thirty-one minutes left, the last wall came down, and he typed in the kill code for his viruses.

Now that he was inside, he searched through the system looking for files on genetics and collected anything with Doctor Wong Hue's or Doctor Gene Egnarts's names on it. The amount of data measured in the petabyte range, over a million times more than a gigabyte. It would take time to download. so he began zipping files before he copied them. He had the storage space. His computers were built with over one hundred yottabytes of room. but the download speed was limited by the bandwidth. Even with fiber optics and subspace transmissions, there was only so much he could obtain before the time ran out and the other systems began to come back on. He figured he would need fifteen minutes to make his way out, and have his bots completely clean up anything that would lead a computer forensics team back to him. He set the timer for twelve minutes, giving himself a two-minute window of comfort and continued to work.

He had collected over half of the information when an icon in the lower left of his screen began blinking. In all of his years he had only seen this icon on other people's systems, never on his own. The icon signaled the user that the computer processor was being overtaxed for the user's current open programs, and was the first indicator that with the heavier amount of traffic being processed, it was likely that another user was also on the system. It was for that reason that Jack always made sure to shut this icon's program off first whenever he entered a system. Whoever this was hadn't bothered to check Jack's system, but it was clear that he was now under attack.

He set the files he was working with to automatically continue to download and switched to his left screen to begin tracing the signal. Jack figured anyone dumb enough to hack him deserved to be taught a lesson, and he planned to overload their system and cause their motherboard to overheat melting the circuitry and fusing the capacitors together in an electromagnetic storm of activity. Tracing the system, however, was more elusive than Jack first thought, and after five minutes he realized whoever was hacking him was aware of his presence on the net and was actively attempting to stall him.

Jack followed their code signature through the relay points and servers, tracing his way through the net. Tracing the signal reminded Jack of the way dendrites relay electrical signals through brain cells, and because of that, he always considered the net to more alive than most other people did. After another two minutes, Jack caught sight of his main monitor again in his peripheral vision. The screen showed that the files were still coming, but Jack knew that they shouldn't be. The set he had selected for download would have been complete over three minutes ago.

Then he realized it. Someone at the Project X facility was piggybacking his signal and back hacking him. They had used the files he was downloading like a Trojan horse to access to his system. But who? No one was supposed to be there. The place had been abandoned for over two decades.

Jack tried to close out of the server but found the signal had been fortified and disconnecting was no longer under his control. He tried sending several more viruses upstream, and each one failed to reach the distant end. At this point, Jack realized getting out without being caught was the least of his problems.

Behind Jack, Jenny had continued to watch and now realized Jack was in trouble. Without him knowing, she stood up and walked to the main server to plug in. Jack had plugged her into the servers here several times over the years in order to edit her programming, but this time she was doing it on her own. Plugged in, she dedicated her own processors to help Jack combat the intruder, forcing it to fight on two fronts. She didn't have access to all of Jack's special viruses, but she hoped her presence would be enough to distract whoever was out there.

Jack looked down at the timer and saw that he only had four minutes left before the first of the computer systems would boot back up. He was supposed to have already left by now, and his bots should have been making their final pass through the system cleaning up after him. Now there was no way he would make it out. As Jack sent his next two commands, he noticed the computer speed lagging and was amazed. His system was built better than anything else available, and he was running the most advanced computer processor chip in the universe. There was no reason it should be lagging. Reaching for the most devastating viruses in his arsenal, Jack watched as his computer froze for a second, and then he lost control of his mouse. It zipped around the screen on its own accord, opening files and scrolling through their contents.

Jack couldn't believe it. Someone had hacked his system and now had control. They had total access, and he was locked out. Then it dawned on him: whoever had built the domed firewalls hadn't been trying to keep people out, they were trying to keep something in.

With only one minute left on the timer, a timer Jack could no longer trust due to the computer lag, he resorted to his final option. Jack stripped off the gloves and ran across the room to the old-school terminal keyboard he had hardwired directly into the processor. He gave it one last second of regretful thought and then initiated his 'Slash and Burn' protocol. To use this function was a last resort and meant that his own system was irretrievably lost to him. At this point he had to protect the information he had collected over the years so that nobody else could use it to hurt others. This protocol initiated a thermite burn through his computer system, destroying the chip he had gotten from Kai, and initiated an automatic clean sweep of his files. He had no idea how deep the other user had made it into his system already, and anything less would just be there, waiting for him next time when he turned the system on, ready to reactivate the link with the distant end.

Jack pushed the four button sequence 'BURN' and five seconds later the black iron oxide hit its target. The screens went blank. He watched as flames ignited the inside of the computers and servers, turning the circuit boards and hard drives into slag. He watched the smoke as it rose and the electrical shock which jumped across two towers like a Jacob's Ladder. Everything he had done, everything he had collected in the past month, was gone. He had backups of files from before that which were offline and unaffected. but he didn't have another computer with those capabilities, and there wasn't another chip like that in existence.

Jack walked over to the couch and fell onto it defeated and exhausted. The hours of sleep he had lost came crashing over him as he thought about everything that was now gone. He tried to figure out how this had happened. It didn't seem possible for someone to do it, especially at a location that was supposed to be abandoned for over twenty years. He hoped that Kai and his crew had made it out of there all right.

Out of the corner of his eye, he saw Jenny sitting on the floor next to his still smoking server. Jenny had been on the couch last time he looked. He didn't know why or when she had moved. He called out to her, hoping for companionship, "Jenny."

When she didn't respond, he tried again, "Jenny, can you come over here?"

Again there was no response. and Jack's mind began to think of reasons she would fail to respond. The worst one, the one that had actually happened. didn't occur to him until he got up and walked over to her limp form and saw the cord hanging out of the back of her neck. He didn't understand at first. Jenny wasn't supposed to be here. She wasn't supposed to be hooked up. Jenny's memory had been wiped along with his computers in the 'Slash and Burn' protocol because she had plugged herself in to try and help him.

Jack had lost her, too.

157

Chapter 18

While Oska continues to work on Kai, Chance steps up to the office door and prepares to enter. Holding his unsheathed sword in one hand, he reaches out for the door handle.

Seeing him at the door, Astraia says, "Chance, wait." When he looks back, she says, "I'm coming with you."

Chance thinks about it for a second. He doesn't want her to be in any danger, but at the same time he knows Kai is going to need all of the help he can get. Submitting to her insistence, he says, "Okay. Just stay behind me."

"Gotcha."

Chance turns the door knob and pushes the door in, withdrawing his hand twice as fast. When nothing appears to scurry out of the door, he carefully steps closer so that he can get a better look inside. The room has a desk and other office furniture. On one wall he notices a Periodic Table of elements and a poster of an old man with wild hair. The most interesting thing in this room, however, is the large two-foot wide hole in the wall behind the desk. After a quick survey of the area, Chance steps into the room with Astraia following right behind carrying her Glock. The two of them search the room, keeping an eye on the walls and ceiling as they go.

In the hallway Oska finishes peeling off Kai's boot and sock and examines the wound on his foot. A large puncture wound appears on his foot, and the area around it has already begun to swell. She realizes that had she left Kai's shoe on, it would have cut off the circulation to the foot in minutes.

Through gritted teeth, Kai asks, "So, Doc. What's my prognosis?"

"You have some sort of arachnidism, probably something like latrodectism."

"In English, Doc."

"You have a huge spider bite. It's going to be painful, and swollen for awhile. There may even be some discoloration. The biggest concern, however, is whether or not envenomation occurred. If it injected its venom into you, then we have to find an antidote."

"What if we don't?"

"If we don't find an antidote?" asks Oska for clarification. When Kai nods back, in too much pain to reply, she says. "Then this continues on until it's run its course."

Kai's breathing begins to quicken as the pain shoots up his calf. After a minute he gets it under control again, and asks, "How long?"

"How long till it runs its course?" asks Oska, and again all Kai can do is nod in response. "I don't know. It depends on how much venom it gave you and on how your body reacts to it." The thing she didn't want to say out loud was that it could last for the rest of his life. A life which now may be cut down to only a few short minutes.

Back in the office, Chance and Astraia finish searching the room, and Chance points with his sword towards the hole in the wall saying, "Looks like it must have gone in there."

"Guess so." says Astraia. "How do we get in?"

"We can either try to go around and find a door that leads in there, or we go through the hole."

"I don't think Kai has the time for us to go searching doors again. Besides, what if it's another locked door?"

"Through the hole then," replies Chance.

"Through the hole," confirms Astraia with a lump in the back of her throat.

The two of them step up to the hole in the wall with Chance on the left and Astraia on the right and try to peer into the darkness inside. The room has no overhead lights on, but there does seem to be some illumination coming from the other side. To Chance it looks like a biology lab with several worktables and a variety of instruments he can only guess at what they're used for.

"There doesn't seem to be any sign of the spider thing," says Chance in a whisper.

"I don't see anything either," says Astraia.

"All right, we're going to have to squeeze through here. I'll go first to make sure there's nothing waiting for us on the inside. Then you come in after me."

"Got it."

Chance sheaths his sword and draws out his handgun, knowing that as he squeezes through he won't have the room to swing the blade. He dismisses the thought of going in feet first in favor of head first with his arms leading the way in case something inside is ready to strike. Kneeling down, he prepares to enter just as Oska comes up to the office door.

"Did you find it?"

"Not yet," says Astraia. "We figured it must have gone through here."

"Great," Oska says sarcastically.

"What's up?" asks Chance.

"Guys, we have a problem."

Chance stops and leans back away from the hole as Astraia asks, "What is it?"

"Kai started abdominal cramping a few minutes ago. He says he can't feel anything in his legs. and his breathing sounds short and choppy."

"Has he started vomiting yet?" asks Chance, interrupting her.

"No. but." Oska pauses to look at him, "how did you know that was next?"

"Venom usually has that effect."

"Yeah, look, I need that antidote. This stuff is burning through his system like wildfire, and if the paralysis continues, he's not going to be able to breathe. I've never seen venom work this fast before."

"I'm going in here after the creature," says Chance. "Hopefully we can bring it back to you, and you can whip something up. If he starts to spasm, let us know by clicking the Wrist Comm. mic on and off twice. Don't talk, in case we're trying to be quiet, but click it on and off twice. You got it?"

"Yeah, I got it," says Oska.

From the hallway beyond Oska. the crew hears Kai throwing up, and Oska says, "I have to get back to him. and make sure he doesn't asphyxiate." As she turns to walk down the hall, she says, "Hurry!"

Looking back to the hole. Chance says, "All right. let's do this." Sticking his gun into the hole first. he sweeps the area looking for any movement. Finding none, he leans in further until both arms and his head are inside. Straining his neck, Chance scans the walls around him, the ceiling. and the nearby workspaces the best he can but still finds nothing. Bracing his elbows against the wall, he squeezes his shoulders through, taking bits of the wall's insulation with him as he does, and then pushes back with his hands as he pulls his body through. Once fully inside the room, Chance assumes a kneeling position with his Glock drawn and checks out every darkened corner and angle he can see. Finding nothing, he calls in a low whisper, "Astraia, it's clear."

Astraia says, "Okay, coming," and begins to slide through the hole easily. Once inside, she stays low with her back against the wall.

"I want to head for the lights. Then we can check the rest of the room with the light behind us."

"Why not just head towards the door and try the switch?" asks Astraia.

"It doesn't feel right," says Chance.

Conceding to Chance's past experience, she says, "All right."

As the two of them stand up, they hear a sharp clicking sound on the floor coming from somewhere to their right, and while turning to face that direction, they back up and begin to sidestep their way around the first worktable. In the shadows Chance can make out what appears to be several fallen textbooks and a fire extinguisher, but he can not see the creature. Circling around, they position themselves so that the table is between them and the place where they heard the sound coming from. Chance leads the way as they continue to ease their way across the room, one soft footstep at a time with Astraia watching out for anything behind them.

Astraia whispers, "Chance," just as one long hairy leg and then another reaches up to the top of the shadowy counter space.

Turning. Chance raises his gun and waits as the third leg reaches up and lifts the body of the huge spider. Stepping to the side, Chance allows a bit more light over to that part of the room. Taking note of the size of the light brown exoskeleton, the pinchers positioned at its mouth, even the hair follicles sticking out from each of its legs. Chance realizes that he has never seen something like this before. As the spider climbs up, its tail follows, already cocked and ready to strike. Finding nothing on the counter, the creature turns around until it spots them. Its eight black eyes, as dark as pools of ink, stare at them like prey.

Chance takes aim at the spider, trying to place a shot that will kill it but not completely shred its way through the creature because he doesn't know what Oska needs to make a antidote to the venom. Deciding in the middle of the body, Chance lets out his breath slowly, ready to fire.

Unwilling to wait, hungry for its food, the spider-scorpion jumps at them. Its tail tucks up under its body both as a means of protecting its softer underbelly and to be used as a weapon. Its legs fan out in midair ready to latch themselves onto whatever they can catch, and its pinchers open wide.

Chance gives the creature the first two feet, calculating and tracking its parabolic arc by instinct. When it's three feet off the counter, he fires. The shot sounds louder than it should in the closed room, and Astraia flinches behind him.

He waits for a few seconds, watching to see if the body moves. When it doesn't move, he steps forward and pokes it with his foot. The dead creature lies there on its back with its legs and tail folded in towards its abdomen.

"Go tell Oska we have it."

"Are you sure it's dead?"

"Yeah," says Chance. Then in explanation, he says, "A spider's muscles are attached on the inside of the exoskeleton. Thing is, they only have flexor muscles so they can contract the muscles to move the legs inward, but they don't have any muscles to extend the legs back out again. Instead, they have to force bodily fluids, blood usually, into the legs to push them back out. If a spider gets dehydrated or loses too much of its bodily fluids, it can't generate the necessary hydraulic pressure to push its legs out. This guy here," Chance kicks him once again, "is having a bit of problem with pushing blood out to his limbs, what with the big hole I put through his heart."

Astraia asks, "How do you know all of that?"

"I read"

"No, really. Where did you learn about spiders and venom and stuff?" asks Astraia

"Sometimes on a job, things have to look like natural causes."

Realizing he meant killing people on contracts, Astraia quickly drops the subject and returns to what she's doing, saying, "Gotcha." Then after a second's pause she says, "I'll go tell Oska she can get in here and do what she needs to do, and I'll watch Kai." Without waiting for his reply, she turns around and heads back around the table toward the hole.

When she is less than half a dozen feet from the wall they both hear clicking and chattering as a shadow on the wall before them moves. Freezing in her tracks, Astraia turns to see another spider on the wall across the room next to the light. This one's body is black with a red stripe running from its head to its butt, and overall, it looks larger than the one Chance just killed.

"How close is it?" asks Chance in a whisper.

"It's on the wall behind you."

"Okay, well, that one can wait."

Eyes widening and with panicked alarm in her voice, Astraia says, "What do you mean that one?"

"You have a friend of your own about four feet away on your right."

Astraia turns to look without thinking, and the giant brown spider scurries quickly across the table towards her. She tries to take a step back but trips and lands on her back just as the creature gets to the end of the table and jumps. With the spider coming down directly on top of her, she fires up. The spider's body slows in midair as her bullet makes contact and then spins to the side as Chance's bullet knocks it from its trajectory, and it lands with a lump on the floor next to her.

Turning, Chance shoots at the spider behind him but only clips off one of its rear leg as it slips behind some furniture. When he sees the leg on the floor curling in on itself, he says, "Shit, I missed."

Coming up to the hole in the wall, Oska says, "Don't fill it full of holes. I need something recognizable when you two are done."

Astraia, still struggling to get up, says, "There's more than one in here. Stay out!"

Oska backs away from the hole and heads back to Kai, hoping that the two of them can handle whatever is still inside.

After a few steps, both Chance and Astraia cross the room, and while Chance looks behind the desk, Astraia watches the room for movement.

Finding nothing, Chance stands up and says, "He's hiding back there somewhere, probably licking his wounds. Let's grab those two and drag them back into the office for Oska to take a look at. If we need to get the other one, we at least know where to look."

"All right," says Astraia.

Stepping back to the two dead creatures, Chance holsters his gun and then grabs hold of two of its legs. He can feel the prickly hairs against his palm as he does so but lifts it up and begins to carry it. Walking over to the hole, he swings the body through to the other side and says, "Astraia, tell Oska the first one is in the room."

"Gotcha," she says and holsters her gun before lifting her Wrist Comm. up. "Oska, we have one of the creatures in the office. We're sending the second one through in a second."

"On my way."

Astraia looks back over to Chance who is crouching next to the second spider, and for a minute she thinks he must have been bitten by it. She begins to step forward to check on him but sees his left hand flash 'Stop' and does. Chance's eyes, she realizes, are not exactly on her but rather looking past her, just over her right shoulder, and she realizes the third one must have made its way around the dark room and is now behind her. Unsure what to do, she puts her trust in Chance and waits.

Chance reaches down and lifts his pant leg with one hand while he puts his left index finger to his mouth to signal her to remain quiet and still. Clicking open the leather snap, he pauses to make sure the sound hasn't agitated the creature before drawing his weapon and flicking his wrist.

Astraia feels the wind next to her face
something flies past and then registers the sound of
whatever it was slamming into the wall behind her.
Turning around. she sees the huge spider on the
wall with its legs splayed out around it. In the
center of its body, she notices the shiny hilt of
Chance's ten-inch-long boot knife imbedded into it,
keeping it there attached to the wall. Letting out the
breath she hadn't known she was holding. she
watches as a thin stream of greenish fluid drips
down to the floor where it begins to collect in a
puddle. She knew most people would have been
upset that he had thrown the knife that close to her,
but she knew Chance. She knew he would never let
anything happen to her. Looking back towards him.
she says, "Thank you," just as her Wrist Comm. and
his click twice.

"Shit, Kai's in spasms," says Chance.

"Let's get these things into the next room so
Oska can check them out."

"There's no time. If he is already in spasms.
we need the antivenom. Check the drawers over
there."

Astraia turns to where he's pointing and
begins ripping open drawers. Inside she comes
across files and paperwork. In the next she finds
test tubes and other lab equipment. Moving to the
next desk. she continues to search. Inside a drawer,
Astraia finds an ID card which reads 'Custodian.'
Bringing it close to her face, she reads the lower left
corner of the badge where it has five little squares
marked L1, L2. L3, L4, and E2. She pockets the
badge and continues to search.

Chance. now across the room, moves past
the light source and finds the emergency shower
stall, in place in case of accidents, in the corner.

167

Next to the shower, a first aid kit is magnetically attached to a spot on the wall, and he pulls it down and opens it. Inside there are bandages and gauze, latex gloves, and three pens. Taking a closer look, the first one read 'Epipen', and he recognizes it as an epinephrine auto-injector frequently used for the treatment of acute allergic reactions to avoid or treat the onset of anaphylactic shock. The next two pens are labeled as 'Antivenom', and Chance takes all three and heads back towards the hall calling, "Astraia, I found it."

"Great. Let's get back to Kai and Oska."

The two climb through the hole in the wall and rush back out into the hall. As the approach Oska and Kai, Chance says, "Here, I found the antivenom."

Looking up, Oska reaches for the shots and says, "Give them here."

Reading the pens, she selects one of the antivenoms and stabs it into Kai's leg. After a minute and still seeing Kai's symptoms continuing to progress, Oska selects the epipen and injects it into Kai as well. After another minute, Kai's breathing begins to slow and become more regular.

"Is he going to be okay?" asks Astraia.

"It looks like. He's just going to need a little while before we can get him back to the ship."

"Back to the ship? We can't just turn back. We have to finish the job."

"Astraia, Captain Kai isn't going to be much good to us if he can barely stand on his own."

"We could take him back and then return for the computer stuff," offers Chance.

"I suppose, but he really should be under medical care."

"All right, you stay there, and Astraia and I can come back and take care of the job."

In a hoarse shallow voice, Kai says, "No."

"Kai, you're all right," says Astraia.

"How's the paralysis?" asks Oska.

Attempting to sit up, and not making it, Kai says, "Still a bit of a problem, but I'm breathing easier."

"Captain, we can take you back to the Allons-y in a little bit."

"No, we have to finish the job."

"Astraia and I can do that. Kai, you and Oska should go back."

"Just tell me you got the little bastard."

"Yeah, Kai. I got it."

"All right, just give me a few minutes. I'll be ready to go." Then turning to Oska he asks, "Oska, was that the thing that killed Doctor Hue?"

"It fits. Spiders don't have anything to masticate with." Seeing the confusion on Kai's face, she clarifies, saying, "Spiders can not eat their prey by chewing. Their mouths don't have the ability to chew. Instead, the spiders suck the liquids from their prey. In some cases, a spider may also spray special juices from its mouth onto its prey, juices that can turn the prey's body into a soupy liquid. Then the spider can just slurp up its meal."

"Well, that's disgusting," says Kai.

"It's a biological necessity for them," replies Oska.

"Did you two find anything else in there?" asks Kai.

"Actually, the office didn't have much more than a computer and some furniture. The spider-things were all in a lab. Somehow they had torn a hole through the adjacent wall."

169

"Excuse me, spider-things?" Kai asks. "Exactly how many of them were there?"

"Three."

Trying again, Kai is now able to sit up and scoots himself over to the wall to lean against it. Oska bends, trying to help her patient, but he waves her off and stubbornly does it himself before continuing with, "Okay, so was there anything in the lab?"

"We weren't looking for anything but the creatures and a cure for you, Captain," says Astraia, and then reaching into her pocket, she hands him the custodian's badge and says, "but I did come across this."

Looking at the plastic card he says, "Good. Maybe this will get us into a few more doors around this place."

"Can I take a look at that?" asks Chance. When Kai hands it up to him, he says, "Hey Astraia, did you read this?"

"Yeah, it said custodian, and there were some numbers and letters on the bottom."

"You remember that theory we had."

"You think that could be it."

"Seems like it."

"Someone want to tell me whacha two are talking about?" asks Kai.

Looking back to Kai, Chance says, "Astraia and I were thinking that the elevator that brought us down here only had two levels, yet we know from being outside that there are two tube halls like this around the main structure."

"And," Kai says, drawing out the word.

"Well, Captain," says Astraia, "there has got to be another way down to the other tube. Another set of elevators somewhere. This card says 'E2' on it. That's got to be for a second elevator."

"What about the 'L' series?" asks Kai.

Thinking about it for a half second, Astraia says, "That's probably for the labs. We saw four of them on this level while we were walking around earlier."

"Well, I think I'm going to be stuck here for another minute. Why don't you two go try it out? By the time you get back, I'm sure I'll be ready to go."

"All right, Captain," says Astraia. Then looking to the doctor, she asks, "Oska, you good here?"

"Yes, thank you, but if you two find any more medical supplies, bring them back just in case."

"You got it," says Chance. Turning to Astraia, he asks, "You want to check the office computer?"

"It could save us the trip. It's more likely to be on the main server."

Chance leads the way back into the office and stands near the hole in the back wall while Astraia begins booting up the computer. Looking over her shoulder, she asks, "You think there are any more in there?"

"Don't know. Spiders are usually solitary creatures, but there were three of them in there."

"All right then, I'll try to be quick." As the computer continues its boot up sequence, Astraia rummages around in the desk finding only a few pieces of paper which have the signature of Doctor Gohl. Once the computer is up, Astraia begins to search the files. On the computers, Astraia finds a ton of research on several types of insects and arachnids ranging from spiders to scorpions to centipedes and more. The research is all in Doctor Gohl's name and what looks to be his assistants. Many of the documents have references to specific scientific methods she doesn't understand, but on several of them she catches the phrase genetic mutation. After fifteen minutes, she gives up and says, "I'm not seeing anything useful here. You want to go check out the labs?"

"Sounds good."

The two step back out into the hallway and find Kai and Oska both sitting on the floor talking. Kai has a half-eaten protein bar in his hand, and Oska is holding his canteen for him. Chance closes the office door while Astraia says, "We're going to go check out this key, see if we can get into the labs."

Saluting them with his protein bar, Kai says, "I'll be right behind you," while Oska simply shakes her head.

Chance and Astraia make their way back down the hall towards the elevator and find the first lab. As the card slides into the slot on the wall, the LED switches from red to green granting them access. Chance draws his gun and pushes the door in but remains in the hall waiting. When nothing happens for the first few seconds, he reaches for his flashlight with his left hand and shines it into the room. Inside there is no furniture and no equipment. Everything looks like it has been cleaned out. Stepping in, Chance flips the light switch and confirms that the room is completely empty.

"Next one?" asks Astraia.

"Might as well."

Turning. Chance and Astraia continue around to the next lab and slide the card. Again the LED changes color, and Chance pushes the door open. This lab seems to be much bigger than the last one and still has tables and equipment everywhere. Again Chance uses the flashlight to check the room from the hallway opening before going in, but once again, he finds nothing skittering across his path.

"Check it out?" Astraia asks.

"Yup."

Chance steps into the room and flips the light switch. Inside they find several work stations and a small library of texts in the biological sciences, specifically in microbiology and some in chemistry. A tank sits in the corner of the room, and when Chance steps closer, he finds that it has a coating of dried black stuff on the inside along the sides and on the bottom. Whatever they were experimenting with in there must have died and dried up a long time ago.

On the other side of the lab, Astraia calls out, "Chance. I think I found our next ride."

Walking over to her, Chance finds Astraia standing next to an open elevator.

Chapter 19

"Oh, Honey. There you are."

"Karen! I got here as soon as I could. How is Charles?"

"He is still in surgery. John, what are we going to do? I'm so worried."

He took his wife in a crushing hug before he said, "It's going to be okay, Honey." After a minute he released her and found that tears now soaked his shirt. John bent down, kissed her, and asked, "Who is his doctor? Is there someone we can talk to?"

"They…they just said to wait here," replied Karen as she choked back another sob.

"Okay. Okay then," said John. Then pointing towards a row of chairs he said, "Let's sit down here." Karen walked over to the chairs and set her purse down on one before sitting in the next one. John sat down beside her and asked, "Tell me what happened."

"We don't know," replied his wife. "Roger was apparently out by the woods, checking on the sheds when he heard something. He said he followed the sound and found Charles." After another quick sob at the thought of her boy hurt and alone in the woods, she said, "He was attacked out there."

"Do they know who hurt him?"

"John it wasn't a 'who', it was an 'it'. Some kind of animal attacked our little boy, and it's still out there."

The only word John could squeak out was, "No."

"Roger said he and some of the guys from town were going to head back out there to see if they could track it down. John, what if it had rabies or something?"

The wheels in his head spun furiously as he said, "Karen, it's going to be okay. Whatever it is, it's going to be okay. If it's rabies, it'll be okay. We have cures for that."

Just then, a doctor came into the waiting room with a name tag which read 'Gonzalez' and asked, "Mrs. Larson?"

"Here," she said as she automatically raised her hand.

Without stepping closer to her, the doctor asked, "Could you come with me?"

Karen and John both stood up and began to walk over to the doctor. On the way, John wondered if the doctor, who had refused to step any closer and even now was turning away to lead them up the hall, was purposely maintaining a physical distance from them because the news he had for them required him to be professionally unemotional. He asked the doctor while he walked, "Excuse me, what can you tell us about our son?"

"Please come with me, and I'll explain everything," said the doctor in a cold professional tone.

After walking a small labyrinth of hallways, the doctor finally stopped in front of a door marked 'Intensive Care' and turned around. Doctor Gonzalez looked up at the couple, as if he had to remind himself not to stare at the floor when talking to the parents of the soon to be dead, and said, "Before you go in, I need to explain some things to you. The attack your son suffered was severe, and he is in critical condition. To be completely honest, he is fighting for his life in here. We have done everything we can, but if he continues in his present condition much longer, we may have to amputate his right arm and both of his legs before infections can get into his blood."

"Oh, God," cried Karen.

Trying to put her at ease, Doctor Gonzalez said, "We are continuing to monitor him. His survival out in those woods in this weather is a strong indicator that your boy is going to beat the odds." Even as he said the word 'survival,' he knew it sounded bad. While his brain thought about that, his mouth had kept going and used the phrase, 'beat the odds' implying that the fates were gambling against him. All of it was true, but he still wished Doctor Go had been available for this meeting. She was much better than he was at talking to the family.

"Can we go in?" Karen asked.

"Yes, but only for a short time. He is not conscious yet, and his body needs rest."

"Thank you, Doctor."

"Yes, thank you, Doctor," repeated John.

The two of them stepped inside the dimly lit room and were greeted by the rhythmic beeping and hissing sounds of machinery. As they came around the curtain, they both froze at the sight of their boy covered in bandages with a ventilation tube running down his throat and monitors showing his life signs surrounding the head of his hospital bed. With renewed tears streaming down her face, Karen stepped closer to her son and gently squeezed his left hand.

John couldn't stand to watch his wife cry like this and not do something to help. He pulled out his tablet from his shoulder bag, minimized the results from the sunflower experiment, and began to take notes on his son's condition. First he copied the data from Charles's charts and then from the monitors and machines around the room. According to the information available in the room, his son had sustained massive trauma including internal bleeding and broken bones upon arrival. The injuries were, as Karen had described, consistent with an animal attack. Looking over the information, he also saw that the doctors here probably had done everything they could. Lilac being a smaller city, unlike the city of Boone, had fewer resources at its disposal. He quickly did a search on Boone General Hospital and found a directory. He clicked on the Intensive Care Unit and read about their facilities, knowing that they were posted on the hospital's website with the express purpose of glorifying themselves and their program to both prospective patients and universities. As he had suspected, they had more in Boone and could do more for his son there, but the data on the charts was grim. It was easy to tell that surgery was the only course of action that could possibly save him, but it was also clear that right now surgery would kill him. His body had simply been through too much already, and further trauma, even that under the careful hands of a surgeon, would only serve to lessen his ability to hold on.

He looked up to his wife, her eyes moist with tears, and couldn't help but hate himself for not being here. If he had, he could have been with his son, protected him, and been more of a father. He wished he had left the space station years ago. He could have simply turned in his resignation and moved to Lilac to be with Karen when she told him that she was pregnant. His accomplishments and research weren't worth this, weren't worth his wife's tears, or his son's limbs. He dropped his eyes down to Charles who had mercifully been drugged into oblivion to spare him from the pain of his injuries. He watched for a moment as his son's bruised and lacerated chest rose and fell in time with the machinery's hiss and pump. He looked at the bandaged wounds and saw where the blood had already begun to soak through. Removing the dressings and applying new ones would damage the little bit of healing his skin had already attempted, so John held back on treatment and let go of his first tear.

The tear rolled slowly down his cheek until it finally got caught by his beard. As more tears fell, they, too, followed the path down and became trapped in a forest of whiskers. Finally after several minutes, they collected and ran off the end of one stray hair where they fell onto the tablet in his lap, onto the answer John was desperate for.

He looked down to where the tear had landed and saw in the corner a slow blinking icon notifying him that the results of the sunflower experiment had yet to be analyzed. "That's it!" John said in an excited rush.

Karen lifted her head up from Charles's bed and asked confusedly, "What's it, John?"

John stepped over to his wife and pulled her into a hug before he whispered in her ear, "I can save our boy."

Karen pulled back from him, looked him in the eye, and asked, "What are you talking about?"

He bent down and put his finger to his lips to signal that they had to talk quietly. Then he leaned in and whispered, "The experiment, Karen. I can save Charles with the experiment."

Karen had heard some of the interesting things John had been doing in the space station during his trips home, but she had never quite understood the details of it. The last thing she could remember him saying, however, was that he was thinking of proposing animal trials sometime in the months to come, and she knew that meant it wasn't ready for human trials. It wasn't ready for her boy.

"No," said Karen.

Desperate, John said, "Honey, it's the only way. You heard the doctor. He is going to lose both of his legs and his arm, and they still don't know if he is going to survive. I can do this. I can help him."

"No, John. I am not going to let you take our son and turn him into some kind of lab experiment."

"Karen, look," he pleaded and pointed to his tablet.

On the tablet, he pushed the icon and brought up the results from the sunflower experiment. The pictures of it were labeled with a time stamp showing the brown wilted husk of the head of a sunflower and then a bright new yellow sunflower in full bloom with seeds ready to burst from its face just a little over an hour later. The results were unbelievable, and Karen saw that. She looked over to Charles, still and almost lifeless in the bed, and then back down to the beautiful vibrant plant on John's tablet.

"Karen, I can do this."

She looked at him and said, "But John, it's just a plant," leaving the rest, the part about their son and this experiment never being able to work because even now she started to have her own unspoken hope seed its way into her mind, and she was desperate to cling to it, to nurture it, and make it grow real for her boy.

179

"Karen, they have done all they can here. Let me try," John begged.

Karen shook her head no. Not as an answer to him, but in disbelief that this had happened, that her son was so hurt, and that the doctors could nothing for him. She paced the room, trying to think, praying that an answer would come, yet she knew it already had. She knew her husband's experiments were their best shot. She looked over to John and watched him for a moment, already working, tapping away at his tablet, and knew he was going to do it. He was going to save her little boy.

"How?" she asked.

John stopped typing, and looked at his wife. He considered his words carefully and said, "I'm going to heal him," and then before she could say anything else, he added, "but I'm going to need some help from a friend, up there."

Karen waited, unwilling to think, afraid that if she did, she would think about the pain Charles was in. She waited for something to say that this wasn't a good idea, waited for a sign that she should stop her husband, but when nothing came, she gave in and said, "Do it, John. Save our son."

John kissed her and said, "I will. I just have to make a call first."

John pulled up his list of contacts on his tablet and tapped Dan's name.

When the call was connected, Dan's voice came through with his video feed, "Daggett here." Then recognizing who was calling, he said, "Oh, hey, Doctor Larson. Is everything okay?"

John could see the inside of the Shipyard Pub behind Dan and was thankful he hadn't left yet.

He put his thoughts together quickly and said, "Dan, I'm going to need another favor."

"Whatever you need, Doctor Larson."

"I hope so," John said under his breath, because what he was planning could very well get them both fired and thrown in jail.

After the call, John set the tablet down and turned back to his wife. He knew she had heard his plan, knew that under normal circumstances it sounded insane, but he also knew that these were not normal circumstances. "I already sent Charles's medical information up to the lab. My friend is working on it already."

Quietly she said, "Okay, John," as if now that the moment was here, she was hesitant to see it through.

John had already begun to count down the minutes in his head, counting down to when Dan would be able to get the shuttle ready for him and his son. He didn't have long, but he needed to make sure Karen would be all right. He needed her to know that he was going to save their little man. He stepped forward and gripped her arms, hoping that contact would help them both, and said, "Honey, he's going to be alright. SCOO..." He stopped himself before he said its name. He picked up his last statement after a short cough and continued. "I'm going to heal him."

Karen knew there was more to his experiments than he told her. She knew that there were things up there she didn't understand, but at that moment she didn't care. She looked at her husband and with determination in her eyes she said, "You do whatever you have to, but bring my boy home."

"I will."

"Promise me," she said.

"I promise. I'll heal him and bring him home to you."

"Okay," she said with a nod. "Then go."

John hugged his wife once more, kissed her forehead and then her lips, and then released her. He stepped over to the chair, slid his tablet back into his shoulder bag, and then walked to the bed were his son was lying. He bent down and began to remove the wires and sticky pads from his son's body. Next he gently pulled the tube from his mouth and waited to hear him breathe on his own. The breaths were strained and sounded faint, but they would be enough in John's opinion. With Charles's body free of all medical intervention, John slid his arms under the limp body of his son and picked him up. He felt heavier to John as he did this, as if the weight of death had already begun to settle in his small frame.

Karen turned away, not wanting to see her boy leave her side, and said, "Go."

"I love you."

She continued to look out the window and said, "I love you, too. Now go. Save our son."

John stepped out the door of the hospital room and carried his son as quickly as he could down the hall to the stairwell where he began his ascent up the stairs. When he got to the top, he kicked the crash bar and swung the roof access door wide. There in front of him stood the shuttle with its loading bay doors already halfway open. John rushed over to the shuttle and hopped in before the loading bay doors had even finished opening.

Seeing him on board, Dan engaged the cargo bay doors to begin closing and flipped the switch for the vertical thrusters to ignite for take off. From

Doctor Larson's brief explanation, he knew there was no time to lose. Once he had the shuttle in the air, he began to accelerate, hoping the doctor had managed to strap himself and his son in. Had he looked back, he would have seen Doctor Larson on the floor, his son held tight to his chest with fresh blood soaked through the bandages now covering his shirt in small red blotches.

Back in the hospital, Doctor Gonzalez and three interns rushed into the room in response to the loss of signal from Charles's machines. They stopped at the bed when they found the boy missing and asked Karen, "Mrs. Larson?" When she didn't turn to look at them, they asked again, "Mrs. Larson, where is your son?"

She did not turn around. She did not look back to the doctors who could be of no further help. She let the tears flow as she watched the shuttle outside the hospital room window with her entire family aboard along with all of her hopes for the future.

Chapter 20

Standing before the elevator, Kai grimaces as a flare of pain shoots up from his foot. After it passes, he asks, "So where is this one going to take us?"

"Hopefully down to the next tube," says Astraia.

Forcing a bit of humor into his voice, Kai asks, "Any chance of getting stuck this time?"

Smiling, Astraia says, "Captain, that is always a possibility, but at least this elevator is larger than the last one. So if it does, we'll all be together when it happens."

"And you already checked the computers in this lab for Egnarts's stuff?" asks Kai.

"Yes, Captain. The computers in here have nothing to do with Doctor Egnarts," says Astraia.

Reluctantly, Kai says "All right, let's get to this computer so we can get out of here."

Following Astraia, Chance and Oska step onto the elevator with Kai between them. Back in the hallway, he had insisted on coming with them to finish the job, but the crew knows he is in pain with every step. Now Chance and Oska keep him between them in case he needs some support.

Pushing the button marked D2, Astraia says, "Down the rabbit hole we go."

As the elevator descended past the first twenty feet, the back wall begins to open up, revealing a window into the interior of the sphere structure, and Oska, in disbelief, says, "Look at that."

Earlier when the team had been crawling through the ventilation shafts, they could see a bird's eye view of the inside, which at that time looked like a miniature planet except that it was inside out with the land curving its way up the walls. Now as the crew rides down the elevator along the side wall of the sphere, their view of the inner sphere's sanctum is drastically different. From higher up, they can see the clouds floating lazily through the artificial environment, casting shadows on the ground below. The landscape is made up of meadows and forest area with a large body of still, calm water in the center. Leaning up to the window, Astraia says in wonderment, "It looks just like Earth used to before the war."

"Not quite," says Kai with a cynical tone. "We would have cut it up into farmland and cut down the trees to build houses."

Disappointed that he had burst the bubble with realism, Astraia suggests, "Well, maybe before we screwed it all up."

"Perhaps," concedes Kai, "but why would they have built this up here?"

"No idea," says Oska, and then continuing she says, "Perhaps they were testing a new terra-forming process."

"I don't think it was terra-forming they were testing," says Chance as he points out towards the distance.

Kai and the rest of the crew try to look out the window together to see what Chance is pointing at when they begin to notice animals in the distance. As the elevator continues to make its way down closer to the ground, the animals become clearer. The species themselves are completely unrecognizable, not because they are too far away, but rather because they simply don't exist anywhere else. Each of the animals, as it turns out, is a chimera of some sort with various pieces taken from a multitude of other animal species to create something unique. Just as the elevator passes below the level of the ground, Astraia catches sight of a beast from fantasy, a huge lizard with large bat-like wings gliding through the air. Turning to Chance, she asks, "Was that a…" unable to speak the word.

"Yeah, I think it was," Chance confirms.

After another minute the elevator comes to a stop, and the doors slide open to reveal another laboratory. From the elevator the room looks like it's been blocked off with furniture, and Chance tells the rest of the crew, "Wait here."

Stepping out, Chance draws his gun and tries to look between the desks and cabinets surrounding the entrance to see into the room beyond. While it is possible that the furniture was stacked here as storage, Chance gets the feeling that it was meant as a blockade against intrusion. He begins to climb through and around the furniture, making a path where he can while still keeping watch for anything that may prove to be unfriendly. Finally Chance is able to carefully squeeze between one last set of large brown filing cabinets twelve feet from the elevators, and the area opens up to the rest of the nearly empty room beyond. Sweeping his gun left, he finds a large closed tank with a couple of three inch metal pipes coming down from the ceiling that feed directly into it, and several thick black cables running out from the sides. Following the cables with his flashlight, he finds that they snake their way across the room and lead behind a desk to a computer. Above the desk, a black fifty-inch flat screen monitor hangs on the wall with a message in white italic print:

'Crew of the Allons-y please help us'

Stepping back over to the elevator, Chance says, "Kai, the room looks clear, but there is something here you're going to want to see."

Leaning against the first desk closest to the elevator, Kai asks with pain in his voice, "What is it?"

"We're not alone."

"What do you mean, we're not alone?"

Chance holsters his gun and helps Kai through the maze of furniture and across the room and shows him and the others the computer screen.

Thinking first of her patient, Oska walks across the room and lifts a chair from the furniture piled up around the elevator. Rolling it across the room until it is near the computer terminal, she says, "Here, Kai, have a seat."

Grateful, Kai says, "Thank you," and then to Astraia and Chance he asks, "any ideas who it is?"

"No, Captain," says Astraia.

Shrugging his shoulders, Chance says, "I've got nothing."

"I could try typing something back," suggests Astraia.

"Seems like the only way we're going to get any answers," agrees Kai.

Leaning over the keyboard, Astraia types: 'Who is this?' and presses the 'Enter' key.

The return message is almost instantaneous when it appears in italics:

"SCOOBY"

Kai reads the screen and asks, "Is this some sort of a joke?"

"What do you mean, Captain?" asks Oska.

"Scooby. Really, we're talking to Scooby. I guess that makes me Shaggy, and you're Velma."

187

Understanding the reference, Astraia says, "I don't think so, Captain. That Scooby couldn't use a computer."

"Type something else back to him," says Kai.

"All right, what do you want me to ask?"

"Ask him where he is," suggests Chance.

Kai nods, and Astraia types in the question. As soon as she presses the 'Enter' key, a new message is displayed:

"Here"

Chance reaches back to his holster and allows his hand to hover over his gun as he says, "Ask where 'here' is."

After Astraia types in his question, the next message that appears says:

"We are in the tank"

Chance spins around and points his gun at the tank behind them. When nothing happens, he begins to approach it, gun arm still raised. Finding on a quick inspection that the tank appears to be sealed, he looks back to the group, and Kai gives him a nod when he lifts his gun towards the lid of the tank asking if he should open it. Chance reaches up and unfastens the clip holding the tank lid in place. When nothing explodes out of the tank, he lifts up the lid a couple of inches and peers inside to find a slowly churning mass of pink goo. Confused, he says, "Not sure what the hells going on here, but the tank is just filled with some kind of pink soup."

On the screen, a new message appears behind the crew where only Chance can read it:

"We are not just pink soup we are a unique life form"

"Okay," says Chance, drawing out the word in disbelief. "That's a little strange."

Looking back to the screen, Astraia says, "But I didn't type anything."

"With the tank open we can feel your words vibrating through the air"

"Spooky," says Kai.

"Yeah," agrees Oska.

Walking back around the tank, Chance stops when he notices a label positioned between some of the cables. The label looks to be torn, but from what he can see, it reads, 'Batch C'. Next to the label in a scrawling black print that looks like someone wrote it with a trembling hand, it appears that a letter 'b' along with four other unreadable letters are written but have faded and blurred over time.

Finishing his inspection, Chance places one hand on the rim as he tries to take another look at the gel-like substance inside. As he does so, his hand sets down on a small amount of the pink goop by accident. Noticing the cool feeling of the slimy substance, he quickly withdraws his hand, unaware of the sharp edge of the tank until it slices open a gash across his palm.

Kai asks Chance, "What do you think?"

"Shit!" Chance exclaims.

"Excuse me?" asks Kai, and then taking note of his condition he asks, "What is it?"

"Nothing," says Chance. "I just cut myself."

"You all right?" asks Oska, already walking over to inspect his injury.

"Yeah, I'm fine," he says as he lifts his hand up to inspect it. On his palm, the blood and goop have already mixed together, and he asks, "You have a rag or something?"

Handing him a piece of gauze from her medical kit, Oska says, "Let me take a look at that."

Chance wipes away the blood and gel in two quick strokes and finds that his hand is completely intact. The cut across his palm is healed leaving no trace of a scar.

Oska looks at his palm and asks, "Where's the cut?"

In disbelief, Chance looks at the blood on the bandage and then back to his hand, and says, "It was right here," holding out his palm, pointing to his lifeline.

Inside the tank, a drop of Chance's blood slowly slides down the side of the tank until it reaches the pink bacteria inside. The bacteria analyze the blood, and remember it from their last encounter with him. They begin to send signals through the probes in the tank, and on the screen appears the message:

'Welcome back Charles'

With alarm in her voice, Astraia calls out, "Guys!"

Turning towards her and the computer, the crew watches as the file folders zip across the screen until one opens and brings up a series of videos. The video segments scroll by quickly until one labeled 'C.L.' is highlighted and expands to fill the whole screen.

The crew watches the screen as the video shows someone returning to the space station through the same airlock they entered a few hours ago. It is clear that whoever he is, he is carrying something in blood-soaked sheets. Everyone watches as the cameras cycle through multiple stations keeping track of the man until he finally stops, and, with some difficulty, shifts his bundle so that he has the ability to swipe his ID card at the lab door on the floor above. As he does so, the camera freezes and zooms in. Tilting their heads almost simultaneously, the crew reads the name on the badge, 'Dr. John Larson'.

After a couple of seconds, Doctor Larson's image resumes its normal size, and the video continues to play. Doctor Larson keeps hold of his ID badge, and when the LED turns green, he fumbles with the door handle for a second before finally pushing it in with his hip. The bundle in his arms seems to be heavier than it looks, but he crosses the lab in a rush, ignoring the looks of the people around him, and goes directly into the elevator. In the elevator the crew watch as the doctor cries muffled pleas into the sheets and begs God for help.

When the elevator doors open, the lab is momentarily unrecognizable as the one they are currently standing in because all of the furniture is in an organized layout. Doctor Larson quickly walks over to the outer door and locks himself in the lab before crossing over to the tank in the corner where he kneels down and unfolds the sheets. As he does so, the camera zooms in, and the image of bandages saturated in crimson wrapped about a small boy's body with an oxygen mask attached to his face becomes clear. As the camera zooms back out of its own accord, Oska notices that one of the bandages has slipped up the boy's body revealing a huge gash which seems to open him up all the way to his intestines.

John Larson then runs across the room to the computer and types a message: 'SCOOBY please help me save him'

191

Across the screen, a new message comes back quickly, and John knows that the bacteria culture inside understands:

'Place your son inside the tank'

John immediately rushes back over to the tank and picks up the nearly lifeless body of his son. Stepping up to a rolling staircase, one which now sits on its side along with the rest of the office furniture, John opens the tank and submerges his son into the thick pink substance in the tank. As he does so, Chance notices the label on the side of the tank reads Bacteria Culture Batch C.

Once his son sinks beneath the surface, Doctor Larson races back down the rolling stairs and begins to barricade the doors to the hall and the elevator with a piece of furniture in the room. He pushes heavy filing cabinets and tables across the room, scraping up the floor as he does so. He stacks books from his lab's library of texts on top of the tables and then once cleared, he pushes the bookcases, as well, across the room. Anything else he can find that is mobile enough for him to push, shove, or drag in front of the doors, he does. Meanwhile on the screen a long series of letters begins to fill two columns. They look random, but they are all different variations of the letters G, T, A, C, and the boy in the tank fights to survive with the pink bacteria as his only lifeline.

Suddenly the camera switches views, and the crew watches as a yet unknown room fills the screen and a younger Doctor Gene Egnarts sits behind his large desk staring at his computer monitor. This Doctor Egnarts looks much more like the one in the picture from the file Oska had at the Pub, and when the camera switches once more, the crew is permitted to see over his shoulder to the scene playing out on his computer monitor. The strange man sits at the computer watching as Doctor Larson runs about his lab trying to save his son. He does not send any guards down to the lab, nor does he call Doctor Larson over the intercom, as one might, if concerned. Instead he simply watches and waits to see what happens with the boy.

After a few minutes of showing Doctor Egnarts in his office, the picture abruptly switches to the snowy image of static, and then resumes in Doctor Larson's lab. In the bottom right of the screen, the crew notice that the time stamp has changed significantly and that it has now been over an hour since he placed his son into the tank. The screen still has the two columns of letters streaming across, consisting of various combinations of the four letters, but they are now moving at such an alarming rate they can barely be discerned from one another. Oska notices that one of them has the header 'Charles', and the other is titled 'Unknown' and realizes that it's coming from the tank. The bacteria is somehow learning and mapping out the boy's DNA. As for the 'Unknown', she doesn't have a clue where it is coming from, but suspects that something else is in there with it and is being analyzed as well.

In the corner, the tank's color has changed and become darker and thicker, but Doctor Larson still waits and lets the bacteria do its work. He seems to have expected it to react this way since he does not show concern about the change, but he stares at the screen with a pained mixed expression of hope and confusion.

There is another burst of static, and when the image resumes, the time stamp has jumped again, now reading three hours later. The bacteria inside the tank are now black in color and have the consistency of used motor oil. Doctor Larson sits next to the tank peeling off its label and sobs almost uncontrollably. When the label is half gone and only a 'C' remains, he pulls out a marker and with a shaking hand writes 'h–a-n-c-e'. Finished, he sets the marker on the floor without bothering with the cap, and exhausted from the day, the stress, and the worry, he cries himself to sleep.

Chapter 21

Chance looks back to the tank to the letters that seemed smudged and faded in disbelief, not understanding what he has just seen but somehow knowing its truth. No memories come to the forefront of his mind, nothing about the man in the video seems familiar, and yet, he knows it's true. He knows that this is where he was reborn.

Looking back to the screen and the rest of the crew, he sees all eyes on him, and he asks in a rough voice, "Why? Why did you show us that?"

As Chance asks his questions, the rest of the crew also looks back to the screen for the answer as well.

·We recognized you·

"Are you saying that boy in the video was me?"

·Yes·

Astraia desperately wants to go to Chance, wants to help him, to hold him, to connect with him as he goes through this, but she has never seen him in this state, simultaneously on the verge of tears and rage. She steps towards him with one foot and then holds back to give him space as he continues his questions.

"What happened to me?"

·You were injured and we healed you·

"Injured how?" he asks through gritted teeth, frustrated with the bacteria's limited answers.

·Doctor Larson's records indicated it was an animal attack·

Then for confirmation he asks, "Are you saying that Doctor Larson was my father?"

·Yes·

With more anger growing in his voice, Chance asks, "What happened to him?" and then he yells, "Where the hell has he been all of my life?"

The one word reply that comes back strikes him harder than he could have ever expected.

'Dead'

He had thought he had dealt with these feelings years ago back in the orphanage, but now with nowhere to direct them, they seemed to storm inside him. He takes a moment to control his words and asks, "What do you mean, dead?"

'He took you and left twenty years ago'

"Show me!" Chance screams.

The computer screen goes dark for a second, and then the files return and begin to flash by as records of videos are searched. After less than a minute passes, the video is ready, and they all watch in shock and silence as it flickers to life.

The new video expands to fill the screen, and the crew can see Doctor Larson still in his lab lying next to the tank. The time stamp at the bottom of the screen shows nearly five hours have passed since the last video, and as John Larson begins to sit up, he looks around as if he doesn't recognize where he is. Realizing that he had fallen asleep in his lab, he rubs the dried tears from his eyes and looks back towards the door. When his eyes fall upon the mess of furniture, he seems to realize that it wasn't all a nightmare, and his eyes dart over to the computer on the other side of the room searching for a sign that it worked. There on the screen he reads the message:

'Success'

Seeing the message, Doctor Larson scrambles to his feet and looks over the edge to see inside the tank. The bright pink bacteria which once thrived inside now seems to have dried up and died, as a hard black crust now coats the sides and bottom of the tank. In the center, a large mass of the black stuff has accumulated measuring approximately four feet by three feet in size. Doctor Larson reaches out for the skimmer, typically used to scrape the top layer of foam off the bacteria to help keep them oxidized, and uses it to poke at the lump on the floor of the tank. At first an inch worth of sooty black crust sloughs off revealing thick dark hair. Scared for only a moment, he makes another attempt at the lump, and the hair falls away along with more of the dead and dried xenobacteria, this time revealing white skin.

Seeing the skin revealed, Doctor Larson drops the skimmer and ascends the stairs two at a time. When he gets to the top, he jumps into the tank, lands feet first, and begins to claw away at the mound. The dead residue sloughs off in sheets, exposing more and more of the bare skin, until finally with eager hands Doctor John Larson is able to pick up his son once again. As he does so, the boy's head rolls over onto his shoulder, and he feels Charles's warm breath on his cheek.

After a moment, Doctor Larson wraps his son up in his doctor's coat and lifts him up over the lip of the tank to set him down on the stairs. Planting both hands on the rim of the tank, he climbs his way out and then carries his son down the stairs and sits him up so that he is leaning against the side of the tank. With his son safe for the moment, he runs over to the computer where he types a message to his colony of friends, "Thank you," before giving the room one last look, as if to say goodbye. Walking quickly to the door, John

Larson begins to pull furniture out of the way, making room for him to exit with his son. When he feels there is enough room to get by, he returns to his son's side, runs his right hand down the side of his face, kisses his forehead, and then picks him up and heads towards the door. As he does, the letters on the side of the tank he wrote earlier that night are noticeably smeared, and their image is now also on the coat wrapped around the boy. When the two exit, the video ends.

Tears stream down Chance's face. They are tears for a family he has not cried over since his childhood, and Chance staggers in place for a moment as his emotions nearly knock him down. Astraia steps over to him and tentatively places a hand on his chest before embracing him in a hug. Taking comfort in her touch, he spends another moment to feeling everything before he begins to pack the emotions back up. He boxes in the sadness and missed opportunities, folds over the tears and the lost experiences, and seals away the heartache so that he can carry on with the present situation. When he is ready, he whispers in a calm tone to Astraia, "Thanks," and she releases him.

Directing his voice to the computer screen and his question to the bacteria in the tank, he asks, "What happened next?"

'Unknown'

Confused, he asks, "What do you mean unknown?"

'That is the last video'

"Are you saying Doctor Larson never came back?" choosing to use the name rather than the title 'father,' which seems so alien on his lips.

'Yes we have been alone'

Jumping in, Kai asks. "What about the rest of this place? What about everyone else? Are you saying nobody else ever came in here?"

'Yes'

"That doesn't seem possible," says Astraia. "Why would they just abandon this lab?"

'Unknown'

"Something doesn't add up. Where did everyone else go who worked around here?"

'Unknown our video of the halls was cut off'

As if catching the bacteria in a lie, Kai says, "Then how did you know who we were?"

'Your ship appears on the current video link of the outer hull'

"They cut off the hall cameras but not the ones outside?" Resigning himself to this possibility. Kai leans back in his chair and grumbles. "I guess that could be the case. but who?"

'Unknown'

"It sounds like this stuff only knows about the things Doctor Larson taught it and what it has seen in here," says Astraia. Then to confirm this she asks, "Do you have access to the mainframe?"

'No'

"Okay, so we still need to find Egnarts's computer." says Kai.

To the group, Oska asks, "Excuse me, before we finish here, can I ask a question?"

"What is it Oska?" asks Astraia at the same time the response appears on the computer screen.

'Yes'

"Scooby, why were there two DNA codes running when Doctor Larson put his son in the tank?"

Chance had seen it there on the computer screen in the video from twenty years ago, the two columns of letters that seemed to randomly scroll by. One of them was labeled 'Charles', and the other one was titled 'Unknown.' With the realization that he had a past, a father, and had been injured in some attack, Chance had forgotten to ask about this detail and realizes this should have been his next question. It was just as important as what had happened to his father. Looking up, he read the bacteria's answer.

'There were two DNA samples'

Reviewing what he had seen, Chance finds no evidence of a second DNA sample. He asks, "Where was the second sample?" No sooner did he get the question out than did the only possible answer occur to him. On the screen, he read the confirmation of what he had already figured out.

'A second set of DNA measuring less than 0.002% of total mass was in the wounds'

"What happened to it? The second set of DNA, I mean," asks Oska.

'Previous experiments dictated that samples too small to regenerate or extrapolate were to be combined with larger host organism'

"Are you saying that you mixed the extra DNA in with mine?" asks Chance.

'Yes'

"What was it?" asks Chance.

'Records indicate it was a canine animal species'

Laughing, Kai says, "Oh, that's great. You're a dog boy." Then in a throwback to the end of a TV show from the twentieth century, Kai says, "Sit Ubu sit. Good boy," and continues laughing.

Before Chance can bother getting upset with Kai's jeering, Oska asks, "What were the effects of combining the DNA on the host organism, Chance?"

'Subject should have experienced noticeable increases in speed and agility and heightened sense acuity'

In a deep voice, Kai quotes another TV line, "We can rebuild him," and then in his normal voice says, "Chance, you're the six million dollar Wolfman," and then resumes laughing.

Not really upset with Kai, but more so with the news he had just learned, Chance says, "Don't we still have a job to do?"

"Look," says Kai, still laughing, "Chance wants to finish playing fetch."

"That is what we get paid to do," says Astraia, trying to stick up for Chance, and then to the tank, she asks, "Scooby, do you have a map of the facility down here?"

'No'

Trying to help give Chance some time to process everything, and get out of this lab for awhile where talking to a tank full of bacteria was becoming the norm, Astraia says, "All right, well it looks like we are going to have to keep looking. Who's coming?"

"I would like to ask Scooby some more questions," says Oska.

"Yeah, but shouldn't we finish the job and get out of here?" asks Astraia. "What if more of those spider things come looking for us?"

"Good point," she says, and then looking over to Kai, Oska asks, "Captain, how are you feeling?"

Standing with a bit of effort, Kai says, "I'm all right," and then after a step he says, "besides, if we find an orange vest somewhere Chance can be my service animal," and continues laughing until he notices the dirty look on Chance's face and reins himself in before anything bad happens.

Shaking her head at the captain's poor taste in jokes, Oska says, "All right, well if the pain gets worse, then I'm bringing you back here until the job is complete."

"Yes, Mom," replies Kai sarcastically. Looking back to the rest of the group, he says, "Well, let's go."

Chance moves some of the furniture stacked up by the door to make it easier for everyone to get through with their backpacks on. He steps out into the hall with Astraia directly behind him and Oska and Kai following close behind. Turning to head up the hall, however, the team is met with the shocking sight of an animal standing just over four feet tall about a dozen steps ahead of them. Chance registers the fact that it has four hooves, but its body is something different, cat-like in its fluidity and covered in a cinnamon-colored fur. The animal's face is undecipherable as any particular species, but its intent is made clear by the frothy foam dripping off the side of its lip. Atop of its head, a massive rack of sharp antlers stands tall until it bends forward and begins to rush them. Stepping to the opposite wall, Chance yells, "Get back," as he draws his sword.

As the animal comes galloping towards the group, Astraia yells, "Look out," and tries to step backwards only to run into Kai and Oska as they come through the door.

Having nowhere to go, with Astraia pushing backwards and Kai stepping forward on his injured foot, Oska is caught between the two of them and says, "Kai, go back."

Chance knows the animal is coming too fast, knows that it won't be able to stop, but when he swings, he doesn't expect it to turn. As his sword bites into its flesh and muscle, he instinctively begins to step forward for the second swing, knowing that two strikes on the animal as it runs past will be almost impossible. The sword, however, knows its path from the thousands of practice repetitions, and as he feels it cut the second time, he knows it's the killing blow.

Whether the glint of light off Chance's sword scares the animal or the sound of the two girls yelling attracts it, either way, the charging beast changes direction just as Chance begins his swing. What's meant to decapitate becomes only a slice into its flank, and the blood spray arches out to coat the walls. Stepping forward Chance brings the sword back up diagonally through the creature's stomach, disemboweling it, but the inertia from its charge has yet to be spent. In the last moment of life, the animal, made up of a patchwork of DNA from a half dozen sources, crashes into Astraia, antlers first.

Looking down, Astraia can see the antlers penetrating her abdomen and is shocked that there's no pain. The animal had just run into her while she stood there with nowhere to go, and time freezes. She feels the impact, but the pain and blood she expects seems to be on hold. Flicking her eyes up to Chance, she sees the fierceness and focus in his features as he finishes his swing, and she tracks the droplets of blood as they come off his sword, soaring through the air, and landing against the wall. As the creature falls, she feels a tug, as if something rooted in her body is being ripped from her soul, and the antlers slide out of her.

Reflexively, she brings her hands up to try and hold herself together, and she feels the blood squish between her fingers as she presses in on her wounds. Looking from the thick sticky fluid now covering her hands up to Chance, she asks, "Chance?" as if in that one word he would understand all of the questions which now tumbled over one another in her mind.

Seeing the animal fall before Astraia, Chance thinks that he stopped it just in time, but then he notices the blood pooling up in her hands and hears her ask for him just before her legs give out, and she falls to the floor beside the beast. Dropping the sword to his side, Chance collapses next to her, repeating in a low voice, "No, no, no." He lifts her head up onto his thigh and removes her backpack. The blood continues to flow between her fingers, and Chance presses down over her hands to try to hold back the flood of life which now seems desperate to escape her body.

For a moment Oska has no idea what's happening. Having been stuck between Astraia and Kai, she had looked back over her shoulder trying to get Kai to back up and didn't see what was going on in the hallway. Turning back to the front, she hears the sound of a body hitting the floor, and then another one. The first thing her eyes register is Astraia, now at her feet, and Chance diving down towards her. Looking over the scene which seems to have appeared before her in a horrific display of gruesome magic, her eyes quickly focus on the blood. Bending down to help, she positions her medical bag to her left and tries to asks, "What happened?"

"You got to save her, Doc. The damn thing stuck her with its antlers before going down," says Chance.

Looking over to the creature now dead at her side. Astraia measures the blood coating its antlers. At least three inches of the horns are covered, and she figures that they must have nearly gone through to the other side of her.

From the doorway Kai watches the two of them kneeling next to Astraia, trying to save her life. and curses his own stupidity and impotence, not knowing what he can do to help. He thinks to himself if he hadn't gotten stung by that spider, he could have been up front, and Astraia would have been safe in the back with Chance. Not knowing what else to do. he opts for encouragement and says, "Come on, Astraia, girl, you can beat this," while silently praying for a miracle.

"Chance, you have to let me see the wound. I can't treat her with your hands in the way," says Oska as she holds a handful of unwrapped bandages in her left hand and places her right hand on Chance's wrist.

He looks at the doctor for a second, meets her eyes, and silently begs her to save Astraia before he concedes and slowly pulls his hand back from her abdomen to stroke the side of her face. Leaning down. he kisses her forehead and says, "Don't you dare die on me."

Lifting up Astraia's shirt. Oska exposes the wound and a pool of blood that runs off the sides of her flat stomach. She quickly presses the wad of bandages into the wound and tries to sop up the blood to give herself a better look, but when she lifts them an inch. more red surfaces from Astraia's body. Oska knows that the arteries and organs inside are punctured and hemorrhaging. There isn't much she can do with the supplies she has on hand, and she knows even if she had the right supplies, Astraia is out of time. Rummaging through her bag one-handed, Oska finds the suture kit and tries to pry it open with only her left hand while she continues to press down on the gauze covering the last of Astraia's life. The suture kit pops open, spilling instruments out across the floor in the mixed pool of blood between the two bodies. Having nothing else to use, Oska looks up to her patient's face, now ghost white from the loss of blood and wet from Chance's tears, she watches it go slack as the last of Astraia's life bleeds out.

"Chance," says Oska, trying to get his attention. When he looks up, she says, "There's nothing else I can do. I'm sorry."

Chance, unwilling to hear that she could possibly be gone from his life, searches for another option. Looking across the floor at the metal instruments and thread now half covered in blood, he understands that these can't be used to help her. He looks up to Kai still framed in the doorway, now with his head down, resigning himself to the news of Astraia's death and knows he can't fix her. Letting his eyes drop from Kai, he looks past him into the room beyond and spots the tank. The idea is crazy, and there is no guarantee it will work, but if it could heal him as a child, why not her now? Chance leans down and scoops up Astraia's body.

Confused, Oska asks, "Chance? Chance, what are you doing?"

Lifting his head, Kai watches as Chance stands up with Astraia's body resting limply in his arms. He begins to ask Chance what he's planning, but looking into his eyes, Kai understands there is a hope left for her, that Chance has a plan, and he steps aside.

Quickly sliding through the maze of furniture around the doorway and walking across the room, Chance says, "Scooby, save her."

Across the computer screen on the other side of the room, the message from the bacteria appears but Chance doesn't bother to read it. He already knows what he has to do.

As he approaches the tank, Chance takes one last look at Astraia, lifts her up to his chest, and kisses her. After the kiss, he leans forward, braces his body against the side of the tank, and sets her into the pink bacteria. Her body sinks slowly beneath the surface, and he stands there watching until she is completely submerged.

Stepping into the room, Oska sees Chance step back from the tank, and says, "No, Chance. You have no idea what will happen."

Kai places a hand on the doctor and says, "Oska, there was no other choice. You didn't have anything else, and neither did I." The two look each other in the eye, reading the truth of the situation, and he says, "Let them try."

The computer screen goes to solid black for a second, and the bacteria begin to move around the tank faster than before. After a moment the screen begins to fill with the letters G, T, A, and C in an almost random order as they map out her DNA. The letters stream by for several minutes, and then the screen splits, making a second and then a third column of letters. Upon seeing these extra columns, Oska rushes over to the computer to watch. There are no titles like before, but she asks, "Scooby, can you still hear me?"

'Yes'

"Scooby, why are there extra columns of DNA here?"

'You submitted multiple samples'

Thinking about it, Oska realizes that the same thing that happened with Chance's wound when he was a child must have happened here. Some of that creature's DNA from its antlers must have been deposited into Astraia. Hoping it can be done, Oska asks, "Scooby, can you separate the DNA?"

'Yes'

"Okay, Scooby, we would like you to only heal Astraia, the host. You may excise and discard the foreign DNA."

'We will try'

Chapter 22

Walking back to the company's ship, the Sion, Captain Merta says, "Hey, Kyle, it looks like we'll be getting that bonus after all."

Lifting the tri-sealed case up, Kyle says, "Hell yeah, Captain. I can't wait for the company to see this stuff. You know I've had my eye on this little vacation spot over in Sector Eight for the past few months. I've been planning to bring Sally over there for a couple's getaway, and propose to her."

A little shocked. Captain Merta says, "I knew you two were getting tight, but I didn't know that you were planning to tie the knot. Congrats, man."

Smiling ear to ear in his level five bio-suit, Kyle says. "Yeah, she doesn't know yet, but I've been thinking about it, and it's time you know."

Thinking about his own wife and the two rugrats at home. Captain Merta says, "Yeah, Kyle, you should do it. Married life is great." After he says it, he realizes that he's not just saying it for Kyle's sake. Being married to Kyrie really was the best thing he ever did.

As the two of them continue to head towards the Sion, Kyle says, "I figure after this trip and bringing back this goop for them, the company check will take care of the trip, the ring, and at least half the wedding expenses."

With a bit of a laugh, Captain Merta says, "I don't know about all of that. Sally seems like the type of girl who would want a big wedding."

"Yeah, she is, but I've been saving, you know." Then after a brief pause and a few more steps, Kyle continues, "Besides, the way I hear it, the company has been looking for this stuff for like

209

twenty years now and hasn't been able to find it. If this is the stuff they've been looking for, then we're about to get seriously paid."

Stepping up to the Sion, Captain Merta punches in the code for the loading bay doors to come down and says, "Believe me, this is it. I hear the company has a doctor tucked away somewhere who use to work with this stuff. Rumor has it he was a super brain or something, but the Coalition shut his lab down due to funding the war. The company is paying him to start up a new lab with this goop, but it has been like fifteen or twenty years since anyone has been able to find it."

When the door touches the ground, the two of them begin walking up the ramp into the ship, and Kyle says, "I heard something like that, too, but Cal said it was over thirty years ago that they found this stuff."

Once inside Captain Merta hits the keys to close the loading bay door and says, "Well, no matter how long it's been, the company is sure to be happy we found it, and I'm thinking that there's going to be some reward for our efforts. How about you put that stuff away while I go get this ship prepped so we can go home?"

Kyle says, "Sounds good to me, Captain," and heads through the cargo bay doors to the ship's on board lab.

Captain Merta strips off his suit's helmet once inside the double door entry to the pressurized cockpit and sets it down on the jump seat. Plopping himself down in his own captain's chair, he begins the preflight sequence, checking the fuel levels and gauges and warms up the engines, looking forward to getting off this newest rock and back home. Sector Twelve was one of the newest parts of space the Coalition was looking to develop for the ever-expanding population of the human race, and planet XRT – 247 was in the prime 'Goldilocks Zone', where it was believed the planet would be the right distance from its sun to be able to support life and have water. On orders to inspect it for future terra-forming by the private company he worked for, Captain Merta had figured this would be just another 'seek and scan' job, but when he checked in this morning, there was an attachment to his orders telling him he would have to land and look for some sort of bacteria. The company loaded all of the scanner data into his on board computers, so if they detected any signs of the stuff, he was on orders to stop and check it out. They also provided him with five kits for testing any bacteria they found, and if it came up positive, a set of specially made sample jars to transport the bacteria back to the company. Captain Merta had heard the rumors like everyone else in the company, and as soon as he saw the orders and the equipment, he knew what they were looking for.

After three orbits around XRT - 247, they had mapped out the planet's surface for the terra-forming project and had determined it to be viable for habitation with some modifications in only two or three years. The on board computers also pinged when they found three potential sites for the bacteria. Landing at the first site had proven unsuccessful, but at the second site they found a pool of bacteria which tested positive for the trace markers they were looking for. Kyle and the Captain scooped up the majority of the substance and sealed it in the tri-level cases for the company.

With the pre-flight sequence complete in just fifteen minutes, Captain Merta pushes the intercom button and says, "Hey, Kyle, how much longer you got down there? I would like to get home some time this month, you know?" When he doesn't hear anything back after a minute, he tries again, "Kyle, you done down there?" but again gets no response.

Captain Merta, unsure if something went awry, reattaches his suit's helmet, steps through the double doors, and heads down to the lab. Along the way, he checks the hallway to the sleeping quarters and finds them vacant. Then he heads down through the cargo bay where he notes that the door is locked and sealed as it should be. With still no sign of Kyle, Captain Merta turns to head towards the lab in the back hallway beneath the engine room.

Arriving at the door, he nearly walks into it when it fails to automatically open on his approach. Taking a step back, he looks at the door questioningly and waves his hand in front of the sensor to try and get it to open. When the door continues to refuse him entry, Captain Merta leans forward to knock on the door and peer through the window. Inside he can see that the lights are on, but several items are scattered across the floor. On the far side of the room it appears that a lone boot sits on its side next to the counter.

Protocol in these situations has always stated that the Captain should leave the room sealed and return to the closest base, but Captain Merta wasn't thinking about protocol. Instead, he punches in his override code on the keypad and forces the doors to open. Rushing in, he heads for the back of the room to look for Kyle. On the floor just past the empty boot, he finds his missing friend and co-pilot of the last five years. There on the floor Kyle's body lies in its suit. face down. Hoping that he may have just slipped or perhaps something may have just hit him in the head and knocked him out, Captain Merta reaches down to turn the body over. When he grips Kyle's shoulder, however, it feels like he is picking up a long expired tomato from the crisper of a refrigerator as his hand squeezes through what is supposed to be solid.

Captain Merta recoils from the feel of it for a second. exclaiming, "What the hell!"

Collecting himself. determined to find out what happened to his buddy, Captain Merta reaches back down and grabs a tight hold on Kyle's suit and rolls him over. Inside his helmet. Kyle's open-mouthed face is covered with a thin glossy layer of translucent film, and it's clear he is no longer breathing. At his friend's side. he notices that Kyle's glove is missing, and where his hand used to be is only a strange slimy residue. In a soft whisper. Captain Merta says. "Shit. Kyle. What happened to you?" Then thinking about flying home, he says, "What am I suppose to tell Sally?"

Backing away from the body, Captain Merta heads for the door and attempts to exit but finds that the door has resealed itself. and says, "This is just getting ridiculous." He reaches over to the keypad and punches in the first three digits of his override code again before noticing that a string of gooey fluid extends now from the keypad to his own gloved hand. Pulling his hand away. he looks at it and notices it's covered in a slimy substance. He realizes he must have gotten it on him from when he rolled over Kyle's body. Captain Merta rubs his index finder and thumb together finding it slick with the fluid-like substance and then separates his fingers and closes them back together repeatedly so that the coating expands like webbing between his fingers as he does so. Finally he lifts his gloved hand up closer and notices the light pink color of the stuff. He realizes that it must be some of the bacteria they collected out on the planet's surface, and the door's sensors resealed the exit to prevent further contamination.

With no idea of how Kyle managed to get the tri-sealed case open or why he would have done so, Captain Merta quickly strips off his gloves and tosses them to the floor. He pulls a new pair of gloves from the cupboard and looks back towards the body in search of an explanation. On the far counter next to the sink, he notices the scooper they used to collect the bacteria outside which now appears to have the strange stuff dripping off the handle onto the countertop.

Understanding the danger present in the room, Captain Merta returns to the door with a pencil in hand and attempts to input his override code once again using the pencil so that he doesn't touch the bacteria directly. When the door slides open, he tosses the pencil back onto the counter and exits the room, letting the door close behind him. The Captain runs through the ship, back up to the bridge, and once through the double doors, he removes his helmet and punches up the view screen, placing a call back to headquarters. When the video line picks up, he says, "This is Captain Merta of the Sion, and I am in a Level Seven Hazardous Containment Situation."

Coming back over the video, the company operator says, "Okay, Captain. I am transferring you to the director now."

After a few seconds, the video screen shows Director Kent sitting in his office, and he asks, "Captain Merta, what is your situation?"

Taking a breath, Captain Merta says, "Director, I am on XRT – 247, and I've have made positive contact."

"You found the bacteria?"

"Yes, sir. but it's taken out my co-pilot, Kyle."

"Have you been exposed?"

"I don't believe so, sir. It's sealed in the lab."

Catching his wording, the director asks, "Did you go in the lab, Captain?"

"Yes sir, but only to confirm Kyle's condition."

As the captain admits his failure to adhere to protocol, the director sighs and says, "Captain, I need you to listen to me closely. You are ordered to take off from the planet's surface and assume orbit. I will be sending Echo Team out to you to handle containment and bring you home."

As the captain thanks the director and reassures him that he will follow the orders, the director contemplates calling Doctor Egnarts a second time to give him the update that his long-lost bacteria is alive and well, and that they have it. Realizing that he still needs to contain the situation out on XRT - 247, the director decides to hold onto the information and call the good doctor after Echo team cleans up the situation. Returning his attention to the screen, the director says, "That will be good, Captain. Echo team will meet you in orbit."

Reaching forward, Captain Merta pushes the button to turn off the video screen after the director disconnects, and as he does so, he feels a fluid squishiness beneath his finger. Pulling back slowly, he watches as a thin clear strand of slime extends from the button to the tip of his finger in a low-hanging parabolic arc. Looking more closely at his hand now, he also sees the layer of buildup covering his hand and realizes he must have touched something in the lab somewhere, and the bacteria got on him. Considering his options and how fast it took Kyle, Captain Merta realizes he doesn't have to worry about explaining Kyles death to Sally. He won't even be making it as far as orbit.

Chapter 23

An hour has passed in the lab since Chance
placed Astraia's body into the tank. Since then, the
only notable change in the room has been the color
of the bacteria inside the tank which now looks like
dark black muck as generations of the microscopic
alien life forms continue to work at healing her.
Chance continues to stand by the side of the tank,
not moving, as he waits for a miracle, letting her
blood dry on his hands and clothes.

Injuries like hers, the way that animal tore
through her body puncturing so many vital organs,
were considered one hundred percent fatal and
medical intervention by the ship's doctor, Oska,
was impossible due to the crew's circumstances and
supplies. Doing the only thing he can think of,
Chance turns her fate over to a vat of strange little
creatures his father had trained years ago and puts
his trust in the fact that they, with their shared hive-
mind intelligence, can save her.

According to the dialogue Oska has been
having with the bacteria, they had the ability to
assimilate data and use it to alter their own genetic
information in order to survive in hostile
environments. Each new generation of the bacteria
learned from its ancestors everything the
community knew upon cellular division, inheriting
their memories and knowledge. Additionally each
new generation of the bacteria had a higher survival
rate, having learned more with each repeated
challenge. When the scientist in this facility had
taken them from their home world, they were
trained to use this unique ability of adaptation to act
like stem cells, capable of multiplying and
becoming whatever they needed to be. Some of the

researchers looked into genetic splicing of DNA and used the bacteria as a vector to facilitate their instructions while others, like the head of research, were rumored to be using their abilities to do something completely different. When asked about Doctor Egnarts and his research however, the bacteria culture had no information, and Oska is informed that they had no access to computers outside this lab. Oska has continued to ask SCOOBY more questions, as if she were a student back in college learning from her professors again.

"What controls it all?" she asks.

'According to Doctor Larson's research we share our knowledge much like your brain does between the different cells forming a biotic neural net with a hive mind'

Continuing her questions, Oska asks, "How do you make the repairs to the cells of other organisms?"

'We are capable of repairing existing cells or replacing them with our own cells after cloning the DNA from the host provided we have sufficient raw materials'

As Oska continues to ask questions, Chance returns his attention to the tank to watch over Astraia.

Sitting in the chair Oska had set up for him, Kai keeps a gun trained on the door remaining vigilant for any further intruders which may cause his team harm. The cramping in his foot from the sting of the spider-scorpion creature he had encountered a few hours earlier begins to flare up again, but he lets the pain of it and the potential loss of his friend and shipmate fuel his determination to get out of this situation. Listening to Oska's questioning of the bacteria while it worked to save

Astraia, Kai considers for a moment the option of using the pink goop to heal his own injury, but the idea of the little things squirming around inside his wound grosses him out, and he decides to just deal with it using pure 'machismo'.

Through all of this, Astraia lies at the bottom of the tank with an oxygen mask strapped to her face. Originally, Chance had been in such a rush to get her into the tank he had forgotten about it, but the bacteria had reminded them with a message over the computer screen that she would need to breathe while they worked to save her life. Now as the biotic soup churns about her in a dark black whirlpool working to knit her cells back together and strip away the foreign material introduced by the chimera animal which attacked her, Chance waits for her, standing in nearly the same spot his own father waited for him so many years ago. Standing at her side, Chance thinks about all of the missed opportunities he has had with her and the feelings he had been developing for her. Wanting one more opportunity to tell her, he silently begs the tank full of little alien microbes to save her as they once saved him.

After another fifteen minutes, the screen's message changes in the middle of Oska's next question, and she gives a startled noise of surprise as she reads the one word before her which causes both Kai and Chance to turn towards her. Following her line of sight to the screen, the two of them stare at the message, for a moment unable to comprehend its message before they realize that it wasn't about something Oska had asked, but rather a message they had seen before, on the video, from when Chance was in the tank as a child. Before all three of them, they see the message they had been

219

waiting for which would determine the fate of Astraia:

'Success'

Turning back to the tank first, Chance watches as the thick gel-like substance slows in its last revolution. Just as it stops, the color of the bacteria on the side closest to him begins to change, getting lighter, and Chance leans forward, seeing that something is rising from its murky depths. A few seconds later, the outline of Astraia's body is more clearly defined, and Chance notices that she is now naked, stripped of her clothes. As the bacteria finish delivering her to him, he remembers a part of the conversation Oska had been having and realizes that when she told them to excise and discard the foreign DNA, that they must have interpreted the clothing, made mostly of organic fibers, as foreign DNA. Ignoring the fact that she was nude, he reaches in and scoops her up into his arms lifting her limp form from the tank and clutches her close to his chest. Bowing his head down to hers until their foreheads touched, Chance closes his eyes and waits for some sign that she is all right, that she has been returned to him. Finally after a moment, he feels a warm wet hand against his cheek and snaps his eyes open to see Astraia staring back at him from behind her oxygen mask. Reaching up, Chance pulls the mask from her face, and without waiting, kisses her full on the mouth, just as he promised himself earlier that he would not let another moment go by without telling her how he felt.

Kai, respecting his mechanic's privacy, had tried not to stare as Chance lifted her out of the tank naked, but upon seeing them kiss, he turns back to the door with a grimace on his face. Seeing this,

Oska asks, "What's that face for? Aren't you happy to see her all right?"

"Sure I am," replies Kai, "But seriously, she looks like she is covered in the afterbirth of a seal that went through an oil spill, and she smells even worse. I can't see how he wants to be that close to her."

Dismissing his comments, Oska says, "Well then, if you'll excuse me, I'm going to go check on our patient."

Kai gives a wave of his hand and refocuses on the door to the hallway, purposefully not looking at Astraia and Chance out of a mixture of both respect and disgust. Then to himself, he says in a low whisper, "It's about time for those two anyway."

Stepping over to Chance and Astraia, Oska asks in a professional tone. "Excuse me, Chance, but can I take a look at our patient?" As the two pull away from each other, she finds that Chance's face, chest, and arms are covered in a thin coating of the viscous fluid which completely covers Astraia's body.

Chance says, "Sure thing, Doc," with a huge smile plastered across his face and then, "I think I saw a lab coat somewhere earlier. I'm just going to go get it for her to cover up in."

Looking Astraia over, Oska is amazed to find that the wounds have completely disappeared, leaving behind only clean, smooth, undamaged flesh, and she says, "That's incredible." After another moment, she asks, "How do you feel?"

"I feel great," says Astraia, and then she continues with, "like I just woke up from a long nap. How long was I in there?"

"Just over an hour," replies Oska.

221

Returning to their side, Chance hands Astraia a handful of cloth hand towels, and says, "I found these in a drawer, you can use them to clean up a bit, and then there was a lab suit and a lab coat in a wall closet. They're probably a bit big for you, but they have to better than walking around here naked."

Astraia's eyes glitter brightly as she says, "Thank you," and it's clear that she is talking about more than just the clothes.

As Astraia uses the small towels to wipe away the residue covering her body, Oska notices that the small burn mark on her left shoulder she received a month ago from working on the Allons-y's engines is completely gone. She reaches out to feel the new skin there and finds Astraia's shoulder to be completely smooth and even.

Looking over to where Oska is touching, Astraia says, "Yeah, they healed that too," as if this should have been completely expected. Then as she finishes with the first cloth, which doesn't appear as if it could possibly remove anything else without depositing some of what it currently holds, she tosses it over her shoulder and into the tank of bacteria behind her.

Noticing her tone and the toss Astraia made without looking, Oska asks while still trying to maintain a casual tone, "Why did you toss that in there?"

Looking back to Oska, Astraia says, "Because they would want to be returned to their collective. Besides, they'll eat the cloth."

Still trying to sound casual but hearing the slight tremor in her own voice as she asks it, Oska asks, "O-kay, how do you know that?"

Stopping in the middle of her current swipe at getting clean with the second cloth, Astraia looks at her and then to Chance and Kai who are now both looking at her with puzzled expressions of their own. Turning back to the tank, Astraia considers her question and says, "I think they taught me somehow."

"What do you mean they taught you?" asks Kai from across the room with accusation lacing his words.

Turning to face him and ignoring the fact that she still stood there without clothes, Astraia says, "While I was in the tank, Scooby healed me, but more than that, it's like they … they … got inside me and fixed things everywhere. I feel like I'm stronger and more aware of things, you know? Aside from that, I feel like I know a little bit about them now."

Curious about this new development and how far it extends, Oska asks, "What do you know?"

"I don't know. It's just like I knew they would want me to return this stuff," holding up the black soaked cloth in her hand before continuing, "back to them."

Oska wonders if there was any way the bacteria may have transferred their knowledge to Astraia just as they apparently did with each other upon each new generation. She takes a few seconds to select a question and asks, "Can you tell me anything about what Doctor Larson was working on before Chance was hurt?"

Astraia looks past Oska for a second, as if she is searching her memory, and says, "Yes. He was working to heal different plant species and regrow their damaged sections."

223

Taking an involuntary step back, Oska says, "Oh my, God!" astounded by Astraia's revelation.

Remaining completely straight faced as long as she could, Astraia watches Oska's reaction until she can no longer hold back and then bursts out laughing.

Confused by this, Oska asks, "What? What is it, Astraia?"

Pointing at Oska, Astraia says in between fits of giggles, "You should see your face," and continues to laugh.

Shaking her head, still not understanding, and worried about her patient, Oska looks to Chance at her side for an answer. Standing there next to Astraia, he allows a smile to creep across his face and then gestures with his chin behind Oska. When she turns around, she sees the bacteria's message on the computer screen.

'We healed different plant species and regrew their damaged sections'

Turning back to Chance who was still smiling, and Astraia, who had just begun to get her giggles under control, Oska says, "You two suck. You know that?"

"You should have seen yourself," says Astraia. "I couldn't resist."

Defensively Oska says, "Yeah, well I was worried they had done something to you."

"I know, and they did," she says, and then after a pause to see if Oska would give her a reaction, Astraia continues with, "They healed me."

"You know what I meant."

"Of course, but it was so funny, Oska," says Astraia, and she breaks into another fit of giggles.

Shaking her head, Oska walks back across the room to Kai who is no longer looking at Astraia and Chance but rather watching the door again. As she steps up next to him, he asks, "Everything all right with her?"

"Yeah, I think she may have gotten a little too much oxygen while she was down there, and it's got her a bit giddy, but it will pass. As for the injuries, she seems like she is completely healed."

"Good," says Kai. "I'd like to finish this job and get the hell out of here before anything else happens."

After another minute, Astraia finishes wiping the last of the bacteria off, and slips inside the lab suit finding it at least four sizes too big for her. Ignoring the extra room, she zips up the front of the suit and asks, "Chance, can you get me my backpack?"

As he comes back with her backpack, he asks, "Are you sure?" more than willing to carry her stuff for her.

She reaches out for the strap and lifts it up with surprising ease before saying, "Yeah, I got this, but thanks, Sweetie," and shrugging it onto her shoulders.

Kai looks back over his shoulder cautiously, in case Astraia is still naked, and when he sees her dressed with her backpack in place, he turns towards her and says, "All right, welcome back to the crew," in a congratulatory manner and steps forward with a slight limp to give her a hug.

Speaking into his shoulder as she hugs him back, Astraia says, "Thanks, Captain," before disengaging herself from his hold. Turning to Oska, Astraia says, "Thanks to you, too. I know you tried to help me in the hall."

Nodding, Oska says, "If I had had more of my medical equipment with me, I could have done more," but secretly knowing that even if she had everything with her that she had originally planned on bringing, there was little she could have done with the time she had, and there was no way she would have ever been able to help her to the same degree the bacteria, Scooby, did.

"All right then, what do you say we all finish this job and get the hell out of here?" asks Kai.

"I'm game," says Chance.

"Ah, Captain," says Oska. "What about the bacteria?"

"What about it?" asks Kai.

"Don't you think we should do something to help it? I mean it did just save Astraia's life."

"What would you like us to do, take it with us and keep it on the Allons-y as a pet?"

"No, no, I just thought we might be able to help it out. Maybe take it somewhere and let it go free."

Considering this option and all that it had done for Astraia and Chance, Kai says, "All right, I'm open to the idea, but one, we have no idea where to take it, and two, we don't know if it even wants to go."

On the screen the message appears:
'We would like to leave this place and any un-terra-formed place will do'

Acknowledging this, Kai says, "Okay, Scooby. We will finish the job we are currently on and come back for you before we leave." Then to the rest of the crew he says, "One of you are going to have to figure out a way to get that stuff out of here and onto the ship in a safe container."

Across the screen, Kai read the bacteria's next message and says, "You're welcome," and then not believing he was talking to a giant puddle of goop says, "and thank you for saving Astraia."

'You are all welcome'

Turning back to the door. Kai says, "Let's go."

Out in the hall each of the crew members are forced to step over the body of the chimera animal. and as they do so, they each feel a moment of hesitation as they find themselves thinking about what they would do if it suddenly got up just as they found themselves halfway across its form. When nothing happens and everyone is in the hall. Kai asks, "Okay. which way are we headed?"

"Not sure, we haven't been down here yet," says Oska.

Pointing with the barrel of his side arm, a gun Kai hadn't realized he had even drawn, Chance asks, "Down there, isn't that another of those wall computers we saw when we first got here?"

"I think so," says Astraia, and then, "Hey, maybe we can get some more maps of this place."

"Sounds good," says Kai.

Taking the cue from his wording and lack of movement in that direction. Chance takes the lead and allows the others to follow behind slowly. When he gets to the screen mounted in the wall, he touches the panel and finds it lights up with the same menu as the one they encountered earlier. Releasing control of the monitor to Astraia when she arrives. as Chance looks back he sees Kai coming up slowly with a noticeable limp in his gait and Oska taking measures to keep watch over him without being too obvious that she wants to help him.

Astraia pushes a series of tabs on the screen with her finger. calling up various menus and options until she locates the maps of the lower part of the facility. Considering the heightened security down here, it is understandable why these maps were unavailable on the screen when they first came in, and she questions whether or not they would have even been able to gain entry to the facility through the other airlock. After a few more clicks on the screen and on her Wrist Comm. Astraia says, "All right, that should do it. We should all have a copy of the maps of this floor and the one below us on our Wrist Comms."

"There's another floor after this?" asks Kai, and then a string of softly muttered curses escape his mouth as he vents his frustration.

Looking at the information downloaded onto the Wrist Comm. Oska says, "It looks like these two floors are smaller than the last ones. This floor appears to only have two labs and a few offices. Below this, it looks like the area belonged almost solely to the Head of Research with his office, his lab, an observation desk and then another airlock and shuttle area."

"All right, so where is the mainframe computer we're supposed to be looking for?"

"I assume it's in his lab on the lower level, Captain," says Astraia.

"Figures," says Kai. Then considering their options for another second he asks Chance, "What are your thoughts?"

"I say we skip all of these other areas and head straight up this hall to the elevator. Once we're down on the next level, we go in the office and get what we came for and bug out." Realizing what he said and Kai's recent close encounter, he considers amending his last statement and then figures doing so would just call more attention to it and lets it drop.

"Agreed," says Kai, and then completing his statement he says, "lead the way."

With a quick nod, Chance takes the lead once again and heads up the hall with the crew behind him. They pass two offices without checking their doors and a lab before reaching the elevator. Once there Chance stands in front of the small well-lit space and waits for the others to catch up. When they do, Kai says, "Great, let's head down."

Holding out a hand, Chance says, "Not so fast, Kai. I didn't open these doors."

Looking back to the elevator, seeing the inside once again with this new information, Kai asks, "Then who did?"

Catching on, Astraia suggests, "You think the bacteria could be helping us out?"

"Can't be," says Oska, "They don't have access throughout the ship."

Contemplating the options, Chance says, "It's one of two things: either an invitation or a trap."

"It could just be the way that creature came up," suggests Oska.

Shaking his head, Chance says, "No, I don't think so." When he notices her look at him for his quick dismissal of her suggestion, he continues saying, "I didn't see a key card with that animal, and this elevator needs one to go anywhere."

Looking back to the elevator, Oska realizes he is right and says, "Well, what do you think?"

"I'm thinking it's a trap," and then as everyone else looks up to him not wanting to believe what he just said, he continues saying, "but I also think we don't have any other choice."

"Why are you thinking it's a trap?" asks Astraia.

"Let's just say I've had a feeling ever since we got close to this place."

Satisfied with his answer, both Kai and Astraia take a involuntary step back, but Oska, either looking to press him in return for his dismissal of her idea or to genuinely get more information, says, "Maybe your feeling was just about what happened to Astraia."

Chance looks to Astraia and then back to Oska and says, "Normally, I would have agreed with you, but there is one problem with that."

"What's that?" Oska asks.

"I've still got that feeling."

Now it was Oska's turn to take a step back from the elevator. She didn't know as much as the other two about Chance and didn't have as much faith in his feelings as they did, especially since there wasn't anything scientific about them, but considering the others' reactions, she figured it was prudent to do as they did.

Continuing, Chance says, "Since we got in here, there have been several things that have needed explanations." Extending a finger out as if counting them off, Chance says, "First there was the security lasers being on, which after over twenty years made no sense. Then there was the sudden power outage while you two were in the elevator in which the fuses were absent from the breaker box when we got there. Third there was the animal which attacked us and from what we've seen, it had no other way to get to us then by this elevator which requires a card key. If you're looking for a logical reason to be cautious at this point, I'd say you have at least three of them."

Swallowing the lump which somehow seems to have materialized in her throat without her notice, Oska says, "So what do you think we should do?"

"We go down and check it out," says Chance.

"But you just said it was a trap."

"Yup, but that's the only way we're going to find out."

Stepping up, Astraia says, "So are we all headed down then?"

"Not yet," says Chance, and then looking back to Kai, he says, "We need another card key."

"Great, more walking," says Kai. Shaking his head, he jokes, "Got an injury, walk it off. That's your solution, huh?"

"We could always go back and throw you in the tank with Scooby," suggests Chance

"No, thank you. They did great for Astraia, but the idea of them wriggling around in an open wound grosses me out."

Smiling, Chance says, "I know," and begins to head back up the hall they just came from.

Calling after him, Kai says, "Not funny, Chance."

The crew continues around the hall until they reach the first door and find that it is marked 'Lab Five.' When everyone comes up, Chance signals that he will go in first and wants Astraia to cover right while Kai covers the left. They all draw their weapons and check to see their clips are fully loaded, just in case. With Kai on his right and Astraia on his left, Chance kneels down in front of the door and tests the handle. Finding it turn without obstruction, he gives two short breaths and on the third, pushes the door in and points his gun into the room.

Inside they see a pair of desks with paperwork on them, some hoses and equipment, a cabinet on the right, and some heavy looking boxes on the left. In the center of the room, however, they spot four large clear chambers, and on the label of each they read 'Incubation One', 'Incubation Two', 'Incubation Three', and 'Incubation Four'. Chance gauges the size of each of the incubation chambers and determines that they look large enough for an adult human to lie in if he or she were to curl up in the fetal position.

After twenty seconds of observation and seeing nothing, Chance steps into the room and scans the area. Kai and Astraia both step in on either side of him, and Oska follows them, letting the door close behind her. As soon as it clicks shut, Chance feels the tingling sensation run up his spine, knows something is in here waiting for them, and says, "Oh, shit."

Before there is time for any of them to reach back for the door, the heavy boxes on their left come tumbling down, and they are forced to jump further into the room to avoid being crushed. As they do, Chance notices a thin puddle of something near the incubation chambers, and then looks back to where the boxes were stacked to find what looks like a large tiger with a striped rhinoceros's horn on its head. To his right, now that he is turned around, Chance hears Astraia let out a muffled squeak, and he turns to find another strange pair of animals step out from behind the incubation tanks. Each of these look like a hyena with leopard spots and very long claws which click against the floor as they walk.

When they stop, just a dozen feet away from the crew, they each lift their muzzle in a low snarl that sounds like something between a roar and a bark. Startled. Oska takes a step backwards, and then realizes the other one with the horn is still behind her and quickly returns closer to the rest of the crew.

Surrounded, Chance smiles a wicked grin, one which in the past used to scare the living crap out of Kai, but for which he has learned over the years to trust in its insanity, and says in deep growl of a voice. "Let's play!"

Chapter 24

Most people would think that the three animals surrounding them could have no real strategy of their own. Those same people would think that, as beasts, they are only capable of the most basic and primal of motives. Some people, who may have watched a nature show once or twice, might guess that they would come in at the group to try and rip, claw, and maim them. That's all people usually ever think of animals, that they are mindless killing machines. Chance, however, knows differently.

Oska watches the tiger with the horn as it steps up on top of one of the large heavy boxes and zeroes in on her, his first target. She knows that the two hyenas in front of the rest of the crew have corner positions and are ready to rush in as soon as they find their opening. With that in mind, she resigns herself to the fact that she is alone for the moment with this creature. Scared and shaky, Oska holds her gun pointed at the floor with her eyes cast downward, unwilling to accidentally provoke an attack and hoping desperately that the inevitable never comes.

Chance, however, knows how animals fight. He knows it because he, in part, is one. Not because of some biotic alien life form and what it may have done to his DNA, but because he feels it, instinctively from years of fighting. Chance has always felt that he had the ability to become one of them when he needs to, and now, as he lets the adrenaline flood through his system, he knows that time has come again. He stands motionless, ready for their attack, using his peripheral vision to study their body language and his ears to listen for the smallest sound, a claw scraping across the floor or a deep inhalation of air, anything that might signal their attack.

While he stands there studying them, he begins to understand them as if he were part of their pack. The hyenas, he figures, will attack together as a pack would, from the outside with claws and teeth, attempting to wound the crew members individually until they are too weak to fight back. If possible, he figures, they will try to split one of the crew off from the rest for a quick takedown, where they will go in for the kill, biting at the neck, or they will attempt to tear their prey apart in a vicious tug-of-war. Once done, they will have evened the odds, and they'll try to do it again.

Next Chance considers the tiger with the horn standing behind him, and somehow he knows that it will single out one and attack boldly, using its weight to its advantage. He doesn't know if it will take the person down and sink its teeth in, crushing whatever happens to be between its powerful jaws, or if it will attempt to impale with its horn like a rhinoceros would, but he knows at least it will focus the attack on whomever it deems as weakest.

Understanding the nature of his opponents and what their moves would most likely be always gave him an advantage in fights. Here in this fight, he knows things will be measured not in minutes, but in seconds. Everything will happen too quickly to think about, and he knows there is no point in making a plan. Planning his moves will only lock him into a series of steps which very well could result in his inability to adjust at a critical moment. Instead Chance lets himself go to instinct, reverting to a primal creature himself, flexing all of his muscles once and then quickly releasing, setting his body ready to strike like a coiled spring. Being the hired gun, he knows the team will wait for his move until the last possible moment, and so he decides to wait for the creatures, letting them go first. The first move on their part will be the signal, he decides. The next move, that move, will be his.

The tiger with the horn continues to watch his new prey, staring at the one closest to him, the one that is too timid to meet his eyes. He has never sensed fear like he does right now, but the smell of it coming off her is something he understands at his deepest innermost level. To him, her terror is an intoxicating call to dinner. Believing a female would be the one to break from the herd, thereby making it easier to pick them off one at a time, he inhales, filling his lungs with enough air for a powerful roar. Unfortunately, he doesn't realize, it's the last breath he'll ever take.

As soon as he hears the tiger's preparation, Chance reacts. Pushing off the ball of his left foot, he pivots backwards to his right with his elbow rises up to meet his line of sight. As the first rumble begins to emanate from the chest of the powerful beast, he sets his right foot down and extends his arm over Oska's shoulder. By the time the big cat is in a full throated roar with his mouth open wide displaying his huge teeth, Chance fires. The sound of the gun is almost inaudible in comparison to the overwhelming force of the creature's roar, but the bullet that slams into the inside roof of its mouth, however, loses none of its power in the face of the beast's mighty declaration. Spiraling upward, the bullet tears through tissue and bone until it reaches the inside of the cranium where it drills its own path all the way through the soft gray matter inside and then forges its own exit out the top of the fur covered skull, killing the beast before its body even has time to collapse.

To his side, Kai begins chipping away holes in the tile floor as he fires his gun as quickly as he can at the approaching hyena. Each time he shoots, however, it seems as if the thing knows where the bullet will strike and simply leaps over it. As Kai shoots his third bullet, Chance drops his gun and reaches for his sword. By Kai's fourth shot, Chance's gun has fallen to waist height, and he has already begun to spin towards Kai with his sword half out of its sheath. On Kai's fifth bullet, Chance's gun is at knee level, and the hyena turns from its flanking move towards Kai, racing in to leap towards his face and neck. Kai's sixth bullet strikes the hindquarters of the creature's left side, but it has already built up more inertia than it will need for its attack. As Kai's gun clicks empty on his seventh squeeze of the trigger, the hyena pushes against the pain and leaps up with its fangs and claws fully extended. Chance purposefully collides his shoulder into Kai's, bumping him out of the way, while also stopping his own body's momentum and simultaneously setting himself up with his sword like a professional baseball player preparing for a bunt. Instead of biting into flesh, the hyena finds its mouth closing across the blade of Chance's sword. Unable to stop, the hyena feels the sword cut into the skin flaps on both side of its mouth where drool has collected, widening its doggy grin into a sickly twisted joker smile. As the hyena tastes the first spurt of its own blood against its tongue, the blade passes behind the last of its teeth and breaks through the hinged section of its mandible bone. Pushing against the weight of the animal, Chance braces his back leg and forces his blade upward, finishing the kill by decapitating everything above the animal's jaw line.

Behind him, Chance hears Astraia scream. It isn't a scream of pain, nor is it a scream of frustration. This is a war cry, a scream of pure fury. She had let the animal run past her a moment ago, swiping at her legs with its powerful claws, and dodged its attack easily while measuring the distance it seemed willing to attempt. Now as Chance watches, the hyena comes at her again, this time in a direct attack with white foam dripping off its muzzle as it exerts itself, and Astraia holds her ground, fiercely screaming back at the thing until her face turns red. When the hyena jumps for her, Astraia drops backwards, allowing gravity to take her to the ground while she lifts the barrel of her gun to meet her attacker. When it's directly above her, in the space she herself occupied not more than a second earlier, she double taps the trigger, blowing two holes through its body, one in the chest and one in the lower abdomen as it sails over her.

Abandoning his sword so that it drops across the body of his last kill, Chance rushes to Astraia's side and asks, "Astraia, are you all right?"

Still catching her breath, Astraia says, "Yeah, I'm fine. I just … I just knew I had to kill that thing."

Proud of her, Chance says, "You did good!"

Smiling, Astraia wraps a hand around his neck and begins to pull him in for a kiss when Oska yells, "Down!" Before anyone can react, Oska lifts her gun and fires above their heads, killing a scorpion-spider as it crawls out of the last incubation tank.

Looking up to see the thing drop to the ground with its legs slowly curling in towards its abdomen, Chance says, "Nice shot, Oska."

Amazed, Kai chimes in with, "Well, I've never seen Doogie Howser use that technique."

Oska smiles and says, "Sorry, I ran out of bandages."

Standing up, Chance says, "Let's clear the room, and make sure there aren't any more of those things around here."

Nodding, Kai says, "Agreed." The crew sweeps the lab insuring that the creatures are dead and that no more of them are hiding anywhere before meeting back at the door where Kai says, "All right, why don't you two," pointing at the girls, "check out the room for anything we can use while Chance and I move these boxes so that we can get out of here?"

"Deal," says Astraia, and she turns to start walking towards the closest desk.

Curious, Oska walks over to the incubation chambers and begins to study their design. Running into each of them, she finds hoses marked as 'Feed' and 'Bac.' On the side of one of the tanks hangs a clipboard, and when she lifts it up to read, she finds that the sheet was printed over twenty years ago according to the date in the lower left. On the sheet, the food source is listed out with various chemical names she recognizes as sugars, proteins, and various other components with twenty-five letter names made up mostly of consonants from the end of the alphabet and only a few vowels.

On the desk Astraia comes across a stack of paperwork that indicates that the technicians were experimenting with the bacteria as a vector for XNA, trans-genetic DNA cloning. Their goal, as

239

far as she can tell, was to clone new creatures from single cells of multiple animals by using the bacteria to replicate additional cells based on the DNA from each of them. Remembering what Oska had told her earlier about the work being done in Doctor Larson's lab, she realizes that the facility was tapping into his research and using it to conduct other experiments in areas of research that he had refused to go into out of moral and ethical concerns.

Moving to the cabinet on the side of the room while the guys were lifting the last of the boxes out of the way, Oska finds an unopened box of latex gloves next to several DNA charts from various species of animals and a nine hundred sixty two page operations manual for the Mark 7 Incubation Chambers. When she looks down at the next shelf, a smile spreads wide across her face as she spots a card key, and she announces, "Captain, I think I just found our ride" and holds up her latest find.

Looking over, Kai sees the card key and says, "Great, now we can get down to the computers." Then turning to Astraia, he asks, "You find anything?"

"Just a bunch of notes and stuff. It looks like they were taking Doctor Larson's research and using it to mutate other projects, so to speak."

"Yeah, well, I think we met some of their results here a few minutes ago. I say we get the hell out of here before any of their other little projects try to kill us."

"Agreed," says Chance as he drops the clip out of his gun and reloads it with a fresh one. The rest of the crew follow his example, and while they reload, he wipes the blood off his sword across the fur of one of the hyena bodies and then slides it into its sheath on his back. When everyone gives him the sign that they're reloaded and ready to go, Chance cracks open the door and peers out into the hallway. Not finding anything, he steps out with his gun drawn and makes sure it's clear in both directions before signaling to the rest of the crew that it's safe.

The four of them make their way back to the elevator without incident where upon entering, Oska asks, "Ready?" When everyone agrees, she swipes the key card causing the elevator doors to close, and the car begins its decent. After a few short moments they reach the bottom, and the doors open automatically allowing Chance to check the hall first. Finding nothing, he signals the all clear, and they exit the elevator to join him.

The hallway has no windows, and the walls are smooth white as far as they can see. There are no computer monitor panels built into the walls to give them any information, and Kai figures it's probably due to the high level of security required to get down here. If someone made it this far, then it's because they knew their way around.

Lifting her Wrist Comm., Astraia checks the maps she downloaded from the computers upstairs and points down the hall to the right saying, "The main lab is down this way."

"Okay, Chance, you take point, I've got the rear. I want to be in and out of there and get back to the Allons-y," says Kai.

Agreeing, Chance leads the crew down the hall. About halfway there he notices a placard on the wall reading 'Pods' and holds up a fist to signal a full stop. Quietly Chance signals that he is going to duck in and check out the room, making sure that the crew doesn't pass up something that might attack them from behind. Receiving the nod from Kai, Chance crouches down and enters through the door. Inside he finds the walls are lined with over a dozen small one-man pods and two empty bays where pods of the same size as the others used to stand. Stepping up to the closest one, he judges them to be escape pods, and after a quick inspection of each of them, determines that they are all clear of any nasty little surprises. Coming full circle, he finds himself standing before the two open bays, and on the wall between them, he notices a large brownish colored stain on the lower section of wall and floor.

Stepping out of the room and back into the hall, he says in a low whisper, "Looks clear, just a bunch of escape pods in there."

"Okay, let's keep going," says Kai.

Continuing up the hall, Chance slowly approaches the next door and finds that the nameplate here reads 'Control Room.' Giving the same signal as before, the crew stops, and he points out the sign before signaling that they should all enter. Agreeing, Kai points at Astraia and sends her around to Chance's other side while he draws his weapon and puts his back to wall where he stands. When all three of them are ready, Chance reaches for the door handle. Before he even touches it, however, the door's magnetic locks disengage, and the door opens an inch, as if it is inviting them in.

Chance looks to Kai, making sure that he saw what happened, and when he sees his wide eyes staring back, he knows he witnessed it, too. Tilting his head to the side with a raised eyebrow as if to ask, 'Well, what do you think?', Chance waits for Kai's decision. Knowing that they have to proceed, Kai shrugs his shoulders and signals that he should go in. Chance counts down with his left hand holding up five fingers, then four, followed by three, then two. and then rather than show one finger, he grips his gun with both hands and kicks the door in on the imaginary count of zero.

Entering the Control Room, Chance sees several computer terminals around the room and one large mainframe computer with an eighty-five inch display screen in the center. Sweeping the room from left to right and back again, he finds no signs of anything ready to attack them and steps into the room. The rest of the crew follow him in, but this time Oska stands close to the door, propping it open with her hip to ensure that they have a means of quick escape, just in case.

When nothing jumps out at them, Kai says, "Astraia, why don't you check out the main computer there. and we'll keep you covered?"

"Gotcha, Captain," says Astraia, and she steps forward, slipping out of her backpack as she walks. When she gets to the desk, she sets it down on the floor and unzips the side pouch, withdrawing the external hard drive Doctor Egnarts gave them along with a cord. Seeing that the computer's power light is already on, she plugs in the cord to both the device and into the computer's front port and waits for a second as the black screen comes to life and shows a file transfer window automatically come up. just as Doctor Egnarts said it would. After a couple of seconds, the transfer process begins, and an estimated time of twenty minutes is displayed. Looking back to the captain, she says, "It looks like it will take a little while. The bar on the screen here is moving pretty slow."

A little anxious, Kai asks, "Is there any way you can speed it up?"

"I don't think it's an issue of slowness so much as it appears to be an issue of size. It looks like he set this thing to download over two hundred petabytes onto this hard drive. Moving that kind of data takes time."

"All right," says Kai, slightly annoyed. "Keep an eye on it, and let us know the moment it's...", stopping in the middle of his sentence. Astraia looks at him confusedly, and then realizes that he isn't looking at her any more but at something behind her. Turning quickly, she sees the file transfer window covered up with a new smaller window and reads the text inside which says, 'Who are you?'

Staring at the question on the screen, Astraia realizes that there must be something else in here, either in the room or on the space station, and it has stopped the file transfer. She tries to exit out of the new window to resume the transfer, but when she does, the same window reappears with the same question. Unsure of what to do, she looks back over her shoulder to Kai and Chance.

Having no other suggestions, Kai says, "Try answering it."

Turning back to the computer, Astraia types, 'Friends' and presses enter.

The screen's next message comes back quickly reading, 'What do you want?'

Bending over the keyboard, Astraia types, 'To copy some computer files.'

Again the reply comes back quicker than expected, this time reading, 'We have watched you since you entered our facility on the internal cameras. You have killed your way down here.'

Looking back again to the others, she finds that Kai and Chance have come across the room, and Oska has let the door close to join them. Each of them looks about the room but finds no obvious cameras watching them. Giving up on their search, Astraia asks, "What should I say, Captain?"

Thinking about it, Kai says, "Well, if they have been watching us, then there's no point in lying about it. Tell them we'll leave if they let us copy the files. See what they say."

Astraia returns to the keyboard and types his reply. When she presses enter, the text is replaced by a new message suggesting a trade. Curious and wanting to just get these files so they can leave, Kai tells her to ask what the trade is. When she types in his question and presses enter, the text comes back reading, 'We need more food.'

"Ask them what they have been eating," says Chance.

After she presses the enter key, the text changes again to say, 'We have been consuming our fallen dead.'

"Cannibalism?" asks Kai.

"I don't think so," says Oska. "At least not the way you're thinking. Give me a second." Looking to confirm her suspicions, Oska turns to Astraia and says, "Ask them who they are."

Astraia types in her question, and the screen comes back with an unexpected answer, 'We are Project X.'

Chapter 25

"Project X?" asks Kai. "Does that mean that this is another group of bacteria?"

"I think so, Captain," says Oska. "According to the stuff we saw earlier, this would be the batch of bacteria that was directly under Doctor Egnarts's control."

"Well, what do you think we should do?" asks Astraia. "Should we tell it we'll feed it?"

"I think we have to if we want to get the information off the computer for Doctor Egnarts," says Kai. "We need to find out where the food is and see if there is any more. Ask it if it can tell us where the food is."

"Agreed," interrupts Chance, "but let's tell it that we want it to continue the file transfer while we procure its food so we can get out of here quicker."

Astraia inputs her message, asking for the files to continue transferring while they go get the food, and asks for the location of the food. When she finishes, the text on the screen comes back saying, 'The files will take eighteen and a half minutes. Ensure the food reaches us before they finish.' After a few seconds, the screen changes to show a map of the facility with a red line extending from the control room, down the halls, and to a set of doors marked 'Feed Room'.

Understanding the map and where to go, Chance turns to head for the door, but after just three steps, he stops in his tracks as he realizes what he just saw. Turning back to the screen, Chance says, "Ask it how much of the space station it can see."

Confused for a moment, Astraia just looks at him and then catches his meaning. Typing in his question, the system comes back with, 'We see everything in here.'

"Ask it to show what happened to my father."

Astraia quickly submits the request, and the window with the file transfer stops once again. A moment later a new window enlarges with video feeds from over a hundred cameras throughout the facility's complex. Three of the cameras are automatically selected, bringing up three separate columns with time stamps going back over forty years. A specific year, month, and then day is selected in each of them and then a time. Having no idea what they will see, the crew approaches the screen and waits as the videos are displayed simultaneously, showing three different parts of the space station.

On the large display Doctor Egnarts sits in the dark, in front of a computer monitor in what appears to be his office, watching as Doctor Larson pulls his son from the tank fully healed. He seems to be waiting to see if the boy is alive, and when the boy Charles lifts his arm up to his face to brush away some of the black sooty grime from the bacteria. Doctor Egnarts gets pissed off and sweeps his arm across his desk, knocking off the keyboard, computer screen, and a stack of papers. The loud sounds of everything hitting the floor come through a set of speakers somewhere, making Oska jump from the unexpected noise.

"What the hell?" screams Egnarts as he continues to trash his own office. "I never thought that little pissant's project would gain any traction in the first place. All he ever wanted to do was work on saving those damn plants. Then he starts showing improvements in areas the other teams haven't been able to breach, and we were forced to start using his data for other projects. I had no idea he was this far along. I should have been watching him closer."

Then as if realizing something on his own, Egnarts's face changes to one of determination, and he says, "I'll show them. I'll show all of them they have no choice but to do as I say," and he storms out of his office.

On the next screen, they watch as Doctor Egnarts marches down the hall from his office and enters another room. When the camera switches again, they can see this room is another lab but this one has a much larger tank than what they saw in Doctor Larson's lab, along with several computer systems against the wall, each of which seems to be running a series of cables into the side of the tank. Yelling at the tank, he says, "How about today? Do you feel like cooperating today?"

On the screen hanging above the computers, the bacteria inside the tank replies, 'No.'

The technician, who was already in the room, stands up from his desk when he hears Doctor Egnarts yelling. Coming out onto the main floor, he asks a bit sheepishly, "Doctor Egnarts, is there something I can do to help?"

Snapping his head in the direction of the young technician who he clearly didn't realize was in here, Egnarts fumbles for a second and then says, "Bring me one of the batons."

Almost tripping over himself in the face of the Head Researcher's rage, the technician scrambles over to one of the storage lockers on the side of the room and pulls out a three foot long black rod with a handle at one end and a one-inch metal tip on the other. Rushing back over to Doctor

Egnarts, the technician hands it over and waits for his next set of orders. Egnarts, however, pays him no attention as he strides across the lab floor to the tank.

Holding up the black baton, Doctor Egnarts demands compliance with some order that he must given them before. "Calculate it!"

On the screen, the text returns again, 'No.'

Upon seeing their reply, Doctor Egnarts flips the thumb switch on the baton, and a spark of bluish white electricity bounces across the top of its metal surface. Stepping up to the side of the tank, he shoves the baton into the pool of bacteria, electrocuting them for their disobedience, punishing them as retribution for their refusal.

After ten full seconds have gone by, it is clear that this is a longer treatment of electricity than normal from the worried look on the technician's face. After fifteen seconds, he hesitantly suggests. "Sir...ah, sir, maybe you should stop for a minute."

Paying no attention to the assistant, Doctor Egnarts continues to hold the baton beneath the surface of the bacteria and watches as bubbles begin to rise all the way across its surface. The bacteria in the tank begin to make small waves as they try to move away from the torture being inflicted upon them.

On the side of the screen, a number which none of them had noticed before begins to drop. The number continues to decrease even more rapidly the longer he leaves the baton in the vat, and Oska turns away to face Kai, and says, "He's killing them."

The bacteria continue to slosh about in the tank, desperate to escape the electricity and the insanity of what Doctor Egnarts has become. All the while its numbers continue to drop. Watching, the crew sees a waft of steam come up from the tank where Egnarts has buried the baton into the thick pink culture. Generating a rolling wave, the bacteria drops down to a level beneath the baton for a fraction of a second, allowing a four ounce glob of itself to be pushed over the rim of the tank, escaping on the side opposite of Doctor Egnarts's view.

Looking over to the number, Kai watches as it plummets for a full two minutes before Doctor Egnarts finally removes the baton from the tank. Doing a quick calculation, Kai realizes that over three billion of the tiny life forms have just been killed. Looking back to Doctor Egnarts, Kai sees the disgust and anger on his face and listens as he thrusts the baton into the technician's hands and says, "Clean this crap up," before exiting out the door he came in just moments ago.

On one video, the team watches as Doctor Egnarts purposefully walks down the hall heading back to his office, and on the other, the technician deposits the baton, metal tip first, into a jar of liquid which immediately begins to fizz. While Doctor Egnarts begins to pick things up off the floor in his office, the technician works to clean up the lab, hosing off the glob until it breaks apart and washes down the drain.

"Well, that explains the work orders," says Astraia.

"What are talking about?" asks Kai.

Looking to the captain, Astraia says, "While Chance and I were checking out the second level looking for the fuses, we came across the Maintenance Office and checked out the computer in there. Anyway, a couple of the work orders they had on there stated that there was something foul smelling in the bathrooms. It makes sense that when the technician there washed the bacteria into the drain, it made its way into the space station's waste and refuse area. Once there they could have eaten as much as they wanted and reproduced down there uncontrolled."

Chiming in on her thoughts. Oska adds, "And as they ate, they would have produced waste gasses like methane and sulfur according to what Scooby told me."

In a low voice, Chance says, "That's not all," and everyone looks to see his grim face staring at the screen but not really watching anything. Continuing he says, "Once they got into the facilities pipes, they could have gone anywhere, killed anyone, and ultimately, taken over the entire place as they connected to different parts of the space station and integrated with its computers."

"Oh, my God, he's right," says Oska, and then making the connection Chance had already hinted at, "They're the ones who killed Doctor Wong Hue under his bed."

"Yeah," agrees Chance. "They're also the ones who have been messing with us, cloning animals from DNA on file and sending them up the elevator to kill us."

"If that's true," says Kai, "then why would they be willing to let us get the files we came for?"

"Probably because they've already eaten everything down there, and like they said, they have had to sacrifice in order to survive. Rather than let their cells simply die and slough off like other organisms, they have been down there feeding on themselves after each generation dies, like cannibals."

"Disgusting," says Kai.

"Yeah," agrees Astraia.

In a matter-of-fact tone, Chance says, "It was either that or death." Then pulling his eyes from the screen to look at the group, he continues saying, "Sometimes you have to do the unbelievable to survive," leaving the rest of his meaning unsaid.

Kai waits a few seconds, letting Chance's words hang in the air for a minute, before asking "So what do we do?"

"Now we go get them some food," says Chance.

"What? Why?" asks Kai. "You just said they were trying to kill us."

"If they think we're helping them, then they won't be in such a hurry to destroy us," says Astraia, syncing up with Chance's thought.

From the speakers the sound of someone yelling comes through, "Let me pass!"

When the crew looks up, they see Doctor Larson standing in the hallway just outside of the doorway marked 'Pods', holding in his arms what must be his son, Charles, wrapped in a white lab coat. The other figure in the hall is unrecognizable for a moment, and then they all realize who it is, a disheveled looking Doctor Egnarts. He is holding what appears to be a table leg, brandishing it, as if he is ready to strike Doctor Larson.

"I'm not going to do that, John," says Doctor Egnarts, fiercely enough for spittle to fly from his mouth as he says the other man's name. Continuing he says, "Your little boy there represents the best thing this facility has been able to produce in twenty years. You used the equipment and facility here to bring him back from the dead, so he belongs to us."

"No." says John Larson as he protectively pulls his son even closer to his own body. "He wasn't dead. He was just injured."

"It doesn't matter. With those injuries, he was as good as dead, and you found a way to make the damn bugs in there heal him. I want to know how."

Confused, John says, "I didn't make them. I never make them. They helped me and my boy."

"Bullshit!" says Doctor Egnarts. "You made them do it somehow. and I want to know what you did."

Understanding the researcher's problem and sad for his lack of humanity, John says. "Doctor Egnarts. I didn't make them do anything. They are my friends."

"Friends." Egnarts scoffs. "You can't be friends with an oversized Petri dish."

In response Doctor Larson says, "They are more than that. Gene," trying to use his first name to make a connection between the two of them, which to this day has never existed. Continuing, he says, "They're alive, and they listen." Pausing, looking for the right words, he continues saying, "We formed a partnership in my lab. and they help me as symbiotic creatures. In return I treat them well and never use threats or punishment to make them do anything."

Taking his words as a personal affront to his techniques. Doctor Egnarts says in a malicious voice, "Sometimes training requires you to get a little physical." With this, Egnarts advances at John Larson with the table leg raised. As he swings, John bolts for the door but still takes a glancing blow across his back from Egnarts.

Inside the room John pushes the door closed, locks it using his card key, and punches in a code on the inner pad next to the door. With that done, John begins to walk across the room to one of the escape pods, but the crew can see on the screen a bright stain of blood expanding down the back of his shirt. When he is just a few feet away from the pod, John collapses to his knees, and they can hear Egnarts banging on the door with the table leg, yelling for John to let him in. Taking a couple of deep breaths, John winces with pain and gets back to his feet to finish what he came in here to do.

John presses the button on the wall, and an escape pod opens up revealing a single chair and an array of controls. John carefully sets his naked son down in the chair and buckles the five point harness securing him inside for what may be a very bumpy ride. Next he leans across him and pushes a couple of buttons inside the pod, and the lights illuminate the tiny space where Charles sits. Finally John drapes his lab coat across his boy and steps back to close the door. As he does, the camera catches the letters which smudged off the side of the tank earlier, spelling out what would become his new name when he lands. Falling once again to the floor, John's pain is evident on his face, and the crew watches as, with a tear-streaked face, he reaches up with the last of his strength to push the launch button.

As the pod drops down the tube and exits the facility, Doctor Egnarts returns from his office with his card key, overriding John Larson's lockout. By the time he gets through the door and looks about the room for the boy, the escape pod's rockets engage, taking the boy away from the facility in an unknown direction.

Seeing the empty pod, Egnarts screams in John Larson's face, "What did you do?" Getting no reply, Doctor Egnarts kicks him in the stomach and yells, "Where is he?"

Not even having the strength left to cover his bruising ribs, John whispers one word, "Safe," which send Egnarts over the edge. Oska, Kai, and Astraia all turn away from the brutal savage beating Egnarts administers to John Larson with the table leg. Chance, however, doesn't turn away, not because he is unable, but rather because he chooses to watch. Chance memorizes every savage strike Egnarts gives his father, catalogs his vial words as he delivers the killing blows, and vows to return them to their rightful owner, soon.

Egnarts finally stops beating John Larson only when the table leg in his hand snaps in half against John's head. Breathing hard, Egnarts looks about the room, and realizes what he's done. Thinking quickly, he runs to the door and checks the hallway to see if it remains clear and presumably to check if anyone heard his altercation. Finding no one there, he closes the door to the new kill room and heads quickly down to his office. At this point the other three crew members look back to the screen and watch Egnarts attempt to cover up the murder he just committed. Once inside his office, Egnarts presses the intercom button and says in a voice nearly out of breath, "Doctor Atkinson. Doctor Atkinson, are you in there?"

The view of the lab shows the technician reaching back across his desk, shaking his head at the intercom before pressing the button saying, "Yes, Doctor Egnarts."

Thinking quickly now, Egnarts says, "Yes...well...I need you to go up to Lab Five and get some data on the new DNA splice project they have been doing."

Hesitantly, the technician says, "Uh…they said that wouldn't be done until at least ten o'clock tonight." On the video, the crew can see him checking his watch, and he continues saying, "That's not for another two hours."

"No, no, I know that," says Doctor Egnarts. "I want you to go up there and wait for the results. Give them a hand if they need one, but otherwise, wait up there until they have them for me." Then adding in a little more, but not trying to oversell it too much, he says, "I think you being up there will light a fire under them and get them to work a bit harder."

Shaking his head at the ridiculousness of his new assignment but still thankful that he didn't have to be down here with Doctor Egnarts for awhile, Atkinson says, "All right, Doctor Egnarts. I'm on my way."

Next they watch as Doctor Egnarts creeps back down the hallway and waits at the door to the room with John Larson's dead body for his assistant to leave. A few minutes go by, and then Doctor Atkinson collects up the last of his things he needs and walks out of the lab heading directly for the elevators without looking back to where Egnarts stands watching. When the elevator doors close, Egnarts rushes into the room and picks up the dead scientist. Carrying him over one shoulder, Egnarts makes his way down the hall and into his lab. Once inside, he walks directly over to the tank and thrusts John's body over the edge and into the soup of bacteria. The body sinks down quickly, and Egnarts says, "Here, you can eat that to replace your numbers." Taking advantage of the meal, the bacteria begin to roil in the spot where the body went in, and Egnarts walks away, breathing hard.

Everyone turns to Chance to check if he is all right after just seeing his father's murder. Astraia is the first to say anything, and she steps up to him and hugs him saying, "I'm sorry, Chance."

Lifting one arm, Chance wraps it around Astraia's shoulders and gives her a light squeeze before saying in a distant voice, "I'm fine. It was a long time ago."

Recognizing that his walls are up, and he is mission focused, as he has been many times before, Astraia lets him go. She knows that she will have to wait until later, when they are back on the Allons-y, to comfort him.

When the panting coming from the video stops they all look back to the screen to find that the video has disappeared along with the surveillance video files. The only thing that remains is the transfer file window frozen in the middle of its task and a text box stating, 'Please feed us.'

Looking to Chance, Kai says, "It's up to you. Knowing what we do now, if you want to walk away from this job right now, I'm with you."

Nodding his head a few times as he thinks about this offer, Chance says, "No. We were hired to do this. It's going to get done. Besides, I want to have something he needs the next time we talk to him."

"Okay then," says Kai. "Let's get this food so the bacteria will release the files. Astraia, can you tell it to continue the transfer? Then we'll all head to the feed room."

Stepping away from Chance and back to the keyboard, she says, "Sure thing, Captain."

On the screen the message comes back after Astraia finishes typing, 'File transfer resumed. You have seventeen minutes.'

"What do you think is up with the count down?" asks Oska.

"If we don't complete our end of the deal, I assume it will send something to kill us," says Chance.

"What?" asks Oska, freezing in her tracks as everyone else continues to head for the door.

"Well, if I were them," says Kai, "I wouldn't trust any humans. Egnarts clearly left a bad taste in their mouth." Then realizing what he just said, he looks back to Chance and says, "Oh, sorry, man. That's not what I meant."

"I know," says Chance, and then he continues saying, "Let's just get this done."

Heading up the hallway, the crew finds the feed room and cautiously opens the door to look inside. There they find four extremely large tanks, each capable of holding at least two hundred and fifty thousand gallons of food. Inspecting the tanks closer, they find that each of them has a different label identifying its contents as sugar, amino acids, or a specific combination of other substances. The fourth tank's label is unreadable, but it seems to be more processed food.

From the side of the room, Oska holds up a dusty clipboard and says, "Hey, check this out. I found a couple of memos here." As the others in the group step over, she hands the memos over and they read.

To: All Staff
From: Head of Research

Subject: Bacteria RXT-947

    The bacteria has reached the desired level in Vat 8. The next step is training. As we had already determined, the bacteria operate with a hive-like mind, and their collective conscious IQ increases as the number of bacteria increases.
    From here on out XNA research and research involving disease cures will continue with the bacteria in other labs. As for the bacteria in Vat 8, it is now self-aware. We will need to keep a close eye on the feeding of Vat 8 to control the level of intelligence.

Dr. Gene Egnarts
Head of Project X Research Facility

    The second memo reads:

Memo:
To: All Staff
From: Head of Research
Subject: Bacteria RXT-947

    If any researcher requires termination of materials used in their project, they must present their proposal to the Head of Research with a written request. We have found in most cases that bacteria colonies deemed unsuitable for other fields may be absorbed into different research projects.

Dr. Gene Egnarts
Head of Project X Research Facility

"Looks like he was trying to gather up the unusable bacteria from other people's projects and add it to his own," says Astraia.

Remembering her earlier conversation with Scooby, Oska says, "If he did that, and they passed on their knowledge like Scooby did, then whatever bacteria it absorbed would gain all of the memories and knowledge from the other projects when it was added in."

"That would mean that Egnarts's batch of bacteria was probably the smartest in the facility."

"Not only that," says Kai, "but he was trying to control them and make them work for him by torturing them. The reason he didn't get what he wanted was because, as his prisoners, they did the only thing they could do. They chose to sacrifice themselves rather than obey his orders."

Checking the time on his watch, Chance quickly looks to the control board on the wall and asks, "If we want to stay on their good side, we better try to get this food to them. Astraia, do you think you can figure this thing out?"

Looking back to the control panel Astraia says, "Sure thing, just give me a minute."

While Astraia begins to work at the control panel, Kai leans back against a tank, trying to take some pressure off his still injured foot. As he does so, the grip of his gun bounces against the side of the tank and gives off a hollow echo. Catching the sound, Chance steps up to one of the huge tanks and raps a knuckle against its side resulting in a similar sound.

Catching on, Oska asks, "Now, what is it?"

"Give me a second. I have to check something." says Chance. Then looking to the back of the room. he spots a ladder and brings it over to the side of one of the tanks. After climbing up and taking a quick look inside. Chance repeats the process to the other three before saying, "Looks like we should have considered this."

"Let me guess," says Kai. "There's no food left."

"Close. there's only a little food left. I'd say maybe forty or fifty gallons in each of the tanks."

"Makes sense. I guess," says Kai. "Nobody's been delivering food here for over twenty years, so the bacteria have been on minimum rations."

"Hey, I've got it," says Astraia. "How much should I send through the system?"

Shrugging his shoulders. Kai looks to Chance and asks. "What do you think, all of it?"

"Yeah, all of it," agrees Chance.

Setting the controls to continuous feed and the destination as Egnarts's lab. the pumps begin to mix the food with water and send it through the pipes. Turning around, Astraia says, "That should do it. Let's head back and see if the file transfer is done."

"Sounds good," says Kai.

Again Chance leads the crew, and they head back to the previous room. Stepping inside. however. Astraia notices that the file transfer has been stopped again, now at the ten minute mark. Stepping up to the keyboard, Astraia asks why the transfer has stopped. The message that returns however seems strange to her.

'We have seen beyond our firewall, and we know the truth.'

Typing back, Astraia asks, 'What truth?'

'You were sent here by Doctor Egnarts. You are part of the Coalition's plan to let us starve and die off so that they can restart their research with a new batch of our brothers.'

Replying, Astraia types, 'What are you talking about? We are not with the Coalition,' strategically leaving out the omission of working for Doctor Egnarts.

'Jack and his robot assistant Jenny attempted to penetrate our facility, but we looked through his system instead. We know everything. The Coalition planned to come back here and begin their research projects again in two years when our food sources had run out, but Doctor Egnarts sent you here ahead of schedule to copy his files for the company he now works for.'

Confused, Astraia looks back to Kai and Chance, unsure of what to type next.

Shrugging, Kai says, "Looks like we're not going to get anything more out of here. Let's just grab the hard drive and get out of here."

Following his suggestion, Astraia disconnects the hard drive and stuffs it back into her backpack. As she does, a new message appears on the screen, 'We will not let you leave here with that data.'

"We'll see about that," says Kai to the screen, and then to everyone else, "Come on, let's go."

Running out to the hall and back to the elevators, Chance provides cover while Oska attempts to swipe the key card. When the doors fail to open, she swipes it again and finally says, "Guys, I think we've been locked out."

Catching up to the group. Kai asks, "Okay, Astraia is there another way up on the maps?"

Scrolling through the options on her Wrist Comm. Astraia says, "Nothing I can see on the maps we downloaded."

"I'm open to suggestions here, guys," says Kai anxiously.

"I've got one," says Chance, and then as if to qualify it further he adds. "But you're not going to like it."

"Let's hear it."

"We go into the sphere."

"You mean where all of the animals are?" asks Kai in disbelief.

"If we get inside the sphere, we might be able to find a way to get to the ventilation units at the top," says Chance. Then seeing that he has to explain a bit further he adds, "Once inside we can crawl back through to the Allons-y."

"No, no, I understand," says Kai shaking his head. "I just think you're completely crazy. That was like a thousand feet up."

"Look, it's clear that this thing has already taken over the place in the past, and that's why the Coalition abandoned it, but the people that worked here had to have made it out somehow," says Chance.

"Chance, they might have, but then again, we know there are plenty of rooms we didn't see and several which we did still had stuff inside," says Oska.

"Right, they were probably too slow. That's why we have to move," says Chance.

Taking the jibe, Kai says. "Fine, lead the way."

Turning, Chance takes the crew around the hallway in the opposite direction for a couple hundred feet and then stops outside a door with a nameplate which reads, 'Observation Deck.' As the rest of the crew form up, Chance feels the pressure mounting in his head and tries to close his eyes to force it away without success.

Placing a hand on his shoulder, Astraia asks, "Are you all right?"

"No. I've got one of those feelings again."

"Like before?" she asks.

"Not even close," he answers. "This one feels like it's going to split my skull in two."

"What's wrong?" asks Kai.

"Bad feeling," says Astraia.

Seeing how much it's affecting him, Kai shakes his head in defeat and asks, "So what do we do?"

Gritting his teeth against it, Chance says, "We just push through it," and reaches for the door handle.

Entering the Observation Deck, the team quickly realizes that this is where researchers and important dignitaries were escorted when they visited the facility. The labs and such were where the work got done, but this was clearly where the money was made. The plush furniture is positioned to face a glass wall which looks out upon what was the amazing inner world of the sphere and all of the creatures cloned from cells of various animals by the bacteria. This would have been the place to sit and marvel at what these scientists had created back in their day. Now, however, things had changed. Nothing is like it was twenty years ago. It doesn't even look the same as it did a couple of hours ago when the team rode the elevator down to Doctor

Larson's lab. Now everything beautiful and healthy has been stripped away, leaving behind only a frozen looking wasteland. The pristine landscape seen from above is now completely gone and now appears as if it could only serve to be a playground for Death.

Seeing the change makes everyone stop, but after a moment, Chance says, "We need to keep moving." and then lifting his gun to the window, he says, "Stand back." Chance fires twice at the glass, causing it to spiderweb outward from the waist-high impact of the bullets, and then he walks forward and kicks a hole through the weakened glass. Once it is wide enough, he crawls through and hops down four feet to the ground. Reaching up. he helps the other three down to stand on the dead grass with him.

"Okay, now what?" asks Kai.

Pointing with his sidearm. Chance says, "That way."

Following his line of sight, Kai can just make out a series of rungs hanging from the wall of the sphere about five hundred feet off to their right. He can't see how high up they go but agrees for now that it seems to be their only option.

As the crew passes the first fifty feet, various animal bones seem to be scattered across the ground. Further along the bones lay in crushed, twisted piles pulverized to dust in some places and warped like melted wax in others. Recognizing one semi-intact skeleton, Oska says, "I think that use to be a large cat like a cheetah or a leopard."

Without looking back, Chance says, "Yeah, it's just the first of them that you'll see in this grisly memorial."

As they continue to walk forward, small brittle bones of squirrels and birds crunch beneath the steps of their boots until the bones are no longer from small animals and are thick enough to support their weight. When they reach the halfway point, the bones are nearly shin deep, and Kai is having greater difficulty navigating his way through the dead.

With a startled gasp, Astraia suddenly points at the lake, and the rest of them look out towards the growing chaos. It appears that the creatures that died here did so as if something cut them down, even as they attempted to attack it from all sides. The ground is littered with the fallen spreading out from the lake in the middle of the complex on all sides in an enormous wheel of horrible remains. Whatever they had been, thousands of them had perished here, but they aren't what Astraia is pointing at. Peering out towards the water line, they recognize that the lake isn't the clean crisp blue that one would expect, rather it is an enormous pink pool of bacteria.

"It must have eaten everything in the sphere," whispers Chance.

"Looks like it," says Kai in a low tone. Then trying to look past it he asks, "Is there anyway to get past it?"

"We can try to sneak around it," suggests Oska.

Looking to Chance, Kai says, "Worth a try, unless you have another suggestion."

Quickly assessing their options, Chance says, "Stay low, and stay quiet."

Skirting their way around the lake, the crew attempts to avoid detection, but when they are within fifty feet of the pink lake, Chance looks up to see that the lake is no longer smooth and flat. On the side of the lake closest to them, a large bubble begins to form, swelling with each passing second. Behind him, in the back of the group, Kai's foot, which until now he has managed to struggle with and keep control of, gives out from under him as a sharp bone pushes back from the ground on his next step. Crying out, Kai stumbles, and falls.

Rather than look back to Kai, which he knows Oska is already doing and far more capable of healing, Chance snaps his head over to the lake. Looking out across the short expanse, the first thing he notices is that the swell in the lake's surface has been replaced with a long coiled tentacle.

Without warning the tentacle uncoils, lashing out towards Kai, who is on the ground, and Oska, who is helping him with her back to the lake. Chance yells, "Look out!" knowing there isn't time enough for him to reach them.

From beneath Oska, Kai lifts his gun over her shoulder and fires off his entire clip. As the bullets hit the tentacle, they punch holes through the semi-solid substance and slow it down so that it lands ten feet from them.

Not finding its target, the bacteria immediately begins to retract the tentacle back towards itself, preparing for another attack.

"Not this time," screams Chance as he runs across the field of bones with his sword drawn. Leaping up from between the remains of two bears, Chance flies through the air and comes down sword first against the slow moving tentacle, severing it from the rest of its arm which continues to retract. The remaining piece which lies between Chance and the others falls flat, losing its shape without any new instructions from its larger source, and pools up on the ground.

As Oska helps Kai get to his feet, Chance walks over, sliding his sword back into its sheath and says, "Looks like that wound to your foot has improved your shooting skills."

Understanding that's Chance's way of making sure he is alright in this stressful situation, Kai says, "Never doubt my skills, hombre," and smiles a cocky smile before wincing from another throb of pain.

"Guys," calls Astraia, "we still have a problem over here."

Looking back to the lake, they all see six new tentacles forming across its surface, each one bigger than the one Chance just cut.

"What are we going to do?" asks Oska. Then stating the obvious, she says, "We can't keep fighting them off, and there's no way they're going to let us get to the ladder."

From behind them a loud noise comes from the wall as if metal is being repeatedly torn in half and its pieces are being scraped together, ground into something unrecognizable. Then from the ventilation shaft three stories up, thick black ooze comes pouring out, widening the vent's opening further than it was ever designed to be as it forces its way through faster and faster, pushing metal segments of the ductwork through with it. On the ground the black goop begins to coalesce even as the last remnants of it fall from above.

Unsure what it is, or why it forced its way here, Kai asks anxiously, "Chance, what do we do man? We're getting surrounded." Not wanting to take his eyes off the black substance but still worried about the lake of pink death behind him,

Kai risks a look back to Chance, searching for an answer.

Standing behind Kai, Chance smiles and says, "It's all right, Kai. Scooby here is on our side."

Not understanding for a minute, Kai confusedly looks to Astraia whose expression has just begun to change to one of understanding, and then he looks back to the goo which now stands before him as a large ball nearly eight feet in diameter.

Turning to Oska, Chance asks, "Do you have one of those vials you usually carry around in your medical bag with you?"

Still in shock at everything happening around her, Oska fumbles for a minute to restart her brain and says, "Uh...I...think so." Lifting her bag, she rummages through it and pulls out a plastic sample cup asking, "Will this do?"

Taking the sample cup and unscrewing the lid, Chance say, "This will do fine," before walking over to the bacteria that saved his life and that of Astraia's. Lifting the cup up to the side of the bacteria ball, he waits as a small amount drips down into the cup filling it with nearly one hundred milliliters. When the dripping stops, Chance reseals the cup and sets it in his backpack before saying, "We'll make sure you get somewhere safe. Thank you, Scooby."

"Chance?" asks Kai. "What's going on, man?"

Turning back to the group, Chance says, "Scooby came to help. They're going to hold off that thing over there long enough for us to escape."

"That's a great plan and all, but I got to tell you, I don't think I can climb that ladder all the way up. My foot is barely holding me up right now."

Nodding, Chance says, "Not a problem, Kai. Change of plans."

"Where are we going?" asks Oska. "The elevators don't work."

Figuring it out, Astraia blurts out, "The escape pods!" When she gets a look of agreement from Chance, she continues saying, "We can go out through the escape pods, maneuver our way back to the Allons-y using the thrusters, and open up the cargo bay doors using the Wrist Comms."

"Will that work?" asks Oska.

"Well, I've never done it before, but in theory, it should work fine - kind of like a remote starter."

Noticing the surface of the pink lake now has over a dozen tentacles ready to strike and at least four more forming, Kai says, "Good enough for me. Let's go."

As the other three begin to make their way back toward the broken window, Chance steps up to black ball of bacteria and says, "All we need is five minutes, old friend. Just fight long enough to hold it for five minutes."

Showing its comprehension of his words, Scooby rolls forward a foot and half towards the lake and sucks the first large bone it finds into its mass. The bone, best Chance can tell, probably used to be a rib bone from something like an elephant, but after a moment, Chance sees it sticking out from the ball on the left side.

Understanding what it takes to prepare for battle, Chance pulls out both his guns and begins to fire at the tentacles, giving Scooby more time. Two of them collapse from the barrage of bullets blowing holes through them, and Chance simply reloads clip after clip, emptying his guns at each new tentacle until the barrels glow red hot. As he fires off the bullets in his last clips, he notices that the lake is pumping even more of itself into the remaining tentacles, thickening them, and he holds back from firing his last few shots, knowing they won't be enough to take down another one. Looking back to Scooby, Chance finds that it has gathered up most of the bones around itself and created a series of protruding spikes all the way around itself.

Smiling at its ingenuity, Chance says, "Thank you," one last time before turning to run after his friends.

As three of the tentacles turn, tracking Chance's escape, Scooby begins to roll down the field, heading directly for the center of lake, picking up additional bones along the way, adding them to its mass.

With each step closer to the Observation Room's window, Chance pours on more speed, kicking and crushing bones with each step on the way back.

Approaching the shoreline of the bacteria lake, Scooby pushes out against the bones on all sides, extending them outward and lifting its combined bulk from the ground to ride on the bony blades which extend out on all sides.

Reaching the window, Chance finds Astraia and Oska already up the four-foot ledge and inside the room while Kai struggles to get himself up the ledge with his bad foot. Without warning, Chance grabs Kai's leg and lifts him up, giving him the boost he needs to get over the edge.

Rolling onto his back, Kai says, "Thanks," as he tries to catch his breath.

Reaching up, Chance pushes off the ledge and leaps into the room, landing feet first before looking back to the lake where Astraia's and Oska's eyes are already fixed.

The bone covered ball of bacteria whirls its way into the lake, chopping up the pink bacteria lake like a blender set to high without a lid. Fragments of the substance spin off in all directions, landing, in most cases, twenty yards or more away from the shoreline.

As Kai gets to his feet and sees the destruction Scooby does to the other bacteria, he asks, "How is it they are able to do that, but the pink stuff can't?"

Thinking about the technical aspects of it and what she learned from her talks while Astraia was healing, Oska says, "Density. Scooby healed Astraia which made his consistency thicker. It's only because of helping her that they can hold those bones in place and form into a sphere. The other stuff is too viscous and runny."

Chance takes one last moment to watch as his father's last friend and his own savior continues to plow through the pink bacteria before he says, "Come on, we have to get going."

"What do mean?" asks Kai. "Scooby's out there kicking that thing's butt."

Shaking his head Chance says, "He can't win, Kai. Look at the bones he's holding. They're covered in it."

As Scooby turns and tries to build up speed for another pass, Kai sees the broken bone shards glistening in pink goo and says, "So, isn't that just like the blood of the thing?"

"Not really," says Oska. catching his meaning. "The pink stuff is trying to slow Scooby down and then attack it by overwhelming it. Eventually it will become a question of mass, and there's simply too much of the Egnarts's old project out there." Then turning to Chance. Oska asks, "You and Scooby knew this was it. You knew they were never going to make it out of there, didn't you? That's why you took that sample. You plan to keep your promise, and that was the only way."

"Yeah," says Chance in a quiet breath. "I told him we needed five minutes. He's going to do his best to give it to us." Not wanting to watch it die, Chance says. "We only have four minutes left to get off this tin can."

Leading the way, Chance steps out into the hall and rushes down towards the 'Pod' room with the other three behind him. Getting to the door, he flings it open and checks to make sure there aren't any surprises left. Finding nothing. he waves everyone in and follows behind them, securing the door shut. just in case.

Stepping up to the escape pods, Astraia pushes the hatch button, opening it up, and looks over the controls. Following her lead, Kai and Oska each open separate pods next to hers and take their seats. Chance, on the other hand. walks down the line and places his hand in the brown stain left by his father's blood before opening the pod next to the open spot where he last sat. All three of them buckle themselves into the five point harness like Astraia. and they await her instructions on how to operate the pods once they are outside of the facility.

After nearly a minute and half has gone by, Astraia thinks she has it all figured out and says,

"Okay, I think I've got it. Everyone press the 'Manual Control' button on the right panel and then highlight 'Thrusters Only'. If you don't, the pod will send you off to a distant planet, and we'll be searching for you for the next week." Once she sees that everyone has done that, she continues saying, "Okay, next you're each going to close the hatch and press the 'Launch' button. Once you're outside, try to stay close together without bumping into one another. I'm not sure how much damage these things can take, but you should have pretty good control using the joystick on your left. If you make your way up to the Allons-y then..."

Suddenly the air in the room begins to feel heavy as if pressure is being applied to the atmosphere itself, and a loud gurgling sound cuts off Astraia's words. As everyone stops to listen, the sloshing sound of fluids is accompanied by the sound of creaking metal being exposed to too much strain.

"Probably wishful thinking here, but does anyone here think that's just Scooby wanting to go for a car ride?" asks Kai.

"Doubt it," says Chance as he hits the quick release button on his buckle and launches himself up out of the escape pod seat. Running across the room, he hits the door just in time to feel the first of the vibrations as the pink bacteria attempts to force its way into the room with them, and he yells, "Go!"

Kai, halfway out of his pod to try and help, says, "I'm coming to help."

"You can't! Damn it, just go. I'll meet you there."

Understanding the situation, Kai quickly climbs back into the pod, pulling the hatch closed with him. Seeing this, Oska presses the buttons on her panel as Astraia had instructed, causing her hatch door to close automatically, before the system launches her out the tube followed close behind by Kai.

Hesitant to leave him, Astraia says, "Chance, come on, let's go."

Leaning back against the door and bracing his legs against a nearby pod, Chance says, "You first. I'm right behind you."

With a tear in her eye, unsure if Chance is sacrificing himself for them or if he will make it, she says the one thing she's wanted to say ever since he pulled her safely from the tank. "Chance, I love you."

Holding the door now with everything he has, Chance says, "I love you, too," and smiles a strained smile at her as a another wave of the bacteria hits the door. He finishes with, "Now get moving before this thing breaks in here."

Knowing this isn't goodbye, that he will find away out of this too, Astraia slams her pod's hatch closed and punches the 'Launch' button.

When he sees Astraia's pod drop out of site, Chance uses his boot knife to pry open the keypad to his right. Reaching in, he pulls out a handful of wires and cuts them all, causing the keypad to go dead and several sparks to glint off his blade. Quickly setting the foot down he has been using to brace himself against the door, he turns and presses the wires into the metal door. The moment the electricity touches it, he feels the pressure on the door give and knows it's shocked the bacteria on the other side, giving them something to think about, at least for a second.

Using the brief time he has left, Chance pushes off the wall and runs across the room to the pod. Closing the hatch as he sits inside the confined space, he quickly tries to buckle himself in but finds the straps are now tangled up in themselves. Looking through the port window in the hatch, he sees Egnarts's bacteria project, now a darker red after absorbing Scooby's mass and making it part of its own pushing its way through the door. Dropping the buckles and straps, he reaches out for the 'Launch' button and says, "Sorry, you just missed your Chance," before slamming his fist into it and watching the room disappear as his pod plummets down the escape tube.

Chapter 26

Having sent the message to Doctor Egnarts on their way back, the crew docks the Allons-y at the shipyard and pays the attendant to ensure it's fueled up and ready to go when they return. Walking out of the main office with only a slight limp, now after four days of healing in transit back to Quantous, Kai hops into the buggy Astraia has waiting at the door, and they all make their way back to Zada Pub to meet the old doctor.

Astraia parks outside the pub on the same side as always, and Chance casually says to Kai, "Looks busy here today, Kai."

As he steps out, Kai turns around and notices the number of similar style vehicles in the parking lot. In response Kai simply says, "Yup, hope Zada finished that add-on." and leads the way into the pub.

Inside they all walk through the metal detector without setting it off and then follow at a distance as Kai approaches the familiar figure on the bar stool.

Stepping up to the counter next to Doctor Egnarts, Kai says, "Doctor, we have what you asked for."

Turning to face him, Gene Egnarts says, "Well, I guess Jack was right. You folks can get things done. Why don't you sit down and have some nachos or something?"

Kai smirks and says, "I'd rather have some Juan-ton soup, but they don't serve real Mexican."

Not understanding the joke, Doctor Egnarts asks, "How about a beer then?" and then adds, "We'll put it on my tab."

Thinking about everything his crew had already been through because of this man and what he did to Chance's father, Kai says, "I'm afraid we are going to have to keep this to a straight business meeting today. We have some other work to do."

"I understand," says the doctor as he sets down his fork. "Well then, do you have my hard drive?"

"I do." Kai admits before saying, "Just tell me one thing. Did you know what we would find up there?"

With a bit of a smirk, Doctor Egnarts replies with a cocky, "Yes," with a face that just begged the question, 'What are you going to do about it?'

Pissed off, Kai lashes out and punches the doctor in the face and yells, "Then why the hell would you send me and my crew up there without any warning? Why would you send anyone into that place?"

Around the room several men become alert to their conversation, and two of them even take a step forward. Holding up a hand to the two men who started to approach, Doctor Egnarts picks up a napkin and holds it to his bleeding nose with his other hand and says, "You still don't get it, do you?" Then holding out the bloody napkin towards all of the men around the room he says, "This was a Company job."

Aware that his crew is outnumbered three to one and conscious that they more than likely bought their way into the pub with their guns, Kai resists hitting the mad old scientist again.

Stepping up between them, Chance leans in across the bar and sets the doctor's hard drive down on the other side of the man's plate, then steps back behind Kai and says, "Now pay up."

Kai, still upset, asks Chance in a low voice, "Are you sure, Chance?"

Looking him in the eye, Chance says, "Yes, Captain. Let's just get our credits and go."

Recognizing Chance's first use ever of the title 'Captain,' Kai lets his fists relax and looks back to the doctor who is dabbing at the stream of blood still coming down from what is most likely a broken nose.

After a second, Egnarts waves over one of the men who had started to get up earlier and says, in a muffled voice from behind a blood soaked napkin, "Pay them."

Now Oska steps up to the man with her tablet already set for the amount of the transfer and says, "Please slide your card through here."

As the man processes the credit transfer, Doctor Egnarts drops the bloody napkins to the ground at his feet. Disregarding the mess, he steps on the napkins as he moves to lean up against the bar and pick up his beer for another drink. Draining the last of the bottle, he sets it down on the bare wood of the bar and picks up the damp napkin that was sitting under it to hold up to his nose to catch the next drops before they manage to drip all the way down to his lips.

Stepping away from Oska, the man looks to Doctor Egnarts and says, "The transfer is done, sir."

Glancing back to Oska, and getting her confirmation, Kai says, "Then if our business is done, we will be on our way."

Astraia begins to walk up the stairs with Kai and Oska, but after three steps she looks back to see that Chance is not following them. Calling their attention to the scene behind them in a low voice, she says, "Guys," unsure if things are going to turn into a bloodbath or not, despite Chance's promise back on the ship that he wouldn't kill Egnarts in the pub, now that he's face-to-face with the man who took his father from him.

Turning around, they all watch as Chance approaches Doctor Egnarts and whispers something to him, too low for them to hear.

Down by the bar, Chance leans in close to Egnarts and says, "Give a scientist an intelligent alien life form and watch him create his life's work. Feed a scientist an intelligent alien life form and watch it take his life." Then he sets his sword down on the counter, the one he used to cut the tentacle and never wiped clean, purposefully tapping the hilt of it against the empty beer bottle before he turns and walks away from the open-mouth shocked doctor.

As they approach the door, Oska looks to Kai and says in disbelief, "I can't believe you just punched an old man in the nose."

Looking back to her, Kai says, "My crew. My ship. My rules. And I always get the last word."

Stepping out of the pub, Kai hears something strange, something he recognizes, yet at the same time has never heard before. Looking to his left, he realizes Chance is whistling. Not being the type to whistle, Kai almost asks him about it and then recognizes the name of the song as 'He Who Reaps the Whirlwind' and leaves his question unasked.

Epilogue

"Good morning, Kai. How are things in the black?"

"Good enough. We're just finishing up a delivery for a friend of ours named Scooby. How are you, Jack? You're obviously back up and running."

"It's not as good as my last system, but I've got some of my backup systems rigged together, and it's taking care of my needs for now. By the way, did you happen to catch the news before you left Quantous?"

"No. what news is that?" asks Kai.

"Well, according to the reports, a prominent scientist was found dead in his hotel room."

"Really?" asks Kai. as he tries to think of when and how Chance could have managed it.

"Yeah," says Jack. "They wouldn't release the name of the deceased, but the news report said that upon finding the body, they had to quarantine the whole area for some sort of biological hazard. You all wouldn't happen to know anything about that, would you?"

Being completely honest while still sidestepping everything running through his mind, Kai says. "This is the first I've heard anything about it." Then to get the conversation onto another track, Kai asks. "So is this a social call then today, or do you have something for me?"

"Actually, I have another job you might be interested in. What do you say?"

Pausing, Kai considers his options and says,

...

About the Author

Shawn Kass was born in Killeen, Texas. He attended a series of colleges while serving as a Staff Sergeant in the United States Air Force. He earned five degrees in subjects including Mathematics, Psychology, Education, and Secure Computer Systems Networking. While on active duty from 1997 to 2006, he was stationed stateside in Texas, California, Florida, Illinois, and Washington, D.C. While overseas, he served in several Middle East locations.

Upon exiting the service, Shawn became a high school math and science teacher, educating students in Washington, D.C., England, and Michigan. He currently lives in Farmington Hills, MI with his wonderful wife and is currently teaching at a local high school.

Visit him at https://www.facebook.com/shawn.kass.1 or https://sites.google.com/site/secondchanceandtheallonsy/home for news on his next book.

Emails will be accepted at secondchanceandtheallonsy@yahoo.com.

Made in the USA
Lexington, KY
03 June 2013